"Virginia Kantra whips up a perfect blend of sexy romance and spine-tingling mystery. Now that I've read this book, I want to move to Eden. Better yet, I want Jarek Denko!"
—*New York Times* bestselling author Lisa Gardner

Just out of her age range and way out of her league.

"You're not married now, but you were once. Maybe more than once. You're straight. You don't smoke, you drink beer, you vote Democrat and think Republican. How am I doing?" Tess challenged the new police chief, her instincts on alert.

"Pretty good...Sherlock."

Maybe Jarek h̶ Maybe she ha̶ ̶e̶ was a real, liv̶ inside the Ice ̶

Tess smiled eng̶ ̶ ̶ ̶ ̶ ̶ ̶u̶r̶ turn."

"A good detective doesn't theorize ahead of his facts."

"What does that mean?"

"It means I'd have to spend more time with you before I developed any theories." And then Jarek gave her a long, slow smile.

Dear Reader,

Once again, Silhouette Intimate Moments starts its month off with a bang, thanks to Beverly Barton's *The Princess's Bodyguard*, another in this author's enormously popular miniseries THE PROTECTORS. A princess used to royal suitors has to "settle" for an in-name-only marriage to her commoner bodyguard. Or maybe she isn't settling at all? Look for more Protectors in *On Her Guard*, Beverly Barton's Single Title, coming next month.

ROMANCING THE CROWN continues with *Sarah's Knight* by Mary McBride. An arrogant palace doctor finds he needs help himself when his little boy stops speaking. To the rescue: a beautiful nanny sent to work with the child—but who winds up falling for the good doctor himself. And in Candace Irvin's *Crossing the Line,* an army pilot crash-lands, and she and her surviving passenger—a handsome captain—deal simultaneously with their attraction to each other and the ongoing crash investigation. Virginia Kantra begins her TROUBLE IN EDEN miniseries with *All a Man Can Do,* in which a police chief finds himself drawn to the reporter who is the sister of a prime murder suspect. In *The Cop Next Door* by Jenna Mills, a woman back in town to unlock the secrets of her past runs smack into the stubborn town sheriff. And Melissa James makes her debut with *Her Galahad,* in which a woman who thought her first husband was dead finds herself on the run from her abusive *second* husband. And who should come to her rescue but Husband Number One—not so dead after all!

Enjoy, and be sure to come back next month for more of the excitement and passion, right here in Intimate Moments.

Leslie J. Wainger
Executive Senior Editor

All a Man Can Do
VIRGINIA KANTRA

INTIMATE MOMENTS™

Published by Silhouette Books

America's Publisher of Contemporary Romance

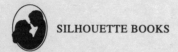 SILHOUETTE BOOKS

ISBN 0-373-27250-2

ALL A MAN CAN DO

Books by Virginia Kantra

Silhouette Intimate Moments

The Reforming of Matthew Dunn #894
The Passion of Patrick MacNeill #906
The Comeback of Con MacNeill #983
The Temptation of Sean MacNeill #1032
Mad Dog and Annie #1048
Born To Protect #1100
All a Man Can Do #1180

*Trouble in Eden

VIRGINIA KANTRA

credits her enthusiasm for strong heroes and courageous heroines to a childhood spent devouring fairy tales. A three-time Romance Writers of America RITA® Award finalist, she has won numerous writing awards, including the Golden Heart, Maggie Award, Holt Medallion and *Romantic Times* W.I.S.H. Hero Award.

Virginia is married to her college sweetheart, a musician disguised as the owner of a coffeehouse. They live in Raleigh, North Carolina, with three teenagers, two cats, a dog and various blue-tailed lizards that live under the siding of their home. Her favorite thing to make for dinner? Reservations.

She loves to hear from readers. You can reach her at VirginiaKantra@aol.com or c/o Silhouette Books, 300 East 42nd Street, New York, NY 10017.

To Damaris Rowland,
who thought a series would be a really good idea.

Special thanks to Lt. Joseph T. FitzSimmons for his
patience with my questions, to Nora Armstrong for
introducing me to her brother in the Chicago PD, to
Pamela Baustian and Judith Stanton for the usual reasons
and to Michael, who has always done all a man can do. I
couldn't have written this book without you.

Chapter 1

The only thing worse than dying on the job was living long enough to retire.

Jarek Denko steered his aging police cruiser with one hand along Eden's main drag. He eyed the empty steps of St. Raphael's Catholic Church, checked out the sidewalk action in front of the Rose Farms Café.

Unless the senior citizens were carrying concealed, the street was quiet.

Jarek had never wanted to spend his retirement on a bar stool at the Joint, nursing a beer and his memories while all around him the active cops talked the job and women. But he sure hadn't figured on giving up the street to become police chief in some backwater town.

His town, now, he reminded himself. It was a good town. And a great place to raise kids. His kid. Maybe the community of Eden could provide whatever was missing from his little girl's life.

His jaw tightened. *Yeah, like a father.* It sure as hell couldn't bring her mother back for her.

He thought with gratitude of his own parents. At least they were trying to support his decision to make a fresh start in a new place. His father muttered about coming up for the fishing. His mother insisted Allie stay with them until Jarek was settled in his new job.

And his brother, who had followed Jarek onto the force and into the most prestigious detective division in Chicago, was laughing his damn fool head off.

"You actually think you'll be happy working in Pleasantville?" Aleksy had demanded.

"Eden," Jarek corrected mildly. "And I can handle it."

He had been a homicide detective for fourteen years. There was nothing he hadn't seen, and damn little he couldn't handle.

Now he cruised past Eden's only movie theater, where a second-run action flick shared the screen with an afternoon cartoon, and turned right, toward the lake. The Town of Eden Police Department stood on a patch of winter-browned grass at the corner of North Lake and Highland. Except for the sign out front and the squad cars parked out back, the department looked exactly like the post office or the library. Trees and two flags softened the squat brick outline and shaded the severe concrete steps.

Jarek pulled into his reserved spot by the rear entrance and keyed himself into the building. The hallway was quiet. The whole building was quiet, even for a Tuesday morning. Just another day in paradise, Jarek thought wryly.

But as he walked to his office, he heard a heavy, genial voice carry from the receiving area.

"Well, well. We haven't seen much of you around here lately. What can I do for you, sweetheart?"

"You can get me in to see Chief Denko," a woman's voice replied crisply. "And don't call me sweetheart."

Jarek sheered off from his office, his attention caught by her tone and the sound of his name. God knew, he could use a diversion from reading files.

Lieutenant Bud Sweet was in the lobby. With his broad red face and thick white hair, he looked like St. Nick's suspicious cousin. His gut strained over his gun belt. Not for the first time this week, Jarek wondered if he would have to requisition new uniforms for his out-of-shape department or order them all into training.

There was a woman with Sweet, dark haired, young and exotic looking in a red sweater and a fitted black blazer. Nothing wrong with her shape at all.

"Lieutenant," Jarek said quietly. With only a week as their boss, he was careful to give his department veterans their due.

Sweet nodded acknowledgment. "Someone here to see you, Chief."

The woman turned, revealing a wide, red, full-lipped mouth and Sicilian gold eyes. The blazer hung open. Well. Wow. Hello. From this angle, the sweater looked even better.

She offered her hand, her golden eyes amused and aware. "Teresa DeLucca. But you can call me Tess."

He shook her hand briefly—hers was warm and firm, with deep red nails to match the sweater—and then thrust his own deep in his pockets. *Look, don't touch,* veteran Joe Arbuzzi used to tell him when he was still a wet-behind-the-ears detective at a crime scene.

"What can we do for you, Miss DeLucca?"

"I want to buy you breakfast," she said.

Breakfast? Like, what two people ate the morning after the night before?

Holy St. Mike. He was a seasoned veteran of the streets. A casualty of divorce court. He knew better than to drool over Miss Call-Me-Tess DeLucca like he was off duty and she was a doughnut.

It was the sweater, he told himself. He'd always been a sucker for…red.

"She's a reporter," Sweet said.

A reporter. Jarek's mental barriers rattled down like the grill over a jewelry store window. He had a cop's natural aversion for the press. Even when they wore red.

"What do you want?" he asked again.

Sweet grinned. "Well, her brother's not in lock-up, and the bars don't close for another thirteen hours, so she can't be here to bail her mama out. She must want you."

Jarek frowned. Surely Sweet was joking? He had to be joking.

But Teresa DeLucca's smile flattened. "Only for breakfast," she said.

Jarek shook his head. "Sorry. I've eaten."

"Coffee, then? The stuff here's terrible."

He raised his eyebrows. "Come here often, Miss De-Lucca?"

"Tess," she corrected. "And, no, not lately. Although I had my first ride in a police cruiser when I was fourteen."

Okay, he was interested. He gestured toward the hallway behind him. "I can offer you coffee in my office."

Her manicured nails toyed with the shoulder strap of her purse. Did he make her nervous? Or was it police stations? *I had my first ride in a police cruiser when I was fourteen.*

"What about the café?" she countered. "I'm buying."

She was a puzzle, with her confident eyes and uncertain mouth. Jarek had never been able to resist a puzzle. It was one of the things that made him so good at his job.

He shrugged. "Fine. You want to come back for your car?"

Her smile relaxed some. She had a tiny overlap in her front teeth that was very attractive. "I'll drive, thanks."

"You'll follow me?"

Those golden eyes danced. "To the ends of the earth," she said solemnly.

He resisted the urge to smile back. Until he knew what she wanted, he couldn't afford to get chummy.

"All right," he said.

Bud Sweet pursed his round, red mouth. "Leaving kind of soon, aren't you, Chief?"

Jarek nodded. "I'll be back in thirty. Page me if you need me."

"We'll manage," Sweet said.

Their eyes clashed briefly. Sweet's fell first.

"Great," Jarek said, careful not to push his point. "Thanks."

Tess DeLucca followed him out of the building, her high-heeled boots making a bold sound on the concrete walk. "I get the impression your second in command doesn't like you much."

Well, there was a scoop, Jarek thought.

"Really," he said noncommittally.

She unlocked her car door and then tossed back her dark hair to look at him. "Did you know he was in line for the chief of police position? Until the search committee decided you were the best man for the job."

"I'd heard something like that," Jarek admitted. It made the lieutenant's antagonism easier to bear. Sweet considered Jarek an interloper. An outsider.

Jarek shrugged mentally. Hell, Sweet was right.

"I'd watch my back if I were you," Tess DeLucca said. "Your lieutenant knows how to hold a grudge."

Jarek frowned, but her face expressed nothing but intelligent interest and a sort of wry commiseration. He muffled another inconvenient spark of attraction. He appreciated her concern, if that's what it was. He admired her frankness. But there was no way he was discussing the deficiencies and jealousies of the officers under his command with a civilian. A reporter, for crying out loud.

"I'll keep it in mind," he murmured, and ushered her into her car.

Tess watched the new chief of police hand his plastic-sleeved menu back to their waitress.

"Grapefruit," he ordered. "And coffee."

"No doughnuts?" Tess drawled.

Denko's eyes narrowed. His face was dark, full of lines and shadows. His eyes should have been dark, too. But they were unexpectedly pale, clear and cool as the lake in March. Tess resisted the urge to rub her arms briskly.

"You want doughnuts?" he asked.

"No. I'll have the pancakes," she told the waitress. She turned back to Denko. "I just thought you might."

He nodded to the waitress—Noreen, her plastic name tag read—and said, "Thanks. That'll be all, then. So." He laced his fingers together; rested them on his paper place mat. All of his gestures were exact and deliberate, Tess noticed. "Do you always draw conclusions about people you've just met?"

She shrugged. "I get impressions. It helps, in my line of work."

"And I strike you as a man who likes doughnuts." His voice was bland. His shoulders were broad. And his stomach, beneath his starched shirt front, wasn't anywhere near the edge of the table. Whatever the new chief's reasons for leaving Chicago, he obviously hadn't spent the past ten years eating doughnuts behind a desk.

She felt caught out by her stereotyping and struggled to make a recovery. "Maybe not," she said. "You impress me as a man in control of himself and his waistline. You're—what?—thirty-eight? Thirty-nine?"

"Forty."

Just out of her age range and way out of her league. She looked at his hands, clasped on the table in front of him. His fingers were long and blunt-tipped, the nails neatly trimmed but otherwise neglected. "You're not married now, but you were once. Maybe more than once. You're straight. You don't smoke, you drink beer, you vote Democrat and think Republican. How am I doing?"

He waited while their waitress, a straw-haired blonde in wilted polyester, filled his cup. "Pretty good…Sherlock."

Maybe he had a sense of humor after all. Maybe she had a shot at a story. She had been so afraid, back at the station, that Sweet's snotty comment or her own impulsive confession had ruined everything. But maybe there was a real, live, warm human being buried inside the Man of Ice.

She smiled engagingly. "Your turn."

He took a sip of coffee. Black. "A good detective doesn't theorize ahead of his facts."

She sat up straighter on the vinyl bench. "What does that mean?"

"It means I'd have to spend more time with you before I developed any theories."

She was deflated. Provoked. "That's an interesting pickup line," she said coolly.

"Just making conversation until our order gets here. Tell me about your ride in a police car when you were fourteen."

The Man of Ice was back. "That was a long time ago."

"But you remember. Were you scared?"

"I'm not scared of anything." But she had been. Oh, she had been.

"So tell me about it."

"It wasn't anything. Kid stuff. Shoplifting." It had been her brother's birthday, she remembered. Mark had had his eleven-year-old heart set on a football, and she'd had her heart set on getting it—on getting anything—for him. Both of them had been disappointed. End of story.

"And you've been on the straight and narrow ever since," Denko said dryly.

She raised her chin at his challenge. "Pretty nearly." No point in pouring out the particulars. She was big on telling the truth. But not about her own past.

The waitress arrived with their food. She started to set the grapefruit in front of Tess when Denko stopped her.

"Other way around," he said. "You've got us mixed up."

Noreen wasn't the only one who'd turned things around, Tess thought morosely. She stared at her plate. A mound of butter slid from the stack of pancakes to plop against the lonely orange wedge. For crying out loud, she was the reporter. She was used to getting people to talk, to confide in her. She was good at it.

But Jarek Denko was better.

She picked up her knife. "So, what brings a big, bad detective from Chicago to our little town?"

"How do you know I'm from Chicago?"

That was a cop's trick, answering a question with another question. Reporters used it, too.

"I asked the mayor," Tess said. "Were you fired?"

He didn't get mad. "No."

She poked a wedge of pancake. "You can't have moved here for the excitement."

He almost smiled. "No."

"Then, why did you move here?"

"Personal reasons," he said briefly.

Tess sniffed. "Oh, that's illuminating. What kind of personal reasons? Breakdown? Breakup?"

A brief gleam lit those remote gray eyes. "What do you want, Miss DeLucca? My medical history or a blood test?"

Oh, boy. He wasn't—he couldn't be flirting with her. Could he? She swallowed a lump of pancake. "If you want to share."

"No."

"Trouble on the job?" she prodded sympathetically.

He eased back in the booth, his gaze steady, his voice calm. "Why don't you ask the mayor?"

"I did. She said you were a regular Boy Scout."

His smile appeared, a thin sliver in the ice. "That would be my brother. I was an altar boy."

"You're Catholic?" Ha. Her mother would love that. Not that Dizzy DeLucca was a saint herself, but she wanted one for her daughter.

The new police chief nodded.

"So, you have a brother. Any sisters?" Tess persisted.

"One of each."

He was answering. This was good. At least, it was an improvement. "And what do they do now?"

"She's a librarian. He's Chicago PD." Jarek took another sip of coffee and set his cup precisely in the center of the saucer. "How about you?"

"One brother."

"Yeah? Older or younger?"

"Younger. Listen, do you—"

"He live with you?"

"I live alone." She moistened her lips and flashed him her best smile. She was not letting him take control of this interview again. "Fishing, Chief Denko? I didn't think you brought me here to hear about my personal life."

He didn't laugh. "I didn't bring you here. What do you want, Miss DeLucca? A favor? A lead?"

"An interview. For the *Eden Town Gazette*."

"Why didn't you ask me back at the station house?"

"Because I was afraid you'd say no."

He nodded again, not saying anything.

Tess picked at the chipped edge of one nail. "Well?" she asked finally.

"No," he said.

She scowled. "Why not?"

"I'm not news."

"You know that's not true. People are always interested in their public officials. Even in Chicago, you'd get a column. Up here, you get the front page and my undivided attention. You're the biggest news to hit town since Simon Ford."

Denko looked blank. So he didn't know everything. Tess found that reassuring.

"Simon Ford," she repeated. "The inventor? He bought Angel Island."

"You mean, he bought a house there."

"No, he bought the island. The point is, you're our lead story. Well, unless my editor decides to run with the new traffic light out at the high school or the Lutheran ladies' zucchini cook-off. But I think we've got a good chance."

A corner of his nicely shaped mouth quirked up. "I'm flattered. But, no."

"What do you have to lose?"

"My privacy?" he suggested dryly.

She arched her eyebrows. "What do you have to hide?"

"Not a thing."

"Well, then…" She let her voice trail off expectantly.

He eyed her with a combination of amusement and annoyance. "You're persistent."

"In my job, you have to be."

"In my job, too. And I'm not convinced letting it all hang out in the *Eden Town Gossip*—"

"Gazette," she snapped, and then scowled. He was just yanking her chain.

"Gazette," he corrected smoothly. "Anyway, I don't like the idea that anybody in town with fifty cents can read all about my life in the paper."

"Haven't you ever heard of spin?"

"I don't need spin."

"Sure you do." She leaned forward earnestly and just missed smearing her sweater in syrup. *Very smooth, De-Lucca.* "You're a stranger here. People aren't going to feel comfortable talking to you. A piece in the paper is like an introduction. It gets your name and face out there, makes people feel like they know you, shows them you're a regular guy. They're more likely talk to you then."

"All the people here need to know is that I'm qualified to do my job."

"And are you?"

He didn't rise to her bait. "Your search committee thought so."

She waited. "That's it?"

"Unless you want to talk to me. Like you said, I'm a stranger here. I could use someone to fill me in on who's who in this town." He sent some subtle masculine signal that brought Noreen scurrying over.

It figured the new chief would be good in restaurants, Tess thought glumly. Probably he could find parking spaces and kill spiders, too. That didn't mean she had to roll over for him.

"If it's gossip you're after, you can get that down the

street at the barbershop. If it's stories about suspicious behavior, you can get those from Bud Sweet."

He shrugged and reached for his wallet. "It always helps to have a civilian perspective. And you're a reporter. An observer. That could make you useful."

"Gee, how nice," she drawled. "If I'd ever wanted to be a police snitch, that would make me feel all warm inside."

He didn't laugh.

Fine. She didn't need the approval of some cool-eyed, tight-lipped cop. She didn't want this attraction to him, either.

She twitched the check from Noreen's hand. "I told you, breakfast is on me." She counted out the money. Too bad *Gazette* reporters didn't merit expense accounts. After the waitress left, she asked, "So, is that the deal? I be your source, you be my story?"

Denko slipped his wallet back into his pocket. A difficult maneuver in the tight confines of the booth, but he managed it gracefully.

"No deal," he said. "I'm interested in developing ties to the community. But my private life stays private."

Tess felt an instant's sympathy. She sure didn't want anyone digging around in her private graveyard.

Her eyes narrowed as she regarded the new police chief. What skeletons was Jarek Denko hiding?

Chapter 2

The Plaza Apartments' one elevator was out-of-order again. Tess shifted the bag of groceries in her arms to open the fire door, propping it with her hip so her mother could walk through.

"I wish you'd let me take you out for dinner instead," Tess said.

Isadora DeLucca smiled shakily. "Oh, cooking's no trouble."

No trouble for who? Tess wanted to ask, but years of protecting her mother's feelings made her bite her tongue. If her mother needed to cook her a high-fat lunch to make up for all the years when Tess had opened cans to feed herself and her brother, well... Whatever her mother needed was fine with Tess.

The hallway smelled like cabbage and mold. No one who could afford to live anywhere else paid rent at the Plaza. The paint peeled, the radiators sweated and the toilets over-flowed. But the aging building provided a first shot at freedom for the very young, a last stab at independence for the very old.

Even on a reporter's salary, Tess could afford better now. Mark thought she was crazy for not buying into one of the snazzy new condos going up by the lake or even moving to a newer, nicer apartment. But Tess told herself this apartment was fine. Mark was back. Her mother was on the wagon. Her life was fine. And if anything happened to make it not fine again, at least she wouldn't be forced out of her home.

Tess had lived at the Plaza ten years, longer than any other resident except ninety-four-year-old Mrs. McMurty on the second floor. Against the advice of her doctors and the pleas of her son, Mrs. McMurty swore she would leave the Plaza only to go to her grave.

On her bad days, Tess imagined she'd escape the same way. Feetfirst and alone, having died of old age.

She unlocked her door.

"I don't know why you don't get yourself a cat," Isadora said as the door opened on Tess's apartment. "You used to love animals."

She still loved animals. But sometime during her twenties, Tess had decided she didn't have the energy left to tackle the care of a house plant, let alone a pet.

"I don't have time for a cat," she muttered, cramming the groceries onto the narrow ledge that passed for a counter.

"You should make time." Isadora puttered around the galley kitchen. She waved a spatula at her daughter. "Love is all you need, you know!"

"Mom." Tess started unloading bags. What on earth was she going to do with an entire bunch of celery? She didn't need celery in her life. She didn't need love, either. Love meant dealing with someone else she was bound either to support or disappoint, and she really, really didn't want that.

She dumped the celery on an empty refrigerator shelf and turned back to her mother. "That was a catchy song. But it's not a very practical philosophy."

"Little Teresa." Isadora smiled in fond disappointment at her only daughter. "Always so practical."

Like she had a choice? Tess had been eight or nine when she figured out that somebody in the DeLucca family had to get the laundry done and the kids to school and dinner on the table. But she didn't want to remind her mother of that. Isadora had been doing so well lately.

The phone shrilled. Her mother stood in the way, poking into a cabinet. Tess sprinted down the hall to pick up in the living room.

"Tess DeLucca," she said breathlessly. Oh, great. She sounded like a phone sex girl.

"This is Butler in News Affairs."

News Affairs. The Chicago Police Department. She had been after them to return her calls for two days.

"Officer Butler." She forced warmth into her voice. "I really appreciate you taking the time to—"

"Sergeant."

"What?"

"It's Sergeant Butler, ma'am."

"Oh. Excuse me. Sergeant." Deliberately, Tess relaxed her grip on the receiver. "Anyway, my newspaper is doing a profile on former detective Jarek Denko, and I was hoping your department could give me some background information."

There was a pause on the other end of the line. "What kind of information?" her caller asked cautiously.

"Well, anything. Everything. Maybe we could start with his employment history, and then—"

"Personnel can give you his rank and dates of employment."

She was hoping for an exposé, not a résumé. Denko was hiding something. Had to be. And it was up to Tess to strip the luster from the police chief's shiny gold star. "I have those, thanks. I was hoping for something more substantial? Commendations, complaints…"

"Let me see."

Another pause, while Tess's mother drifted into the living room. "Don't you have any garlic powder?"

Tess covered the mouthpiece of the receiver. "You didn't tell me you needed garlic powder."

"Well, no, dear, I just assumed you had some."

"I don't cook, Mom. Why would I have garlic powder?"

"You still there?" Sergeant Butler asked.

Tess turned her back on the kitchen and grabbed for a pad and pen. "Yeah, I'm here."

"Okay. Well, Detective Denko received an Award of Valor as a patrol officer."

She tapped her pen against the blank page. "Thanks. Yes, I found that on your Web site. And that was fifteen years ago. Can't you give me something a little more current?"

Like, Chief Check-Out-Those-Biceps Denko beat his ex-wife. Or was on the take. Something, anything, to make the man less of a saint, and this story more than a board member's bio in a corporate newsletter.

"You want current, talk to Denko," Butler said. "I don't have anything for you. You understand."

Oh, she understood all right. She understood no cop in Chicago was going to rat on one of their own to a reporter from Eden.

She could let it go.

Or she could go digging for the truth and deliver more dirt than a home and garden feature on Big Boy Tomatoes.

No neon sign hung over the door of the Joint on Belmont Street, only a black-and-white ad for Old Style: Bottles And Cans. The bar's patrons—cops and police groupies—didn't need more. Either you knew what waited beyond the heavy wood door, or you didn't belong.

Jarek belonged. One week away didn't change that.

Responding to a tip, a middle of the night phone call, he'd left his king-size bed and tidy three-bedroom house to drive an hour and twenty minutes south to Chicago. When he opened the bar door, the warmth and the smells, the smoke and the noise, swirled to greet him. He breathed them all in, let them wrap him like a favorite old sweater.

The place was full. The four-to-midnight shift had ended two hours ago. Four-to-fours, they called it, because most cops didn't roll home until four in the morning. His ex-wife had hated that part of the job. Had hated most parts of his job, actually.

Jarek scanned the room. His brother Aleksy—Alex—was sitting in a booth by the pay phone with a beer in front of him and three off-duty detectives beside him. Catching Jarek's eye, he raised his beer in silent salute before tipping the neck of the bottle toward the bar.

Jarek looked where his brother pointed. And there, perched on a bar stool like any badge bunny, sat Teresa DeLucca in black leather pants and a midriff-skimming top that raised the temperature in the crowded, narrow bar another twenty degrees. She was talking with his former partner, Steve Nowicki, a good detective with the biggest mouth in Area 3. And Stevie, who looked like he couldn't believe his luck, was pouring out his heart and practically drooling down her cleavage.

Hell. Jarek ordered a beer and considered his options.

Aleksy slid out from the booth and sauntered over, still in his street suit. His dark hair was ruffled and his eyes were wicked.

"It took her fifteen minutes to zero in on Nowicki," his brother informed him, "and he's been bending her ear for over an hour. Who the hell is she?"

Jarek accepted his beer with a word of thanks to Pat behind the bar. "Teresa DeLucca. She's a reporter for the local paper."

Aleksy raised his eyebrows. "No kidding. You actually have news in Mayberry?"

A reluctant smile tugged Jarek's mouth. "Brother, in Eden, I *am* the news."

"So, her interest in you is purely professional?"

Jarek took a careful sip of his beer, pushing away an inconvenient memory of Tess's soft lower lip and candid eyes. He had a department to run and a daughter to raise. A relationship with any woman would be a distraction. A preoccupation with some puzzle of a reporter would be a disaster.

"Absolutely," he said.

"And your interest in her? You get to put her in handcuffs yet?"

Jarek narrowed his eyes in warning.

Aleksy backed off, raising his hands in mock surrender. "Just asking, big brother. *Something* got you out of bed in the middle of the night."

"You did," Jarek reminded him. "You called me."

"Yeah, and as soon as you heard this babe was here asking questions, you hotfooted it down. I told you I could handle things for you. In fact," Aleksy waggled his eyebrows, "I'd be more than happy to handle her."

Jarek's burst of male territorial instinct surprised him. If he wasn't careful, he was going to find himself marking trees and pawing at the ground. "Holster it, hotshot," he ordered briefly. "She's too old for you."

"Are you kidding? She can't be a day over twenty-five."

"Thirty." He'd run her driver's license. "And you date nineteen-year-olds."

Aleksy shrugged. "Only when they ask me nicely."

Jarek smiled faintly, his attention still fixed on Nowicki and Tess at the other end of the bar.

Aleksy's dark eyes danced with mischief. "Anyway, isn't she a little old for you, too? I thought you were totally involved with a nine-year-old these days."

"Ten," Jarek corrected him absently. "Allie's ten. And I'm not getting involved with the woman."

"Really? What are you going to do with her? Arrest her?"

Jarek's jaw set. "Like you said, she's over twenty-one. She has a right to drink in a public bar."

"She's still invading your space, bro."

"My turf," Jarek said, setting down his beer. "My rules."

Quietly he moved along the bar. Under the drifts of conversation, the bursts of laughter, his former partner's voice carried plainly.

"—was always the calm, collected one," Nowicki was saying, leaning forward earnestly to look down Tess's top. "Like a computer, you know, storing up all these names, pictures, little connecting things you'd think wouldn't matter to anybody and then—*click, click, click!*—the picture comes up and he's put it all together, who, why, how, the whole puzzle." Nowicki took a long pull on his bottle. "Working with somebody like that makes it a pleasure just to show up in the morning."

"You must miss him," Tess observed.

"Hell, yeah, we all miss him. He was a terrific guy. A great detective. We miss him a lot."

"You can stop the commercial, Nowicki," Jarek said. "I don't think Miss DeLucca's buying."

His partner turned, genuine pleasure lighting his broad face. "Ice Man! We were just talking about you."

"I guessed," Jarek said. He looked past Nowicki to Tess on her bar stool, her casual posture a pose, her eyes a challenge. His libido flared. Annoyed with himself, he spoke coolly. "Hello, Tess."

Nowicki's head went back and forth. "You two know each other?"

"We've met," Tess murmured. "How's it going, Ice Man?"

She didn't miss a trick, Jarek thought, torn between admiration and annoyance.

He spoke without moving his gaze from hers. "Would you give us a minute, Steve?"

Nowicki laughed, four beers past discretion. "Don't be a spoilsport, Jare. We were getting somewhere here."

"Someone was getting something," Jarek said. He jerked his head slightly, an unmistakable signal to his partner to get lost.

Nowicki sighed. "Okay, okay. I'm gone."

Jarek stepped back to let him pass and then slid onto his abandoned stool. "This is a hell of a place to be at two o'clock in the morning," he said quietly.

Tess arched her eyebrows. "You're here."

"We're not talking about me."

"No," Tess agreed. "That was the problem."

"It doesn't have to be your problem."

"It's my story. And you're still holding out on me."

"So what?"

"So, it's a challenge." She flipped her dark hair over

her shoulders and shot him a look that dried his mouth. "I've never been able to resist a challenge."

He sipped his beer, which bought him some time and lubricated his tongue enough so he could talk again. He didn't need any more challenges. He had all he could handle sleeping tucked up in his old bedroom under the eaves of his parents' house. A ten-year-old challenge with his eyes and her mother's scowl.

Teresa DeLucca was playing with fire. He had to find a way to prove to her that she could get burnt. "You're wasting your time, Tess."

"No, I'm not. Your partner's not like you. He answers my questions."

"Honey, at two o'clock in the morning, the bearded lady could walk into this bar and Nowicki would answer her questions. Most cops are easy when they're coming off shift. Of course, it didn't hurt any that you're wearing those pants."

She stiffened defensively. "So, they worked. I got what I wanted."

"You were lucky. You could have gotten something you didn't want."

"Like what?"

Jarek drew a short, sharp breath. He could do this, he told himself. He would prove to both of them that he was scorch proof.

"Like this," he said, and leaned forward, and covered her mouth with his.

He surprised her, and Tess prided herself that very few men could do that anymore.

His mouth on hers was warm and sure. She recoiled slightly—from shock and the faint taste of beer—and then let herself be persuaded, let her mouth be taken, by his. He was disarmingly direct. Devastatingly thorough. Competent, she thought almost resentfully, before her brain shut down. He angled his head and used his tongue, and she shivered and melted and sagged on her bar stool, seduced by the nearness of his firm, warm chest and that hot, bold mouth moving on hers.

Oh, boy.

He raised his head. Maybe he had surprised himself, too, because his eyes, that she remembered as gray and cool as midwinter ice, were dark and hot.

She blinked.

He eased back. "Didn't your mother ever warn you not to come on to strange men in bars?"

Indignation warred with…oh God, was that disappointment?

She cleared her throat. "Obviously you've never met my mother." She picked up her drink, pleased when the ice cubes did not rattle. She was still shaking inside from his kiss. It was just her bad luck Chief Law-and-Order Denko could kiss as well as he did everything else. "Anyway, you kissed me."

He shrugged, not denying it. "That may have been a miscalculation."

"Gee, thanks," she drawled. "Worried it will ruin your reputation?"

His teeth glinted in a brief smile. "No. Kissing you will do wonders for my reputation."

She refused to be charmed. "Thank you. I think."

And then he spoiled it by adding, "Besides, now every guy in the place knows you're off-limits."

Tess set down her drink and glared at him. "Is that why you did it? Because you thought you were making a point?"

"I did make a point. It's not safe for a woman looking

the way you do to walk into a cop bar and imagine the only thing she's going to leave with is information. But that's not why I kissed you.''

"Oh, yeah?" she asked, very nastily because her body was still humming and her feelings were all mixed up. "So, why?"

"I must have wanted to." His eyes were dark and direct. "I think I've wanted to kiss you ever since I met you."

Her heart thumped in excitement. She straightened defensively on her bar stool. "And being a police officer, you figure you can take what you want, no questions asked?"

He frowned. "No. Don't theorize ahead of your facts, Tess."

The fact was, she didn't trust cops.

The fact was, she was attracted to this one.

And she didn't like that one bit.

She raised an eyebrow. "Are you trying to tell me you're an honest cop?"

"I'm not telling you anything," Jarek said evenly.

No, he wasn't. The only thing he had admitted to was wanting to kiss her.

She nodded toward a booth by the door, where his former partner had joined a table of other off-duty detectives. "They seem to think you walk on water."

He shrugged. "I did my job."

"More than that, I heard. Ice Man? Cool under pressure. You took a gun away from some psycho commuter on the train—"

He looked uncomfortable. "That was years ago. When I was a patrolman. Detectives don't get written up for stuff like that."

"But didn't you face more dangerous situations as a detective?"

He regarded her silently for a moment. "You're the oldest in your family?"

She was confused. He confused her. She wasn't used to men remembering what she said. "Yes. How did you—"

"As the oldest, there are things that are expected of you, right?"

Tess squirmed on her wooden perch. She didn't like thinking about her adolescence, the years she struggled to keep Mark fed and out of trouble, the mornings she woke for school already dog-tired and sick-to-her-stomach worried and overwhelmed. She certainly never talked about them. "What's your point?"

"My point is, you don't make a big deal out of meeting your responsibilities. You just do your job." He met her gaze directly. "Same thing if you're a detective. I did my job."

Tess fought the seductive tug of understanding. He was a cop, she reminded herself. They had nothing in common. "Very macho," she said dryly.

His mouth curved. "Damn straight."

She caught herself smiling back and thought, *Uh-oh.* She didn't need these little sparks of connection. She couldn't afford this tingle of attraction. She didn't like the way Jarek kept turning this interview around. She was the reporter, wasn't she? Dispassionate. Objective. In control of the conversation and herself.

Sure she was.

"What made you decide you didn't want to be a detective anymore?" she asked.

"Circumstances."

"Would your decision have anything to do with your wife's death a year ago?"

He set down his beer. "Who told you that?"

She'd caught him off balance, Tess thought, cheered.

Good. It made up, a little, for his uncomfortable perception, his unexpected understanding, his devastating kiss.

I think I've wanted to kiss you ever since I met you.

She pushed the thought away. "Nowicki," she said.

"Nowicki has a big mouth. And you should check your facts."

"She didn't die?"

"She wasn't my wife. Linda and I divorced eight years ago."

Well. Tess wasn't sure if she was relieved the new police chief wasn't still grieving or disappointed that she had lost her story hook. "So, your loss wasn't a factor in accepting the job in Eden?"

Jarek stopped looking impassive and started to look annoyed. Score one for the Girl Reporter.

"Why don't you just write that I liked the idea of making a fresh start?"

"I understand that part," Tess said. "What I don't get is why you'd choose some little resort town on the edge of nowhere."

"The Wisconsin border."

"Same thing."

His guarded smile reappeared. "Not a fan of small town living, are you?"

"It's all right. If you don't mind wearing the same label you got stuck with in the second grade for the rest of your life."

"Then why not get out?"

"Oh." Nobody asked her that. She'd given up even asking herself. Everyone knew, or thought they did, how things were with the DeLuccas. "Well, my father split on us. Maybe I didn't want to follow his example. Besides, my brother needed me."

"Both your parents are gone?"

"No. Well, my mother—" She stopped.

"Your mother?" Jarek prompted gently.

Her mother was a drunk.

"She needed me, too," Tess said. Sure, Isadora DeLucca was sober now. But what would she do if Tess left her?

Tess picked up her drink again. "Anyway, here I am, thirty years old and living two miles from home, defending truth, justice and the American way for twenty-two thousand a year." She laughed self-consciously. "Now you'll tell me I have a Super Girl complex and I'll have to slug you."

"No," he said quietly. "I'm not going to tell you that."

"Right. You'll just think it."

He gave her one of his straight, cool looks. "You have no idea what I think of you."

Her heart slammed into her ribs. She had a slow-motion moment when the smoky, raucous bar swirled and faded and refocused with Jarek as its center, his calm eyes and his firm mouth and his blunt-tipped hands turning the bottle.

She felt the heat crawl in her cheeks, and then a new voice rattled between them like ice cubes dropped into a glass.

"Are you going to introduce me to this seriously hot-looking babe, or do I need to find an excuse to drive to Mayberry?"

Tess blinked.

A man stood at Jarek's shoulder. She recognized one of the detectives from the booth by the door, the young one with the ruffled hair and creased jacket.

Jarek looked resigned. "Tess, this idiot with the suit and no manners is my brother Aleksy."

The Boy Scout. She recovered enough to offer her hand. "Tess DeLucca."

"Alex. It's a pleasure." His smile was wide, his hand-shake firm, and his eyes assessing.

She let him hold her hand two beats too long, aware of the look that passed between him and his brother.

"You don't mind if I join you?" he asked.

Jarek stood. "Actually, we were just leaving."

"There's gratitude," Aleksy complained. "You owe me."

Jarek tossed two quarters on the cloudy surface of the bar. "That's for the phone call. We'll settle the rest later."

"Wait a minute." Do not overreact, Tess told herself. "He called to tell you I was here?"

Jarek hesitated.

"Take the fifth, bro," Aleksy advised him.

Tess stiffened with sudden certainty. Of course he called. Her stomach sank. Cops stuck together. Why else would Jarek show up at two in the morning at a cop-and-groupie bar on Belmont? Because he'd been drawn by some magical, electrical connection between them? What a joke.

But not nearly as big a laugh as the fact that somewhere at the back of her pathetic, needy little mind, Tess had accepted that he must have done exactly that.

Because *he* drew *her*.

"What did he tell you?" she demanded.

"Aleksy mentioned there was a woman here asking questions," Jarek admitted quietly. "From the description, I thought it might be you."

"And you drove down here to shut me up."

"Actually, he drove down to shut Nowicki up," Aleksy said.

She waited for Jarek to deny it. He didn't.

She straightened her spine. "Excuse me. I'm going home."

"Let me take you," Jarek offered. "We can argue in the car."

She wouldn't go home with him if he were the sexiest man alive and she hadn't had sex in a billion years. Which was a good thing, because at least one of those was true.

"I have my own car," she said.

His gaze went to her drink. "Are you okay to drive?"

"It's soda water," she said through her teeth.

He nodded. "Fine. I'll follow you, then."

Aleksy raised an eyebrow. "You're not spending the night at Mom and Pop's?"

"Why?" Jarek asked.

"To see Allie."

"What's the point? She'll be busy getting ready for school in the morning. She won't have time for me."

"Who is Allie?" Tess wanted to know.

"His daughter," Aleksy said.

Tess sucked in a breath. "You have a daughter? Who lives with your parents?"

Jarek's eyes narrowed at her tone.

"Just since Linda died," Aleksy explained. "That's why he took the job in Pleasantville."

Jarek shoved his hands in his pockets. "Okay. I think we're done here."

"I guess we are," Tess said.

He had a *daughter*.

And he hadn't shared even that much of himself with her. Not over breakfast, when they'd talked about their families, not tonight when she had asked him directly about his reasons for moving to Eden.

Maybe he didn't think the daughter was important.

Maybe he didn't think the interview was important.

Maybe—and this was depressingly likely—Tess wasn't all that important, either.

She slid off her bar stool. Well, the hell with him. It wasn't like they had a personal relationship. She didn't even want a personal relationship. Not with any man. Certainly not with Officer Frosty here, with his hot kisses and his cool silence and his family secrets. Tess had more than enough family and plenty of secrets of her own.

She tugged her sweater down over her suddenly cold midriff. Jarek Denko was only another story. Twenty column inches and maybe a picture above the fold. And she wasn't about to let his tall, dark and silent routine stop her from doing the one thing she did well.

"Nice talking to you," Aleksy said cheerfully.

"I'll bet," said Tess.

She stalked out of the bar.

Chapter 3

He could have handled that better, Jarek acknowledged as he drove north.

He watched the baleful gleam of Tess's red taillights five car lengths ahead. She'd indulged in one short burst of speed and temper as they merged with a couple of trucks making an early morning run on Highway 12. But she settled down quickly enough. He had no trouble following her car. He wished he could follow her thought processes as easily.

His hands tightened on the steering wheel. On the job, he was known for his ability to take all the facts of a case into account. But he'd sure miscalculated with Tess. He'd underestimated her determination to make him a news item. He'd misjudged the timing and the amount of the personal information he'd needed to give her to keep control of her story.

And he definitely hadn't reckoned on his own reaction to their kiss.

He practically broke a sweat just thinking about it. About her. She was hot. And unexpectedly sweet. When he kissed her, his body went hard and his mind went blank. For a minute there, kissing her, he'd felt hot, too. Hotter and more dangerous than a stolen pistol, and about as likely to go off. Heady stuff for a disciplined cop and responsible family man.

He unrolled his window to let the cool, damp night stream in over his arm. Living like a monk for the past eight years had obviously made him susceptible to pushy reporters in black leather pants. And the potent contradiction posed by Tess's curl-up-and-die looks and little-girl-lost mouth would tempt a saint.

But his loss of control wasn't her fault. Her voice echoed accusingly in memory, her flip tone not quite hiding the insult to her feelings. *Anyway, you kissed me.*

She was right, Jarek acknowledged fairly. His frustrated body was his problem. Her hurt feelings were his responsibility.

And if Tess, in a typical female snit, decided to smear him in the paper and stake him out for the local gossips to feed on, then the resulting loss of public goodwill would be his headache.

Jarek frowned as he watched Tess's tin can compact zip toward the off ramp. He signaled his intentions to the empty lane behind him and then followed her down the exit to Eden. He was determined to keep his private life private. His failed marriage and his unhappy daughter were off-limits as topics for the press. But ticking off the reporter assigned to introduce him to the town was bad public relations.

Maybe he should agree to that interview Tess wanted. He could steer the talk away from his hopes for his family and onto his plans for the town.

He would have to be nice to her, he decided. If he wanted her cooperation. It was practically his duty.

His mind drifted to all the ways he'd like to be nice to Teresa DeLucca. His body buzzed with anticipation.

He did his best to ignore it.

Tess's fingernails beat a nervous, angry tattoo against the steering wheel. Every time she looked up, she saw Denko's car in her rear view mirror, a dark blue, unmarked Crown Victoria. Nothing new, nothing flashy, nothing to signal whatever midlife crisis had triggered his move to Eden.

His driving was like the rest of him: patient, dogged, steady. She told herself these were not qualities that appealed to her. He probably made love the same way. She pulled a face at her windshield. Nothing kinky or exciting for Chief By-The-Book Denko.

She passed the brightly lit Gas-N-Go and turned under an arch of trees onto a dark residential street. Of course, Denko would still get where he was going that way. She bet he made sure his partners did, too.

The barred moonlight ran over the hood of her car. She shivered a little, with temper and lust.

The Plaza parking lot was quiet, all the seniors' cars tucked in safely for the night. Tess found an empty space and cut her engine. In the silence, she heard the rumble of Jarek's engine as he pulled in behind her. His door slammed.

She took a deep breath and got out of her car. "You want my license and registration, Officer?"

"I'll pass, thanks." He strolled toward her. "I wouldn't say no to a cup of coffee, though."

The moon had ducked behind the trees. The glare from the building's security lights could hardly be called romantic. That was okay. She didn't want romance. Particularly not with a tight-lipped cop who came equipped with a school-age daughter.

"Oh, no," she said. "Offering you coffee is what got me into trouble in the first place."

His eyes narrowed. "What kind of trouble are we talking about here?"

Tess cursed her big mouth. One of these days she was going to learn to think before she spoke. *Yeah, and then she'd probably never talk at all.*

"I just think we should keep things on a professional footing," she said weakly.

Denko nodded, his gaze still fixed on hers. "I wasn't suggesting anything else."

Disappointment and a lack of sleep made her incautious. "Sure you weren't. I bet you invite yourself up to women's apartments at three in the morning all the time."

Maybe his lean cheeks reddened slightly. Under the sodium security lights, it was hard to tell.

"You wanted an opportunity to talk," he said.

"So I'll call the station and make an appointment."

"You might not catch me in. I'm in and out a lot."

She raised her eyebrows. "Fighting our big crime wave?"

The creases deepened around his mouth, but he didn't smile. "More learning my way around. Trying to get a feel for things. You could help."

His intensity pulled at her. He wasn't a big man—lean and only average height—but she still felt threatened.

She shook her head. "Not in my job description, Chief."

"Then…as a friend?"

"I'm not feeling very friendly at the moment."

He took a step closer, close enough that she could smell the wickedness that clung to his hair and clothes, the tang of beer and cigarettes from the bar, the scent of his skin. "Maybe we should work on that," he murmured.

Possibility quivered through her. *Don't be dumb, De-Lucca. You don't want this. You can't want this.*

"Sorry," she said. "It wouldn't work. You held out on me."

He watched her closely. "Would it help if I apologized?"

"I don't think so. You're not exactly my type."

"Want to tell me why?"

"Well…" She could think of a million reasons. Couldn't she? She moistened her lips. "For one thing, you're a cop."

"I won't apologize for that." He sounded more amused than upset.

She stiffened with annoyance. "And you have a kid. I don't do men with kids."

"Why not?"

Because she needed to keep him at a distance, she told him the truth. Part of it, anyway. "I raised one family already. I'm not interested in taking on another."

He stepped back. "Got it. We'll keep it professional, then."

Obviously he wasn't crushed by her rejection. Tess tasted flat disappointment. "I think we'd better."

But she didn't object when he walked with her across the parking lot to the Plaza's cheerless entrance. At three in the morning, she wasn't up to arguing either about her building's negligent security or Jarek Denko's outdated notions of male courtesy. The anticipation she'd felt earlier that evening driving down to Chicago in pursuit of a story had evaporated. She fumbled for her keys, feeling flat and tired.

She was completely taken aback when Jarek stooped and

brushed her cheek with his lips. Pleasure fizzed along her veins.

"Professional courtesy," he explained blandly. "Sleep well."

Oh, right. Tess staggered up the four flights to her empty apartment, her hormones churning and her brain in turmoil. She'd be lucky if she closed her eyes at all tonight.

She prowled into the kitchen, fueling her nervous energy with some stale chips from the bottom of the bag. She ate standing at the counter, listening to the hum of her refrigerator and the persistent gurgle of her leaky toilet. She licked her finger and pressed it to the seam to catch the last salty potato crumbs.

It was only the late hour that made her notice the silence, that made her feel so alone.

Jarek's car swooped onto the lake bridge north of Eden and over a sea of mist. His eyeballs were gritty. A headache had been building at the base of his skull since the radio call that jarred him awake almost half an hour ago.

As a rookie detective, Jarek had learned to go for days without much sleep. His new schedule gave him hours alone on a brand-new, super firm, double-wide mattress. But for the past three nights, he hadn't slept so well. Maybe it was the new job.

Or maybe it was the woman. Tess DeLucca.

Should he have called her?

She'd been crisp and professional yesterday when she phoned the station to set up this morning's interview. Jarek lifted a hand from the steering wheel to rub the back of his neck. She was going to be really ticked if he blew her off. But right now her feelings were not his top priority.

Besides, she was probably still sleeping, he thought, and

then had to push away an inconvenient image of her dark hair and ivory skin against the white sheets of his bed.

He had enough trouble already.

The early-morning sun barely cleared the pines. Jarek followed the hidden shoreline past the gated driveway of the grand old Algonquin Hotel, heading toward the Bide-A-Wee vacation cottages, relying on the police scanner and his own imperfect knowledge of the town. He missed Chicago's numbered grid.

Bud Sweet should have called him, damn it.

But even without coordinates, Jarek found the scene of the crime without any trouble at all.

His mouth compressed as he took in the stretch of road. From the look of things, he was about the only person in town Sweet hadn't called. If some enterprising burglar decided to hold up Main Street this morning, the downtown merchants were out of luck. Vehicles spilled along the asphalt under the pines. Yellow tape meandered in a haphazard rectangle around a white Honda Civic with Illinois plates. Red and white lights rotated and flashed from three patrol cars, two EMS vans, and—Holy St. Mike, was that a hook-and-ladder truck?

Jarek pulled his radio car in thirty yards behind the mess and parked on the shoulder. As he got out of the car, he saw a woman pressed against the yellow tape, bright and exotic looking against a background of dark uniforms.

His body reacted with quick enthusiasm.

Tess.

Jarek groaned mentally. With the exception of Bud Sweet, he couldn't think of anyone he'd like less to find at a crime scene.

He approached the huddle of cars, automatically putting his hands in his pockets. *Look, don't touch.* The pine needles edging the road muffled his footsteps.

"Tess," he said quietly.

She started. Turned. Something in his chest tightened at the early-morning pallor of her face, the unexpectedly serious set of her mouth.

"What are you doing here?" he asked.

Her eyes, that had been wide and welcoming, narrowed. She hitched her purse strap on her shoulder. "Getting a story."

He felt a muscle jump in his jaw. He didn't want her here. She would be upset. And he couldn't be distracted.

He looked past her to the white car, its doors gaping open. No body that he could see, but there were enough uniforms crowding around to block his view of the interior. "I don't have time to talk to you now."

Tess shrugged. "Okay. I'll wait. You can give me a statement later."

That wasn't what he wanted, either. In his book, the public's right to know took a poor second to the victim's right to justice. But he couldn't spare time to argue.

He nodded once. "Suit yourself. But you need to step back from the tape. We have to worry about contaminating the crime scene."

She looked at him, and then at the chaos surrounding them, and then at him again. She raised her eyebrows.

"Yeah, I can see how that *would* be a worry," she deadpanned.

He resisted the urge to grin. There was nothing funny about a screwed-up investigation.

Behind Tess, Patrol Officer Stan Lewis—who should have gone off duty an hour ago—quit arguing with the paramedics around the ambulance to run over and consult with the mob around the car. Jarek shook his head. He didn't care how hard up his officers were for excitement. A crime scene was not a Lions Club picnic.

"Excuse me," he murmured to Tess, and ducked under the police tape.

Bud Sweet stood guard by the white car, flanked by all four members of the day shift and rookie patrolman Tim Clark. When the lieutenant saw Jarek, his face crumpled like a disappointed Santa Claus's.

Jarek let his gaze travel slowly along the lineup to the flashing police cars and the hook-and-ladder truck still half blocking the road.

"Somebody want to tell me where the fire is?" he asked mildly.

Sweet drew himself up. "No fire. We have a roadside assault. Clark here caught the call on an abandoned auto. Only when he came to investigate—"

Jarek held up one hand to silence him. "Just a minute. How's the victim?"

"Stabilized," Sweet said.

"She's still *here?*" Jarek couldn't keep the anger from his voice.

"I was going to question her."

Jarek pivoted and strode quickly to the nearest EMS van. A tiny uniformed technician moved to intercept him, her dark eyes snapping.

"We need to get her to the hospital," she said. "Now."

Jarek nodded. "Do it."

As the tech climbed into the ambulance, he swung in after her and crouched down next to the victim.

Young. Blond. Pretty. Or she had been, before the attack. She was swaddled in blankets, an IV running into her arm.

Jarek put his head down close to hers. "Honey, can you hear me?"

She opened dull blue eyes. Whimpered.

The tech reached around him to moor the cot.

Jarek tried again. "Honey, do you know who did this to you?"

"Police," she whispered.

His heart nearly broke for her. She was really young. Maybe eighteen? "Yeah, I'm with the police," he said gently. "You're safe now. Did you see who hurt you?"

"We've got to go," the tech interrupted.

Jarek's jaw set. He started to crawl out of the ambulance.

"Lights," the girl on the stretcher volunteered suddenly.

Jarek leaned back in the open door. "What, honey?"

"The car that stopped me." She licked cracked lips. Blue eyes met his and then slid away. "Red lights. Like police."

Jarek felt as if he'd just been thumped in the stomach with his own nightstick.

Red lights. Hell.

He stood like a block while the female tech slammed the doors and the van drove away, its turret lights flashing. On Jarek's home turf, in Chicago, the police were identified by blue flashers. Ambulances and fire trucks operated with red. But in Eden and for most of Illinois, all official emergency vehicles were identified by red flashing lights. Only volunteer firefighters used blue.

And the victim in his most recent case had just identified her assailant's car as showing red lights. *Police* lights.

Jarek swore again, silently, viciously. And then he turned and stalked back to the officers clustered around the white car.

Tess still waited too close to the yellow tape, her usually animated face soft and serious.

Her absorption in the scene hit him like another slam in the gut. He had a red light assault on his hands *and* a reporter underfoot. What a godawful mess.

Routine, he reminded himself. Do the job.

He looked down the row of police faces. "Anybody get pictures before the body was moved?"

"This isn't a homicide," Sweet objected. "The girl's alive."

Jarek lifted one eyebrow. "And are we sure she's going to stay that way?"

Sweet's red face got redder.

Jarek dismissed him. "Lewis, take photos now. I want someone to go with the ambulance. Is Baker on?" Laura Baker was the department's only female officer.

A patrolman shifted in the line. "She's out today."

Sweet tugged on his gun belt. "This isn't Chicago. We don't have the manpower to waste on an ambulance run."

Jarek held on to his temper. "I don't see a shortage of manpower here. I want an officer with the victim at the hospital."

She needed police protection. Jarek frowned. Unless she needed protection *from* the police.

He did a rapid mental review of his department. Who could he trust? Who the hell did he know, really?

"Call Larsen in," he ordered. "Tell him to make sure that they do a rape kit in the E.R. And I want all nonessential personnel cleared off this scene. Have you called the state police yet for crime lab support?"

Sweet scowled. "We work with the county."

"Not on a possible homicide," Jarek pronounced. "Call. Johnson and White, I want you to move all vehicles out of here. See my car? I don't want anything parked closer than that. And recordon the crime scene, divert traffic to— what's the nearest parallel road?"

"Green's just west of here," Clark volunteered.

Jarek turned back to the rookie patrolman. "Right. Green it is. You found the victim?"

"Yes, sir. I—" The young officer swallowed hard. "She

didn't want to talk. I tried to get a description of her assailant, but... Anyway, I finally just wrapped her in a blanket and left her alone.''

A compassionate action that had effectively wiped any trace of the son of the bitch who attacked her from her skin. Hell.

''All right,'' Jarek said. ''Did she give you her name?''

''No, sir.''

''How about her purse? Do we have an ID?''

''Her wallet's missing. I ran the plates,'' Bud Sweet said. ''Car's registered to a Mr. and Mrs. Richard Logan of Evanston. So the car could be stolen.''

''Or she could be their daughter,'' Jarek said grimly. ''Find out. And find out what she was doing up here.''

''She was a student at Bloomington,'' Tess said from behind him, her voice flat. ''Taking a break from exams.''

His gut tightened like a fist. He turned. Tess had moved to *this* side of the crime tape, but he couldn't object to her presence now. He wanted to protect her from the ugliness of the scene. He needed to protect his department from the force of her determination, from those wide golden eyes that saw too much. But this wasn't Chicago, where he could canvass half-a-dozen surrounding buildings for witnesses. If Tess knew something, he had to talk to her.

''You know the victim?''

Tess's slightly crooked teeth caught her lower lip. ''Her name is Logan? Carolyn Logan?''

''I don't have a first name. Can you describe her?''

''Oh...'' Tess frowned in concentration. ''Medium height, nineteen years old. Blond, shoulder-length hair. Her eyes were blue. Or maybe gray?'' She shook her head. ''Light, anyway.''

Okay, so her being a reporter wasn't a total loss, Jarek

thought. It was a good description. And, for good or bad, it fit the battered girl in the ambulance.

"How do you know her?"

"I don't know her," Tess corrected him. "I met her last night."

"Tell me."

She fidgeted with her purse strap again. "My story for yours?"

His jaw set. He didn't make deals. But he knew how to get what he wanted from an interview. "It could work that way."

She snorted. "Oh, now, that's something I can stop the presses for."

She wasn't as tough as she made herself out to be. He waited.

"Oh, all right," she said crossly. "What do you want from me?"

Too much. He shoved the thought away.

"I want you to wait for me over there," he said quietly, "while I finish talking with the investigating team. And then I'd like it if you'd go with me to the station house so I can take your statement."

"You can't take it here?"

He could, of course. But he wanted her away from the crime scene. A vicious sexual assault might be news in sleepy Eden. But to a town that depended on tourism, it could also be a public relations disaster. And to the new police chief, the attack at the beginning of his watch was a personal and professional spit-in-the-eye.

Especially if his own department was implicated.

He met her gaze steadily. "No point in being uncomfortable. You want to give the station house coffee a shot?"

The memory of her words trembled between them. *Of-*

fering you coffee is what got me into trouble in the first place.

Tess hugged her arms across her waist. Lifted her chin. "Maybe I'll let you buy me a drink instead."

"It's a little early for that."

"Why don't we see how long this takes? I'll just get my butt back on the other side of your police tape until you're ready for me."

Jarek watched as she walked away and bent back under the yellow crime scene tape. Her butt. Yes.

Sweet coughed. "Looks like you've got yourself a hot one, Chief."

Jarek stiffened. "Excuse me?"

"Hot lead," the lieutenant said. "If DeLucca really knows anything worthwhile, that is."

Sweet was a jackass. Tess was a complication. And Jarek had never felt more like an outsider in his life.

"We won't know that until I take her statement," he said calmly, and turned back to the scene of the crime.

Chapter 4

Tess slid into the dark booth at the back of the Blue Moon and pushed a coffee mug toward Jarek Denko. Her own stomach cramped with hunger and nerves. She should never have skipped breakfast.

"We've got to stop meeting like this," she said.

The creases deepened on either side of his hard mouth. "Over coffee?"

"In bars."

Denko looked around at the empty tables. Sunlight slanted through the shutters, gleaming on the bottles, dimming the neon beer signs along the walls. "I didn't know this place even opened at ten."

"Depends on who you know," Tess said smugly.

He blew on his coffee before sipping it. *Cautious,* she thought.

"And you know everybody," he said.

"Pretty much."

"Convenient," he remarked.

She shrugged. "As long as you don't mind everybody thinking that they know you."

"Is that a problem for you?"

Tess wondered if the gloomy booth was dark enough to hide her wince. She flashed him a smile, in case it wasn't. "It's a problem for anyone growing up in a small town."

"Don't tell me that," he complained mildly. "I just moved here."

"I think you'll be okay. You look pretty grown-up to me."

Grown-up. Yes. Hard and assured and competent. Tess had enjoyed watching him take command away from Bud Sweet, admired his immediate concern for poor Carolyn Logan.

Jarek set down his mug. "Honey, I'm past the age of worrying what other people think of me. But I'm planning on raising my daughter in this town."

Tess toyed with objecting to the "honey" and then gave it up. Three days ago, she'd swapped saliva with this man in front of his brother and a bar full of cops. She supposed that kiss created a bond, of sorts.

"Is she coming to stay with you soon? Your daughter?"

"For the weekend. Next weekend." He glanced at the bare table in front of her. "Aren't you getting anything?"

Okay, not much of a bond, she thought wryly. He still wouldn't discuss his family with her. "Tim's bringing me orange juice."

On cue, the bar owner appeared, a well-built, closely shaven man in his forties.

He offered her a tall, cold glass and a smile. "Here you go, Tess. You get home all right last night?"

Tess thought of Carolyn Logan and shivered. "I… Yes, I did."

"Just wanted to be sure. It was pretty late when you left." He turned to Jarek. "How's the coffee?"

"Fine. Thanks. You Tim Brown? The owner?"

Tim looked surprised. "That's right."

"Jarek Denko."

"The new police chief," Tess contributed.

"Yeah, I heard," Tim said. He stuck out his hand. The two men shook.

"Well…" Tim hesitated. "Can I get you folks anything else?"

"We're good, thanks," Jarek said.

Tim went back to the register. Tess waited for Jarek to say, "Nice guy," which is what everybody always said when they met Tim. When he didn't, she said it for him.

"Tim's a nice guy."

Jarek took another sip of coffee. "He grow up here, too?"

"No. He moved here from Chicago. He did something for the city. Sanitation? Firefighter? But he married a local girl. A cheerleader, even." Jarek raised his brows slightly. Tess explained. "Heather Brown went to school with my brother."

"Wouldn't that make her a little young for him?"

Tess thought so. But she said, "Not really. Tim had the looks to attract her and the money to keep her. The bar does very well during the season."

"And the rest of the year?"

"It pulls in enough locals to stay open. The after-shift crowd from the paper mill, mostly. There's not much to do in Eden on a Friday or Saturday night. Except the Algonquin lounge, and most people can't afford to drink there. I can't, anyway."

"Is that what you were doing here last night? Drinking?"

Tess suppressed a flash of annoyance. "No. I was meeting someone." When Jarek didn't react, didn't say anything at all, she sighed. "My brother. I was meeting my brother. He's a bartender here."

"What's his name?"

"Mark." Tess scowled. Jarek had actually taken out a little notebook and was writing stuff down. "But he doesn't have anything to do with this."

"Was he here?"

"Yes. He was working."

"Did you talk to him?"

"Well, yes. I told you, I came here to meet him." Because Mark, irresponsible, unreliable and infuriating as he was, could always make her feel better. And since her abortive kiss with Denko on Wednesday night, Tess had been feeling pretty lousy.

None of which she was confiding to Jarek Denko.

"Was that before or after you saw Carolyn Logan?" he asked.

"Before. We were talking, and then I went to the ladies', and when I got back, she was sitting at the bar."

Denko scratched something down. "What time would that have been?"

Tess did her best not to be intimidated by the damn notebook. Reporters used notebooks, too. It wasn't as if anything she said was going to be used against her. "Ten? Around then, anyway."

"Was she with anyone? Friends? A boyfriend?"

Tess shook her head. "She was alone. She had plans to come up with her roommate, but they fell through. She told me she didn't want to waste a guaranteed reservation, so she decided to make the trip alone."

"A reservation? You know where?"

Tess frowned. "The Bide-A-Wee, I think. In the lodge."

Jarek made another note. "Anybody hit on her while you two were talking?"

"I…" Tess stared into her orange juice, trying to re-create the scene in her mind. At the cash register, Tim Brown hunched over a calculator and a legal pad, reconciling the previous night's take. "Not really. She left a couple of times to dance. We both did. But mostly we just talked."

"We? You and Carolyn?"

No point in muddying the waters, Tess thought. "Yes."

"And your brother?"

Tess felt sick. *Stupid.* She had nothing to worry about. The years when she had to protect Mark were over. He was a grown man, a former marine who had returned from overseas with a chip on his shoulder, a tattoo on his arm and training in weapons and self-defense. None of which she needed to share with Denko. "I told you. He was tending bar."

"Right. He drive you home?"

"No. He lives at the other end of the marina. He's got an apartment over one of the boathouses."

"But you stuck around, maybe? Till he got off work."

"No." She wished to God that she had. "I left early. Around midnight."

"And was the victim, Carolyn, still there at 'around midnight'?"

"Yes."

"Still alone. Sitting at the bar?"

"Yes."

"And you don't know what time she left."

Tess picked at her paper napkin. "No."

"You okay?" Denko asked gruffly.

She straightened defensively against the vinyl seat back. "Why wouldn't I be?"

"Maybe because an hour ago you saw somebody you knew, somebody you'd talked with, hauled off in an ambulance?"

She was getting used to his perception. She wasn't quite as prepared for the way it made her feel: naked and warm.

But then he spoiled it all by adding, "Or could be there's something you'd like to tell me you haven't gotten around to yet."

"You have a nasty, suspicious mind, did you know that?"

His smile glimmered like a break in the ice. "Goes with the job."

"I'm not sure I like your job."

"Are you going to tell me about your ride in the police car when you were fourteen?"

Ouch. "No. Are you going to tell me why you cleared all your officers from the scene and called in the state crime scene investigation team?"

Something gleamed in his eyes. Respect, maybe. Or annoyance. "Noticed that, did you?"

"Yes. Is it relevant?"

"Relevant to what?"

She pulled out her own notebook. Let him see how he liked being the one questioned for a change. "To my story about the attack."

"Police blotter stuff," he said dismissively. "Not much of a story."

She tapped her pen against the blank page. "Maybe not in Chicago. But if tourists are getting raped by the side of the road in Eden, it is definitely a story."

She thought he tensed, but his voice remained calm as he corrected her. "One woman was attacked. That hardly constitutes a crime pattern, even in Eden. You shouldn't sensationalize."

She glared. "I don't call it sensationalism to warn the community."

"That's very public-spirited of you."

"You have a problem with that?"

"Not at all," he replied. "If the public interest is your actual objective."

"Excuse me?"

"Are you really interested in getting a warning out there, or do you just want to get a headline with your name under it?"

She rolled her eyes. "Oh, yeah, I'm a real glory hound, writing for the Eden *Gazette*."

"Big stories get picked up by bigger papers," he observed.

Her heart hammered. "And do you think this could be a big story?"

His lips firmed. "I think you might make it into one. If it suited your purpose."

She ran a hand through her hair in frustration. "Look, I'm not acting from sinister motives here. I just don't like secrets. I especially don't like the police keeping secrets." Boy, there was an understatement. She pushed away a sixteen-year-old memory. "And I don't appreciate you standing in the way of a story."

"Understood. I don't like secrets, either." His eyes, cool and steady as rain, met hers. "And I won't tolerate anyone standing in the way of an investigation."

Mark DeLucca had a face like an archangel on a cathedral wall and an assassin's flat, black gaze. It was a look likely to appeal to a lot of women, Jarek figured. Daring ones. Dumb ones. It remained to be seen if the victim, young Carolyn Logan, fit into either category.

"Your sister mentioned that Miss Logan spent a lot of time at the bar last night," Jarek said.

Mark continued to brush paint on the bottom of a skiff with sure, even strokes. Around the graying wooden dock, sunlight sparkled on dark water. The wind swayed the pines and tattered the white clouds high overhead. The whole scene was straight out of one of Pop's fishing magazines or a glossy Great Lakes travel brochure.

DeLucca looked almost as at home in this environment— a fallen angel in Eden—as Jarek felt out of place.

The younger man dipped his brush in a can of blue paint. "She was there."

His response didn't make it clear whether he meant his sister or Carolyn Logan. But at least he was talking.

Yeah, and if he said something incriminating and Tess found out about it, she'd likely murder them both.

Jarek shook his head. He had enough troubles with this case without worrying about Tess's reaction to him questioning her brother.

"Did you serve Miss Logan?" he asked.

Mark's mouth twisted with bitter humor. "I don't violate the underage drinking laws, if that's what you're asking. I carded her."

"And?"

"I gave her a Coke. She was nineteen."

A baby, thought Jarek, and imagined his daughter, his Allie, reaching nineteen. Damn it, Eden was supposed to be a safe place to raise children.

"Notice anything else?"

"It was an Illinois license, and she lied about her weight." Mark DeLucca shrugged. "Nothing unusual about either one."

"What about her conversation with your sister?"

"What about it?"

"Do you remember what they talked about?" *Did you talk with Carolyn Logan? Flirt with her? Rape her?*

"Why don't you ask Tess?"

"I'm asking you."

Mark DeLucca's eyes glittered with black amusement. "Well, now you can ask her. Because she just got out of her car, and she's coming over."

Jarek turned. Tess's car was parked in the shadow of the boathouse, and Tess herself was striding down the dock.

His headache returned with a vengeance. But despite his pounding head, he admired the picture she made, flying toward them with all the elegance and wicked intent of one of those black-necked geese defending its young. She wore jeans, and boots that were more suited to Michigan Avenue than a dock in the lake district, and an expression between hope and fury.

He caught himself stuffing his hands deeper into his pockets and smiled in wry recognition. *Look, don't touch.*

She stopped beside them, her breath quick through parted lips, her golden eyes bright and narrow with suspicion. "Mark."

Her brother straightened, wiping his hands on the thighs of his jeans. "Tess." His dry tone was a parody of hers.

Not a lot of love lost there, Jarek thought. But then she reached out and touched his jacket sleeve, and his hand covered hers in quick reassurance before they both turned to face Jarek. Now he saw the family resemblance he had missed before: the dark, straight hair and the dark, arched brows and the go-to-hell tilt of the jaw. Only Tess's mouth was full and soft, and Mark's eyes were black and cold.

"You didn't waste any time getting over here," Tess said to Jarek.

He met her gaze and her accusation calmly. "Neither did you."

"Do you two know each other?" Mark asked.

"We've met," said Jarek.

Tess's mouth flattened. "He pulled me out of a cop and groupie bar on Wednesday night."

Mark went as still as a coiled snake.

"Just keeping her out of trouble," Jarek said evenly.

"That's usually her job," Mark said.

Jarek raised an eyebrow. "Is that what she does? Keeps you out of trouble?"

Mark slanted a sharp grin at his sister. "When we were growing up, yeah. Not so much since I got back to town."

"You were away?" Jarek asked, deceptively polite.

"Six years."

He didn't elaborate.

"Prison?" Jarek asked.

The grin broadened. "Marines. So I figure I'm big enough to watch out for myself now." DeLucca looked at Jarek, and the amusement left his face. "And for her."

He was being warned off, Jarek thought. Fair enough. If his sister looked like Tess DeLucca, he'd bristle, too. But, Nora, bless her, had never been the black leather pants type.

Tess elbowed her brother in the ribs. "Stop it," she said. "So, what did you tell him?"

"Same as you, I bet. I met the girl last night. I didn't know her personally. I'm sorry some son of a bitch hurt her, and I don't know who did it."

Jarek persisted. "You can't remember who else she spoke with?"

"A bunch of rich kids came over from the Algonquin. I thought she was with them at first." His shoulder jerked. "Frankly I was more concerned with what my customers were drinking than who they were groping on the dance floor."

"And was Miss Logan groping anyone?"

Mark DeLucca's dark brows drew together in thought. "No," he answered at last, slowly. "No, she wasn't. She shot down Carl Taylor."

Who the hell was Carl Taylor?

"Taylor's Gas-N-Go," Tess offered before he could ask. "Married, two kids."

It was the kind of background information that Jarek desperately needed and sorely missed. And, because of Tess's undisguised partiality for her brother, the kind of lead he couldn't depend on.

"Thanks. So, she left alone...what time, Mr. DeLucca?"

"Late. Twelve-thirty?"

"That fits what I told you," Tess said.

Jarek threw her an annoyed look. She smiled back, both challenge and apology bright in those wide gold eyes. Why had he thought life would be simpler in Eden?

Do the job, he told himself. "You were responsible for closing up?" he asked Mark.

"Not last night, no. I clocked out around one."

"Also alone," Jarek said.

The gleam again. "If I'd been in the mood for company, I could have had some."

Okay, that was probably true. The DeLuccas were a good-looking family. "So, you weren't in the mood. Did you drive?"

"Are you kidding? I live five minutes away."

"But you do have a car."

"Sure. Right over there by the boathouse."

Jarek followed his nod. Parked beside Tess's tiny compact was a black Jeep Cherokee with dings in the side and mud on the tire guards. Very macho.

"Mind if I take a look?"

Tess cocked her chin. "Do you have a search warrant?"

Jarek understood family loyalty. Hell, he admired it, and

the stubborn angle of her jaw, but he wasn't going to let either one get in his way.

"Do I need one?" he asked Mark.

"If I say yes, will you go away and never come back?" Mark met Jarek's eyes and smiled slightly. "Yeah, that's what I thought." He gestured toward the Jeep. "Be my guest."

Jarek waited for Mark to pull out his keys and slouch ahead along the dock. Tess fell in beside them. The wind flattened her shirt against that amazing chest and plucked at her hair. Jarek caught a whiff of her shampoo, musky and incongruous against a background of diesel, woods and rising water.

"Did you tell him he could have a lawyer?" she asked.

Jarek's headache screwed up a notch. "No, I decided to skip that part."

"He has a right to a lawyer."

"I don't need a lawyer," Mark said.

Jarek tried to sound reassuring. "I haven't arrested your brother, Tess. He's not in custody, he's not obliged to answer any questions, and he's free to go at any time."

"After you look in his car," she said with disgust. "This is ridiculous, you know. I don't know what you've heard, but Mark would never hurt a woman."

He hadn't heard anything yet. He didn't know these people. A detective had to rely on his knowledge of a neighborhood, its feuds and alliances, its racial and religious makeup, its individuals' schedules and quirks. For the first time since he'd left Joe Arbuzzi's protective wing, Jarek was operating alone and blind.

He set his jaw against a surge of frustration. Based on Carolyn Logan's whispered testimony, Jarek couldn't even trust his own department.

Mark DeLucca unlocked the Jeep. "Tess, shut up," he said affectionately. "Let the chief do his job."

She glared at them both, her mouth mutinous. "I'm trying to *help* him do his job. He's wasting his time going after you."

Jarek hoped she was right. He liked Tess, with her hard attitude and her soft mouth and her instinctive defense of her brother. He sensed Mark DeLucca was a much tougher nut than his sister, but he didn't particularly want to arrest the guy for assault.

He stuck his head in the Jeep, looking for something really obvious to suggest that Mark DeLucca could have lured Carolyn Logan into his car, like a long blond hair or a missing earring or...

His heart rate jumped as he spotted it. Or a red-and-blue, dual-head strobe light mounted on the visor over the passenger side.

Jarek eased his shoulders out of the car, careful not to brush against the seat or the door.

"Do you mind if I get my kit from the car? As long as I'm here, I might as well do this properly." He looked directly at Mark. "You understand."

Mark went very still. His eyes went blank. "Yeah, I understand."

"I don't," Tess complained, her gaze darting between them. "What's going on?"

Jarek had a potential break in his case, and he hated it. "I just want to make sure I'm following procedure. I appreciate your cooperation," he said to Mark. "You must be in law enforcement yourself."

"No," Mark said flatly.

"My mistake. I just figured—" Jarek gestured. "You've got the signal lights."

"For rescue emergencies. I'm a Wofer."

''Wilderness First Responder for the county,'' Tess said. It was the second time that morning that she had explained something to him. Maybe she genuinely was trying to be helpful.

The possibility didn't make Jarek feel any better about what he had to do next.

Chapter 5

"Sorry, Tess." Sherry Biddleman looked up from the computer screen behind the nurses' station. "Immediate family only."

Tess dangled the white box in her hand by its string. "I brought hazelnut crescents. From Palermo's."

"Dang." The pretty, round-faced nurse stuck a pen behind her ear. "Are those for me or the Logan girl?"

Tess set the bakery box on the high counter that separated the nurses' desk from the hall. Her heart beat faster. "These are for you. I just want to see how she's doing."

I want to ask what she remembers.

I want to prove Mark wasn't involved.

"Not so good," Sherry said. "She came in with rib fractures and severe pulmonary contusion. They gave her a chest tube in E.R., and she almost bled out."

Tess's quick shudder was for real. "How is she now?"

"Better. Calmer." The nurse pulled a face. "Drugged."

Tess tapped a fingernail on the bakery box. "Look, I

know her. Couldn't I go down to her room and pop in for just a minute? Maybe until her family gets here?''

''There's a policeman sitting outside her door.''

Tess lifted the lid of the box. The scent of chocolate hovered in the air, briefly banishing the hospital smells of fear and sweat and disinfectant. ''Which policeman?''

''Paul Larsen.''

Tess bit her lip, considering. She remembered the middle Larsen boy. Fifteen years ago he played rowdy and unrefereed football in the park with her brother. He had married Connie the Eternal Virgin Kolicki, but even that hadn't soured him. He was a good guy, a likable guy. For a cop. Maybe he would even let her in to talk to Carolyn.

''I think I'll go say 'hi.'''

Sherry shrugged and helped herself to a hazelnut crescent. ''Sure. Give him a thrill. Just don't tell Connie I sent you.''

A big man erupted from a room at the other end of the hall. ''Where's a damn nurse?''

''Dang,'' Sherry said, and dropped her pastry.

''Emergency?'' Tess asked.

Sherry rolled her eyes. ''He thinks so. His wife's got some idea a stay in the ICU should come with room service.'' But she moved away smoothly to deal with the problem.

Tess eased in the opposite direction. ''Down here?''

''And right at the corner,'' Sherry called as she intercepted her patient's husband.

Right. Okay. Tess fought the flutter in her stomach as she hurried down the gray linoleum.

Jarek Denko was new in town. He might not automatically assume that trouble with a girl meant Mark DeLucca was involved. But somebody would tell him. Some outraged father or disgruntled boyfriend or jealous husband

would let him know that Mark DeLucca couldn't be trusted
around anyone wearing mascara, and after that it was only
a matter of time before Jarek came after her brother.

Who was she kidding? He was out to get Mark already.
She just didn't know why.

Tess slowed as she neared the end of the hall. What was
it about Mark's car? Because something had provoked Jarek's sudden wariness at the marina, the abrupt return of his
nightstick-up-the-back attitude. Something had made him
decide to attack her brother's Jeep with his scary black case
and plastic sample bags.

Mark told her not to worry about it. Mark said she was
overreacting.

Mark was a shortsighted idiot.

It was up to Tess to fix things. It was always up to Tess
to fix things.

She rounded the corner. But first she had to get past Paul
Larsen.

Back in the days when he used to collect bruises in the
park with her brother, Paul Larsen had been a skinny,
cheerful kid with a dark cowlick and a toothy smile. He
was old enough to shave now, and he was thicker around
the middle, but he still had the cowlick and the grin.

When he saw Tess, he smoothed the first and flashed the
second. ''Tess DeLucca!''

''Hey, Paul.'' She smiled back tentatively. ''I didn't
know Connie let you out on weekends.''

''I'm working,'' he explained, as if that weren't perfectly
obvious with him in uniform and guarding the open doorway. Beyond his molded plastic chair, Tess could see the
foot of a hospital bed. An observation window opened onto
the hall, but green-striped curtains blocked her view of the
room inside.

''Really? On a Saturday?''

He nodded importantly. "Patient protection."

"Wow. Big deal, huh?"

"Chief Denko asked me to come in," he confided. And then, as if even the name was enough to recall him to a sense of duty, he frowned. "What are you doing here?"

She looked at the decent young face of Mark's childhood friend and thought, *I can't do this.* "Oh, I brought Sherry some Palermo's crescents."

He whistled in appreciation. "She must have been a good girl."

She *had* to do this. For Mark's sake. Tess gave Paul her best let-me-out-of-this-ticket-officer look and said, "And have you been a good boy?"

He laughed and colored. "Pretty good."

"You should go get one. I brought extra."

He glanced at the open doorway behind him. "I don't know," he said doubtfully.

"Sherry could really use your help. And I don't just mean with the pastries. Some big guy was hassling the desk when I left."

Paul stood, straightening the crease in his uniform pants. "Well, that's no good."

"I could call you," Tess offered. "If I, like, hear anything in there."

"Yeah, okay." He took a few steps down the hall. "I'll be right back."

Tess nodded encouragingly. "I'll be waiting for you."

She watched him disappear around the corner to the nurses' station. Impulse warred with nerves in her stomach, already churning with the hazelnut cream she'd bolted down earlier.

Oh, boy. Jarek Denko was going to be royally pissed if he ever found out she'd decoyed Paul into deserting his post. Not to mention the chief's reaction if he discovered she'd butted in on his investigation.

But really, she was helping him, Tess rationalized. She knew this town better than he did. She knew Carolyn—okay, not well, but better than he did. And in her heart, she knew better than anyone ever could that Mark absolutely could not have done whatever Jarek suspected him of doing.

Tess shot one more look down the empty hall. She wouldn't break her word to Paul. She would wait for him.

"But not out here," she muttered.

Delivering bad news never got any easier, Jarek thought as he escorted the Logans onto the elevator. It didn't matter how many times you did it. It didn't make any difference if you were breaking the heart of an old man whose wife didn't survive a blameless trip to buy bread or a single mother whose son wouldn't be getting into trouble any more.

There was always the pain.

There was always the anger.

There was always the feeling in his gut that he could or should have done some damn thing to prevent the tragedy.

He knew different, of course. Common sense told him he wasn't responsible for every attack that took place on his watch. Almost twenty years on Chicago's streets had convinced him that no power or police force on earth could stop the stupid, wicked, crazy things human beings chose to do to one another. But if Jarek no longer believed he could stop bad things from happening, he made damn sure whoever did the bad things paid.

In Carolyn Logan's case, he didn't even have that reassurance.

Beside him, Dr. Richard Logan stared at the bank of

elevator buttons, his face carved like a Roman senator's and his eyes shattered. His wife Angela was talking spasmodically, in spurts of fury, bursts of grief.

The pressure at the back of Jarek's neck built with every restless rise of her voice. And when the elevator doors slid open and Jarek saw Officer Paul Larsen chatting up the round-faced nurse at the desk, it threatened to explode.

He balled his fists in his pockets. "Larsen," he said coldly.

The patrolman jerked like a trout on a line. "Chief! I was just—"

Jarek raised his eyebrows, conscious of Richard and Angela Logan listening anxiously beside him. "—asking about Ms. Logan's medical status?"

"I— Yes, sir."

"And how is she?"

"I—"

The nurse stepped forward, eyes sharp and smile bright. "Mr. and Mrs. Logan? Carolyn's doctor must have told you her surgery went very well. She's recovered from the anesthesia, but she's been sedated to relieve the pain of the rib fractures and to calm her down. Waking up unexpectedly in the hospital is a little upsetting for most patients."

So was being raped and beaten to the point of death, Jarek thought but did not say.

The grooves dug deeper in Richard Logan's face. His wife pressed a hand to her mouth.

"Can we go back now?" Jarek asked.

"Of course." The nurse—Sherry Biddleman, her ID tag read—smiled sympathetically. "Down the hall and to your right."

Jarek shot Larsen a look that pinned him to the gray linoleum tiles. "Would you wait for me here, Officer Larsen?"

"Yes, sir. Sir—" he began urgently as Jarek started after the Logans.

Jarek checked his stride. But he'd already spent too many hours today on damage control. He'd blown precious time that could have been put into the case running interference between his new department and an amused and superior state investigative team. He'd wasted focus sparring with Call-Me-Tess DeLucca and her bad news brother. Whatever Larsen had to say could wait until Jarek had reunited the Logans with their daughter.

"Save it," he ordered.

"But, sir—"

If he had to listen to any more explanations or excuses he was going to blow, and that wouldn't be good for Larsen, the Logans or the case.

Jarek strode down the hall, hands still clenched in his pockets, and caught up with the Logans as they turned the corner. An empty chair sat vigil in the hall outside Carolyn's room. The green curtains over the observation window were drawn.

Jarek hung back to give the Logans a moment alone to adjust to the sight of their daughter.

And then he heard Angela Logan's voice rising in bewilderment from inside the room. "Who are you?"

Busted.

Tess stared across Carolyn Logan's hospital bed. The thin woman with the uneven lipstick and expertly frosted hair must be Carolyn's mother. The upright citizen type with the kicked puppy expression would be her dad. And behind them, glaring at her with cold murder in his eyes, was Chief Jarek Denko.

Oh, boy.

With the heel of her thumb, she swiped hastily at her

tears. Her other hand still rested on Carolyn's. As surreptitiously as possible, she drew it back through the metal guard rails of the bed.

She was embarrassed at being caught. She hated being caught crying. She was here to give comfort, not receive it. Besides, streetwise reporters didn't break down at victims' bedsides.

Clearing her throat, she dredged up a smile. "Mrs. Logan? I'm Tess DeLucca. I stopped by to see how Carolyn was doing."

The woman's mouth worked. "Are you—are you a friend of Carolyn's?"

Conscience pinched Tess. "I— Actually we met last night. I was with her at the bar."

Mr. Logan scowled. "Carolyn was at a bar?"

The girl on the bed opened her eyes. "Daddy?" she whispered.

"Oh, my baby!" His wife stumbled across the room.

"Well." Tess stood awkwardly. "I'll just leave you to—"

"What do you know about what happened?" Mr. Logan demanded.

"Miss DeLucca has already given her statement to the police," Jarek said calmly. "We're following all available leads, Mr. Logan."

Tess sidled past them. "If you want to ask me any questions—or anything—I'd be more than happy to meet with you." She stopped to dig in the bottom of her bag. "Here's my card. You can call me."

"I'm sure the Logans will want to spend some time alone with their daughter first," Denko said. His voice was smooth and warm. His gaze, meeting hers over Logan's shoulder, cut like a saw blade in February.

"Right," Tess said, fighting a shiver. "Well, I really should be getting along. Nice to meet you. Both of you."

Mrs. Logan stroked her daughter's hand, completely ignoring Tess. Tears streaked her foundation. Tears leaked from the corners of Carolyn's eyes and ran into her hair. Mr. Logan looked at Tess as if he hated her.

Oh, God. Had Jarek told them about Mark?

She edged toward the door. "Call me if you need anything. I mean, I know you're from out of town, so if there's anything I can do—"

"Besides back off?" Denko murmured, very quietly.

She glared at him and tried for a dignified escape. But she should have figured the chief of police would track his man. Woman. Whatever.

He followed her into the hall. "I can't believe anybody would exploit a situation like that to get a story."

His low opinion stung. He was wrong about Mark. He had to be. And he was wrong about her.

She turned on him. "Is that what you think I was doing?"

"You gave him your card."

"In case they wanted to talk. Trauma can take the family of the victim that way. Sometimes talking is the only way to make what happened manageable. Bearable. You're a cop. You must know that."

Jarek's mouth thinned. "Is that what you were doing in Carolyn's room? Encouraging her to talk?"

Tess's heart hammered. "I wanted to see how she was doing."

Jarek tipped back his head and stared down at her. If he was trying to intimidate her, he was doing a great job. "I won't have you interfering with a witness."

She crossed her arms defensively. "I wasn't interfering."

"You didn't talk to her about the attack? You didn't question her?"

"Of course, we— I wanted to know if she remembered anything that could help."

"Help who?"

"Well…you," she said. And Mark, but now didn't seem like a real good time to bring that up.

"You want to help me," Jarek said without inflection.

She would not be bullied, however politely. All through her childhood, Tess had resisted the adults who looked down on her because she was a DeLucca. All her life, she'd fought the interference of patronizing teachers and meddling social workers and hostile cops.

"You ought to be glad that somebody wants to," she said. "I don't think you can rely on your department for this one, Chief."

"What are you saying?" Jarek asked, very quietly.

Oh, boy. "Carolyn said—she told me the car that stopped her, her attacker's car, had flashing red lights."

"And you suspect someone in my department."

"That's as likely as you suspecting my brother."

"Did Carolyn Logan tell you he didn't do it?"

Tess shook her head in frustration. "No. But she would have recognized Mark."

"Unless his face was covered."

Tess flinched.

Jarek went very still. "Is that it? Was her attacker wearing a mask?"

Tess nodded miserably. Had she just made things worse for Mark? "She thinks so. One of those stocking things. Like a bank robber on TV? She didn't see it at first, the headlights were behind him as he got out of his car. And by the time she got a good look at—at his face, she'd already unrolled her window. He unlocked her door."

"Did she see the vehicle? Was it a radio car?"

"No. She assumed it was an unmarked police car."

"Did she recognize the model? The make?" Jarek grilled her.

Dark and big and boxy, Carolyn's broken voice whispered in the back of Tess's mind. The description fit the chosen transportation of every weekend warrior in McCormick county. Half the population of Eden drove SUVs.

Or Jeep Cherokees.

"No," Tess said.

Jarek raised his eyebrows. "I'll talk to her."

"She thought she was getting pulled over by the police," Tess insisted. "That's at least as good a theory as saying my brother did it."

"Except that we know your brother had contact with the victim before she was attacked. There's no clear link between any member of the Eden police force and Carolyn Logan."

"That you know of. Yet."

"Police lights do not mean that the police are involved," Jarek said through his teeth. "EMTs have lights. Emergency responders like your brother have lights." He paused a moment to let that sink in and then said, "Chicago's only an hour away, and every fire fighter in the city has red flashers. Not to mention that any punk with a credit card and a hankering to play cop can buy signal lights over the Internet. We have to look for another connection."

Tess bit her lip. Okay, so the problem was bigger and more complicated than she'd thought. That was no reason to feel daunted. She was good at problems. "I could help."

"No."

"What are you afraid of? That I'll prove Mark is innocent?"

"You're the one who should be afraid," Jarek said

roughly. "Look at Carolyn Logan. You think if her assailant suspects you're involved in this case he won't come after you?"

She was mad at him for trying to frighten her. Madder because—oh, admit it—for a second he succeeded. "Make up your mind, Chief. You can't have it both ways. Either my brother is a suspect, in which case you can't possibly believe I'm in danger. Or he's not a suspect, in which case I won't compromise your investigation and I could conceivably help. Which is it?"

"I told you before, I don't theorize ahead of my facts. And I don't need you playing amateur sleuth on my watch."

"I am not an amateur sleuth. I am an investigative reporter."

His eyes gleamed. "Fine. Go report something."

"No gag order?"

"What?"

She angled her chin. "Am I allowed to report on Carolyn Logan's assault in my paper? Or would it be too damaging to the public's confidence in our fabulous police force if people in Eden knew that some joker with red lights was pulling women to the side of the road and attacking them?"

Jarek's mouth was a grim line. For a moment, he looked so serious that he almost revived Tess's moribund faith in the justice system. "It's not an issue of public confidence. It's a matter of public safety. Print your story. But leave the girl's name out of it."

Tess pulled herself up. "You can trust my discretion."

"No," Jarek said. He sounded faintly regretful. "I can't. I can't trust anybody."

How lonely. She pushed that thought away.

"That's mighty cynical of you," she said.

"Not cynical. Practical. I've worked with the media before." His gaze met hers in direct challenge. "You're not after the truth. You're after a story."

Chapter 6

"Terrible thing to read about in the paper," George Tompkins proclaimed as he rang up a customer at the hardware store.

Jarek, puzzling over paint samples one aisle over, stiffened. Despite his determination to put the case aside for a few hours, he caught himself listening for the unseen patron's reply.

"It was a terrible thing to happen," George's customer answered dryly. "Whether I reported it in the paper or not."

Tess DeLucca. Jarek recognized her husky drawl. He stared at the pink-striped paper in his hand, his insides churning with a whole mess of emotions. Anticipation. Regret. And a profound caution.

The feature story in yesterday's *Gazette* had painted a wincingly clear picture of his inexperienced officers trampling the crime scene. But if Tess hadn't spared his department, she hadn't pilloried it, either. The article stated plainly that the victim had been pulled over by an un-marked car flashing red lights. Tess had included Jarek's warning that female motorists signaled by any unidentified vehicle should drive to a well-lit, attended area before stopping. But she had made it clear that the unknown assailant was more likely to be an imposter than a member of Eden's own police force.

Jarek admired Tess's objectivity. And was grateful for it. He hadn't counted on her being fair, not after he'd ticked her off by vacuuming out her brother's car and making that crack about the media.

"The Chamber of Commerce is talking. An attack like that is bad for the town," George Tompkins was saying.

Tess's voice sharpened. "It's worse for the victim. Or are you suggesting we hush it all up and let the tourists take their chances? Not to mention the women who live here."

Jarek was tempted to applaud, which surprised him. He'd never really gone for the outspoken type. His ex-wife, Linda, had been the quiet sort.

Until she decided she wanted out.

He pulled another card at random—Cotton Candy through Dogwood Dream—and compared it with the one in his hand.

George Tompkins cleared his throat. "All I'm saying is, we didn't have this kind of trouble when Walter was police chief."

Jarek's hand tightened on the two strips of paper. Hell.

"Good thing, too," Tess replied smartly. "Because Walter Dale couldn't have solved a serious crime if his or anybody else's life depended on it. At least Denko has experience."

"He had to leave his job in Chicago. For personal reasons, I heard. You think maybe he drinks or something?"

The store owner's voice shifted suddenly. "Oh, sorry, Tess, I—"

She cut him off. "Where did you hear that?"

"Dick Freer."

Jarek frowned. Richard Freer—owner of Liberty Guns and Ammo—had been on the search committee that selected him.

"Well, I checked with Chicago, and our new chief is clean," Tess said. "You can tell that to Dick Freer."

Jarek heard the rattle of the cash register and then Tess swung around the stacked cans of paint at the end of the aisle, brown bag in hand, heading for the door with her long, get-out-of-my-way stride.

Jarek moved deliberately in front of her. "Thanks," he said.

She stopped. He watched, fascinated, as color swept from her throat to the tips of her ears. "You heard?"

He nodded.

Her hands fidgeted with her purchase, and then her chin went up. He admired her swift recovery. "If you really want to thank me, you can stop hassling my brother."

Jarek squashed his brief regret. "Your brother has already cooperated fully with the investigation. I don't have any reason to bother him again."

Unless and until the results came back from the state crime lab putting Carolyn Logan in Mark DeLucca's car on the night of the attack. But Jarek didn't see any reason to belabor that point now. He did not theorize ahead of his facts.

Tess raised an eyebrow. "Really? So it's just some odd coincidence that Bud Sweet has been by the marina six times in the past four days."

Jarek frowned. There was bad blood there. He wished he knew why. "I'll talk to him."

"I'd appreciate it." She edged around him.

He caught the scent of clean soap and musky perfume as she passed, and his lower body tightened. He wasn't ready to let her go, Jarek realized. Not yet. He hadn't spoken to her since that one unsatisfying phone interview three days ago when she'd checked the details for her newspaper article. He hadn't kissed her in over a week.

He jammed his hands into his pockets, and then pulled them out again when he remembered the paint samples.

"Nice job with the story," he said.

She looked unexpectedly vulnerable. "Are you kidding me?"

He wondered, with a funny fissure in his chest, if she wasn't used to compliments from anybody or if she just didn't expect them from him.

"No, it was good. Accurate without being inflammatory. And I appreciate you printing that list of cautions for motorists."

She shrugged, as if she didn't want him to see her pleasure. "That's me. A real public servant."

He met her gaze directly. "Maybe we have something in common after all."

Oh, boy.

The bottom dropped out of Tess's stomach as she was scorched by those intense, light eyes. How did he *do* that, render her speechless and yearning when she wanted to be quick and cool and angry with him?

She flipped back her hair. "Great. So now we're pals. Want some friendly advice?"

She felt his slight, polite, unmistakable withdrawal. Jarek still wouldn't tolerate her interference. Okey dokey. This was better. Anyway, it was safer. But she missed his heat.

"Thanks, but I don't need your help," he said.

With the investigation, he meant.

Her heart beating faster, she nodded at the strips of paper in his hand. And took a chance. "You do if you're planning on painting your house pink. I've got to tell you, folks around here are conservative. Pink flowers, pink flamingos, maybe even pink shutters, you could get away with. But no pink houses. This isn't Miami, you know. It isn't even Gary, Indiana."

He studied her a moment. When he smiled, the warmth reached right across the aisle of Tompkins Hardware and made her face glow.

"The samples are for my daughter's bedroom," he explained.

She grinned foolishly back. "Well, that's a relief. What is she, eight?"

"Ten."

Tess shook her head. "Then, no. She won't put up with pink, either. I mean, not that it's any of my business, but—"

"Actually," Jarek said gravely, "Allie wants to paint her room black."

Tess bit her lip. "I take it this is a problem?"

He gave her a twisted smile. "One of several recently."

She didn't want to know. She didn't want to care. *I raised one family already. I'm not interested in taking on another.* But when she looked at Jarek, the humor curling the corners of his mouth, the frustration lurking in his eyes, her resolve slid away.

"What about a compromise?" she suggested.

"What did you have in mind?"

"Does she have a favorite color? Besides black," Tess added.

The frustration deepened. "I don't know," Jarek said.

What kind of father didn't know his little girl's favorite color?

Hers hadn't, Tess reminded herself. Of course, most days Paul DeLucca hadn't remembered her name, either.

Jarek frowned at the samples in his hand. "She's staying with my parents now. Her room at her mother's was pink. I thought it would help Allie feel at home here if I painted her new room the same color."

"Okay." Tess decided. "You can have points back for that."

He raised his eyebrows. "Are we keeping score?"

She flushed. "Sorry. That was rude. It's no concern of mine."

"No?" His voice was gentle. "How old were you when your father left you, Tess?"

"I—" —*don't talk about it.* That was one of the rules in an alcoholic household. Everybody in town knew her story anyway. But Jarek just stood there in the middle of the paint aisle, strong and silent as a rock and about as immovable. She gave up trying to get around him.

"Nine," she said finally. "I was nine."

"That's tough," he said.

She couldn't bear his sympathy. She couldn't trust it. It made her feel things, want things, she was better off without.

She shrugged. "I'm a big girl now. Does your daughter have a favorite shirt? A favorite dress? Could you ask your mother?"

He accepted her change of subject. "Allie's favorite shirt is blue." She must have looked surprised, because he added, "I'm a detective, Tess. We notice things like clothes. We just don't talk much."

"I figured that out," she said dryly, resisting him.

He smiled again, and her breath caught even though she didn't want it to.

"So, what about blue?" she asked hastily. "For her room, I mean."

He hesitated. "Blue would be okay. I guess I wanted something more—"

"Feminine?"

"—special," he finished.

Her heart melted. Her imagination grabbed hold. What would a special bedroom have meant to her, twenty years and a hundred broken dreams ago? "You could stencil something. Or sponge-paint clouds. Or—" She broke off.

Jarek was shaking his head.

"Sorry," Tess said stiffly. "That's probably not what you had in mind."

"It's exactly what I had in mind." His gray eyes were rueful. "I just can't paint worth a damn."

She grinned. "You're not telling me there's something the Great Chief Denko doesn't know how to do."

"I'm telling you there are some things I know better than to try."

"Chicken," she teased.

"Would you do it?"

"Sure, I—" Too late, she saw the trap he had set for her. "I don't think that would be a very good idea."

"Why not?"

"I thought we agreed we had a professional relationship."

The crease deepened alongside his mouth. His eyes gleamed. "You could consider this another professional courtesy."

Right. She remembered the angles of his face in the moonlight and the warmth of his lips on her cheek, and her heart boogied in her chest.

Don't be dumb, DeLucca. Jarek Denko wanted something. And it probably wasn't her.

"What about my brother?"

"What about him?" Jarek asked steadily.

"Come off it. I watched you vacuum out my brother's Jeep. You can't tell me he isn't a suspect in the Logan case."

An edge crept into his voice. "Tess, at this moment half the population of McCormick County is a suspect in the case. Including the officers under my command. If I avoided everyone who had or might have a personal connection with this crime, I'd be commuting from Canada and taking my meals in Wisconsin."

He was alone in this. *Just like she was.*

And then he added, "Besides, you told me Mark didn't do it."

Hope lurched inside her. "Do you believe me?"

She thought his disciplined body tensed. But his voice was calm and even. "That's not the question. The question is, do you believe it enough to take a chance on painting my daughter's bedroom?"

Good question. Tess looked down at the brown paper bag that held the new valve system for her toilet. Maybe he was right. Maybe she did need to trust more, in Mark or in herself. She certainly didn't want Jarek to think she had doubts about her brother's innocence.

And maybe that's what he was counting on.

Jarek couldn't really think she was going to blurt out incriminating evidence against her brother while she daubed clouds on his daughter's walls. Could he? She snuck a look at his face. It didn't give her a clue.

"You're holding out on me again," she complained.

"I hold out on everybody," Jarek said.

She narrowed her eyes at him.

He sighed. "What do you want to know?"

She tried not to let her surprise show. "Well… Um, how is the investigation going? Are you close to making an arrest yet?"

"Is this a private conversation or am I going to read about it in the paper?"

She put her chin up. "You aren't going to trust my discretion?"

"No."

"Okay." She couldn't blame him for that, she supposed. At least he was talking to her. "It's private."

He glared up and down the deserted aisle. At the register, George Tompkins discussed crabgrass with a customer. Jarek lowered his voice. "Then—not for the record—this investigation is going nowhere fast," he said.

"That's bad." Bad for Carolyn Logan and her family. Bad for Jarek, dealing with the weight of the town's expectations. And bad for Mark.

"It's not good," Jarek acknowledged. "But we're dealing with a traumatized victim with short-term memory loss, a compromised crime scene and no witnesses. It's going to take some time."

"The people at the bar…?"

"I've got a statement from your brother and a list of customers from Tim Brown. I'm working my way through both of them."

Tess nodded to disguise that the thought of Jarek taking Mark's statement didn't make her very, very nervous. "Well, that should be productive," she said brightly.

"Not really." Jarek started sorting the pink paint samples back into the correct slots in the display rack. Tess blinked at this evidence of his thoroughly orderly mind.

"Most of the kids Carolyn met from the Algonquin were only in for the weekend," he continued. "It's taken my officers three days just to track them all down. And not all of their families have been what you'd call cooperative."

"Rich, nervous daddies with lawyers?" Tess guessed.

Jarek smiled in acknowledgment. If she didn't watch it, she'd start imagining there was some kind of bond between them. "You met them?"

"I know the type." She had even dated a few, smooth boys with fast cars and nice clothes, before she learned better. "One of them might have had trouble hearing 'no.' Who else?"

"Carl Taylor."

"What does he say?"

"He claims he was home at the time of the attack. His wife backs him up. But she was mighty unhappy to hear he was at Tim's that night instead of working the late shift at the Gas-N-Go."

Tess frowned. "You can't think Valerie Taylor—"

"I don't," Jarek assured her. "Though if I were old Carl, I'd be prepared for some hot words and cold meals over the next couple of weeks. What do you think of this blue?"

She glanced at the strip in his hand. "Nice. Are you speaking from experience?"

Those remote gray eyes studied her. "Do you want to know if I spent my married nights out drinking with the boys, Tess?"

Yes.

She flushed. "No. Just making conversation."

"Fine." He turned back to the paint samples. His shoulder, hard and warm, brushed hers.

She should drop it. It didn't matter. She didn't care.

She stared at the ranks of blue on blue until, needled by the memory of her parents, she blurted out, "Did you?"

"Did I what?" Jarek sounded distracted.

"Spend your nights in bars?"

He carefully replaced another strip. "More than I should have," he said quietly. "Making detective— It's not like when you're on patrol. Working cases takes more out of you. More time. More commitment. And if you're good at it, you start thinking like the safety of the city depends on you. You get a promotion. You get a reputation. You start believing you are one hot son of a bitch."

"Ice Man," Tess remembered.

"Yeah. Only—" He broke off.

"You start drinking," Tess said flatly. The sinking disappointment she felt surprised her.

"Just a couple of beers," Jarek said. "To take the edge off, you tell yourself. Once you make Area 3, you get cases you would never in a million years want to take home with you. Real bizarro stuff, race crimes, sex crimes, crimes against kids... So even when you get off the job, you don't go home. You go to the Joint with the guys to talk it out or drink it away, and you leave your wife home alone with the baby."

His behavior was understandable. Excusable, even. Except that Tess had heard enough excuses growing up to last her a lifetime.

"Are you telling me that's the way 'it had to be'?" she asked bitterly.

"No," Jarek said. "I'm telling you that's how it was. I'm not proud of what I put my family through."

"Then why stick with it? I mean, you're willing to make a life change now. Why not then?"

"Because by the time I figured how much damage the

job was doing to my marriage, Linda had decided that the only thing she liked less than my absence was my company.''

Ouch.

"You still could have made time for your daughter,'' Tess said stubbornly.

"Maybe I could have. Only Linda convinced the judge that I couldn't provide Allie with the stable home a little girl needed.'' He shrugged. "Well, she was right. She wanted me out of their lives. It seemed kinder to give her what she wanted.''

"Or easier,'' Tess said.

Jarek turned his head. His face was set. His eyes were bleak. "Not easy,'' he said.

And even though Tess knew better than to trust in regrets and promises, she believed him.

He selected another blue-striped card. "Anyway, I learned my lesson. I'm not going to make the same mistake with Allie.''

"What does your daughter think about you moving up here without her?''

"She knows it's only temporary. Just until the school year is over. I figured she's had enough disruptions in the past twelve months.''

He still didn't say how Allie felt about it, Tess noticed. But she admired his apparent determination to do right by his daughter. Jarek Denko was a decent guy who was obviously ready to shoulder his responsibilities, put his past behind him and settle down.

Too bad that was the last thing she was looking for.

"So, how about it?'' Jarek met her gaze, his smile warm and his eyes coolly challenging. "Want to join my house painting party? Sunday, four o'clock. I should be done with the walls and ready to start on clouds by then.''

It wasn't her house, Tess rationalized. It wasn't her daughter. She could see Jarek again without really committing to anything at all.

But the very temptation she felt to say 'yes' warned her she was already too involved. ''I, um, I'll have to let you know.''

Jarek nodded. ''Fair enough.''

If her answer disappointed him, Tess thought crossly, he hid it very well.

''They're not coming,'' Aleksy said, lowering his paint roller.

Jarek pulled another long strip of masking tape from around the bedroom window. ''Who's not coming?''

''Whoever you keep hoping to see out there.'' His brother stepped back to examine the wall's new coat of sky-blue paint. ''Okay. We're done. So, who are you waiting for?''

Jarek frowned at the ball of sticky tape in his hand, vaguely embarrassed both by his brother's perception and his own disappointment. He didn't like thinking his attraction to Tess was that obvious. ''I thought Teresa DeLucca might stop by.''

Aleksy raised dark eyebrows. ''The babe? Way to go, bro. It's about time you got back in the game.''

''Don't get too excited,'' Jarek said dryly. ''We bumped into each other when I was picking out the paint, and she happened to mention she had some experience.''

Aleksy grinned. ''Better and better.''

''Painting experience, moron.'' Jarek wadded the trash into the bag in the center of the room. ''Neither one of us is interested in anything else. Besides, like you said, she's not coming.''

"Too bad. I wouldn't have minded getting to know her better. Since you're not interested.''

"Go to hell,'' Jarek said amiably.

Aleksy grinned.

They worked a while in companionable silence, collecting brushes and stripping the last masking from the white trim.

"So, any breaks in the Logan case?'' Aleksy asked.

Jarek poured paint from his tray back into the can, carefully controlling his frustration. "Nope.''

"Did you hear from DCI?''

The Illinois Department of Criminal Investigation. Since Eden lacked its own forensics department, Jarek had turned the lab work in the case over to them.

"Not yet. Seems they've got bigger fish to fry than my nonfatal assault. I did get the serologist's report.''

"And?''

"The only blood he identified from the car or kit is Carolyn Logan's. Her attacker was either really careful or my officers contaminated the scene before I got there.''

"You still beating yourself up about that?'' Aleksy asked.

Jarek smiled wryly. "I don't have to. I've got the entire town council in line waiting to take a swing at me.''

"It's not your fault the responding officers screwed up.''

Good old Aleksy. But Jarek shook his head anyway. "It's still my responsibility. At this point, I'm hoping that either DCI will identify latent fingerprints in the car or that the trace and fiber evidence will match with one of the suspects.''

His brother frowned. "Look, bro, I don't know your people. Are they that incompetent? Or could one of them be tampering deliberately with the scene?''

Jarek had forced himself to face that possibility already. ''A cover-up, you mean? Because there's a chance Carolyn Logan's assailant could have been on the job.''

''Maybe.'' Aleksy knocked the lid back on the paint can. ''Or maybe some jackass just wants to make you look bad.''

Jarek shifted the empty tray and wiped his hands on a rag. ''I don't know. That's the worst of it,'' he said honestly. ''Not knowing. I've got a couple of veteran officers who don't trust the way I do things and a bunch of rookies who want to imprint on the first suspect they see like a bunch of baby ducks.''

Aleksy snorted with laughter. ''And who do they like for Mama Duck?''

Jarek dropped the paint rag into the trash. ''Mark De-Lucca.''

''DeLucca, huh? What is he, like, a cousin?''

''Brother.''

Aleksy whistled. ''Close family?''

Jarek thought of Tess reaching for her brother's arm and the quick way his hand covered hers on his jacket sleeve. ''Very.''

''Hell. He do it?''

It was an echo of Jarek's own words. *You told me Mark didn't do it.*

And Tess's question, taut with hope: *Do you believe me?*

Jarek rubbed the back of his neck. ''If I listen to my lieutenant, I'd say yes. If I went with my gut like you do, I'd have to say no. But I don't theorize ahead of the facts, Aleksy. You know that.''

"Guess it's a good thing she decided to blow you off, then."

Yeah. But...

Jarek looked out the window at the bare little yard and empty sidewalk in front of his new house. "I like her," he admitted.

"Hey, I like her, too, bro. That doesn't mean I want to see you mixed up with the suspect in an ongoing investigation."

The truth stung. "Tess isn't a suspect. And she could be useful. She knows this town."

"So, get a guidebook."

"She's loyal."

"Get a dog."

Jarek turned sharply.

"Okay, okay." Aleksy raised both hands in surrender or apology. "That was out of line. But, jeez, Jarek, couldn't you find someone less—" he caught his brother's eye and changed whatever he'd been about to say "—complicated?"

Jarek shrugged. "Maybe I like complicated."

"Right. If she were a nice quiet girl from a good Catholic family you probably wouldn't go for her."

His observation was accurate enough to make Jarek uncomfortable. "I married Linda, didn't I?"

"Yeah, and we all saw what a raging success that turned out to be."

"Not her fault," Jarek said automatically. "My head was in the job."

"Exactly my point. It's not like you to put a woman before a case."

"That's not what I'm doing."

"What the hell are you doing, bro?"

"What the hell business is it of yours?"

"Look." Aleksy stabbed his fingers through his hair, leaving a streak of blue paint behind. "When I moved up to detective, you made sure I knew the score and kept my nose clean. I owe you. Don't screw this up."

Jarek grinned in appreciation. "Thanks, but I'm good."

"You're going to have to be." Aleksy held his brother's gaze a moment and then shrugged. "Okay. Your call. At least the babe will keep you—"

"If you say young, I'll have to hurt you," Jarek warned.

"You can try. Anyway, I was going to say, 'on your toes.' But keep your head down."

"Don't sweat it, hotshot. Like you said, she's not coming."

The doorbell chimed in the hall.

Aleksy raised his eyebrows. "Sure about that?"

Jarek ducked downstairs without answering him.

Chapter 7

It was her. Tess.

Jarek could see her waiting on his front porch, her image unmistakable through the flat security glass on either side of the door, looking like something he'd dreamed up to go with the house. With her smooth dark hair and tight dark jeans, she plainly hadn't come prepared to paint anybody's bedroom.

Though Jarek sure wasn't going to object if she decided to inspect his.

He opened the door, so damn glad to see her he was practically speechless. "Hi."

Her eyes were wide and gold. Her smile was nervous. "Hi."

He gestured to the paper sack she clutched in front of her like a tackle dummy. "What's this?"

"Oh." Collecting herself, she thrust the bag at him. "I brought you a housewarming present."

He took it. Sniffed. The mouthwatering aroma of fresh

baked bread escaped from the top of the bag. Pleased by her thoughtfulness, he asked, "You make this yourself?"

Her ivory skin turned a dull red. "No. The bread's from Palermo's, the olive oil's from my pantry and the wine is from the bargain bin at The Hop and Grape."

"Great," he said. "Thanks." He didn't care about the bread. Or the wine. "Why don't you come in and I'll see if I can find a corkscrew?"

Her lips parted. "Well, I—" Her gaze went past him to the stairs. Her face changed. "You didn't tell me the Boy Scout was going to be here."

Jarek turned as Aleksy sauntered across the tiny foyer, his face sharp and his eyes skeptical. Swell. And here Jarek thought Tess's brother was going to be the problem.

"Aleksy." It was a command. "Come say 'hi' to Tess."

"You bet. Hi, Tess. How's the family?"

Tess stiffened. "Just fine. What have you told him?" she asked Jarek.

He sighed. "We discussed the case. Very generally."

Her eyes betrayed her hurt. Her lips firmed. "Well, *generally,* I don't stick around while someone disses my brother. Enjoy the wine." She started to back out.

"Watch yourself." Jarek caught her elbow before she tumbled down the steps. "Aleksy, go into the kitchen and find the corkscrew. And see if you can locate your manners while you're in there."

Aleksy hefted the bag with the bottle and went.

Jarek tugged Tess gently forward. "Can we try this again? Hi, Tess. Nice of you to stop by. Can I offer you some wine?"

She tossed her dark hair. "Is your brother planning on adding anything to my drink?"

"I'll watch him," Jarek promised.

"And that's supposed to make me feel better?" Tess muttered. But she let him lead her into the living room.

She sat on the edge of his wide leather couch and looked around appraisingly. The room was fully furnished with his parents' comfortable castoffs and some overstuffed favorites from his bachelor apartment.

"Wow. You look moved in," Tess said. "I was expecting boxes."

Jarek shrugged. "I've been here two weeks."

Her gaze traveled over the framed family photos along one wall. "Is that your family?"

He glanced over his shoulder at Allie's school portrait and a snapshot taken in front of the Grand Canyon when he was twelve. His pop had his arm around his mom. His little sister Nora was mugging for the camera. Nothing he could see should have put that deep suspicion in her voice. "Some of them. Why?"

Her thumb fretted the nail polish on her index finger. "I'm just saying I've been in my apartment for ten years and I don't have all my pictures hung up yet."

Okay. He already knew she wasn't a nester. He couldn't seem to bring himself to care. "Did you come over to point out how we're different? Or to give me a hand with Allie's bedroom?"

She shifted awkwardly against the fat leather cushions. "Neither one, actually. I came to give you this." She dug in her over-the-shoulder bag and handed him a few folded sheets of paper.

"What is this?" he asked quietly, not opening them.

"A copy of your profile for the *Gazette*."

He frowned. "I agreed to help you with the motorist safety piece instead."

"That was last week. This week I'm introducing Eden's new police chief to the town."

He hated to rain on her parade. "Tess—"

"Read it," she urged. "It's good."

"I'm sure it's well-written," he said carefully. "But it's not news. I thought you understood that."

"Let me worry about what's news. You can concentrate on what's good PR for your department."

"Right now I want to concentrate on this case."

"Well, a little spin won't hurt you or the case. In fact, it could help."

"And what's this help going to cost him?" Aleksy asked from behind them.

Jarek twisted around to see Aleksy standing in the living room doorway with the bottle of wine in one hand and a bouquet of glasses in the other.

"Can it," Jarek said briefly.

His brother hunched one shoulder. "Hey, don't get mad at me. I found your corkscrew."

"But not your manners."

Tess straightened on the couch beside him. "You can't honestly think I'd write a puff piece for you because I want some kind of favor."

She looked indignant. Worse, she looked hurt.

Jarek wanted to reassure her. But his memory was very good. And what he remembered at that moment was Tess standing in the aisle of Tompkins Hardware saying, *If you really want to thank me, you can stop hassling my brother.*

"My God, you do," Tess said slowly. "That's exactly what you think."

"I haven't formed an opinion one way or the other," Jarek said evenly, doing his best to be fair.

Wrong answer.

Tess stood. Her eyes simmered. "Well, this has been fun. We must do it again sometime." She stalked to the door, and even Aleksy was smart enough to get out of her way. "Like when hell freezes over," she said, and left.

The door shook in its frame behind her.

Aleksy propped one shoulder against the doorway. "So, you're good with this one, huh?"

Jarek rubbed the back of his neck. "Shut up," he said.

Ungrateful, suspicious, cold-blooded *pig*.

Tess yanked the toilet's shutoff valve and smacked her head against the bottom of the sink. Tears sprang to her eyes. She blinked fiercely.

She would not cry. Just because her toilet leaked and Jarek Denko was a dyed-in-the-wool traitor rat fink was no reason to cry.

She was a grown woman. She was responsible for her own plumbing. She was responsible for her own feelings. Maybe she hadn't had a lot of experience with—she squinted at the package from the hardware store—with floating-cup ballcocks, but she had plenty dealing with unreliable, two-faced men. Any pain she felt was her own darn fault, for thinking Jarek was any different.

She flushed the basin and dropped a towel into the tank to soak up the remaining water. He should have been—maybe grateful was too strong a word, but she sure hadn't done a hatchet job on the man. It wasn't easy conveying why this cool-eyed, tough-minded homicide cop from Chicago belonged in sleepy Eden. But she had. He did. He had the sense of place and love of family to become a part of this community. He had the grit and integrity to protect it. Tess had drawn on his partner's stories and her own observations to write about both sides of Jarek Denko.

And in return she'd hoped, she'd expected...

You can't honestly think I'd write a puff piece for you because I want some kind of favor, she had told him.

His cool reply burned in her memory. *I haven't formed an opinion one way or the other.*

Tess grabbed the old water inlet pipe and twisted. The hell with him and his opinions.

The pipe came off in her hand, water dribbled on the floor, and she looked around frantically for the directions.

Twenty minutes later when her intercom buzzed, she was fed up enough to cry. She was sure she'd positioned the new unit in the tank correctly. The flapper chain was connected, the overflow tube was hooked up...and water still gurgled into the toilet in a noisy stream.

The buzzer nagged her again.

Tess tripped over a plastic utility bucket on her way out of the bathroom and mashed down the intercom button. "What?"

"It's 'who.' Denko."

Heat swept her chest, her face. She pressed her forehead against the cool plaster wall.

"Tess? Can I come up?"

Yeah, sure. That's all she needed to make this evening perfect. A visit from the Ice Man.

She buzzed him up without answering and padded barefoot to the door to let him in. She would not dash to change her clothes. She wasn't even going to brush her hair. She hadn't asked for company. Especially not his.

Taking a deep breath, she yanked open the door. Jarek was standing back a few feet, so that if she'd bothered to look through her peephole she could have seen him. It was a nice gesture. A cop's move. He looked great, calm and dry and solid in faded jeans and a navy-blue sweater.

Tess clutched the edge of the door, suddenly conscious of her old gym shorts and tangled hair. Irritation raised her chin.

"I have a wrench," she said, "and I'm not afraid to use it."

"I can see that," Jarek agreed, laughter sparking in his eyes.

"What do you want?"

Down the hall, a hinge creaked as old Mr. Nelson kept an eye on the comings and goings in the hall.

Jarek rubbed his jaw. "That was a nice piece you wrote for the paper."

She struggled to hide her pleasure at his compliment. "I know."

"I wanted to tell you."

"Thank you."

He lowered his gaze a moment. "And I wanted to apologize."

"Okay." Oh, God, was he looking at her undershirt? Was it wet? She crossed her arms over her wildly beating heart. "Make it good."

Jarek looked up again, and he was definitely smiling. "I apologize."

Her elderly neighbor shuffled into the hall in his even more ancient bathrobe. "You all right, Teresa?"

She cleared her throat and called, "I'm fine, Mr. Nelson, thanks. Harry Nelson," she explained to Jarek. "Used to be a security guard at the paper mill."

He nodded in acknowledgment. "Look, do we have to talk out here? I could do without an audience."

Tess sniffed. "I thought you didn't care about public opinion." But she opened the door wider and stepped back.

Maybe not far enough. His hard, curved shoulder brushed her arms as he came in, and she caught a whiff of his aftershave. Bay rum. It should have struck her as old-fashioned, but he just smelled clean and nice.

He stuck his hands in his pockets and looked around the

dingy hall to her living room, strewn with newspapers and decorated in Early American Garage Sale. She waited for him to make some crack.

"Got a problem?" he asked.

"What's that supposed to mean?"

"You've got a bucket out. Tools. I thought maybe you were having a problem with your water."

Heat washed her face. "Oh. Yes." But she wasn't ready to throw the towel in yet. Unless it would stop the leak. "I'm working on it," she said.

He nodded. "Want me to have a look?"

She liked that he offered. She liked that he *asked,* instead of just taking over. And what harm could it do? Let Chief Never-Let-'Em-See-You-Sweat Denko get his hands wet and dirty for a change.

She shrugged. "You can if you want."

He wasn't a big man. But her tiny bathroom seemed even smaller with two adults maneuvering inside. Distracted by their close quarters, it wasn't until he had the top off the tank and his sweater pushed back to the elbows that she told him, "I already replaced the float cup. But the water won't stop running."

He had great forearms.

"That's because you've got mineral deposits on the valve seat," he said.

How did he know?

She retreated to the doorway and watched as he detached, scoured and replaced things. Under the navy sweater, the long muscles of his back bunched and stretched as he reached to turn her water back on.

Water gurgled, ran...and stopped. No drip. No leak, Tess thought with relief. But the silence that bubbled up to replace it was nearly as noticeable.

"That should do it," Jarek said, and washed his hands at her sink.

"You didn't tell me you used to be a plumber."

He sent her a slow, sideways grin that scrambled her breath. "You have no idea the things I can do."

Oh, boy. The tiny bathroom felt humid and close. She could smell her soap on his skin.

In a panic, she backed into the hall. "So, what else did you do today?"

His hard face lightened with amusement. "We had one funeral procession, four driving with suspended licenses, and one criminal trespass. Didn't need the SWAT team at all."

Why did he have to be able to laugh at himself? It made him too likable. And much too attractive.

Tess retreated to the living room and barricaded herself behind the couch. "No progress on the Carolyn Logan case?"

Jarek strolled after her. "That's the third thing I came to tell you. The results on the trace evidence came in. None of the carpet fibers recovered from the Logan vehicle match your brother's Jeep."

Hope tightened her throat. "Does that prove Mark didn't do it?"

"It doesn't prove he did do it," Jarek answered carefully.

He was honest.

That was something.

It wasn't enough.

She arched her eyebrows. "Disappointed at losing your favorite suspect?"

"Not really. And your brother isn't my lead suspect."

"Just Sweet's."

Jarek's mouth compressed. "Is Lieutenant Sweet still giving you a hard time?"

"No," she said fairly. "At least, Mark says he didn't stop by the marina today."

"And you? Is he bothering you?"

"He always bothers me," Tess said without thinking, sweeping up an armload of newspapers.

"Why?"

"Oh." Damn. She was rattled. Jarek's closeness, his questions, his concern, rattled her. "It doesn't matter."

"It might."

She was increasingly afraid that he was right. But she didn't want to go there, even in her own mind. Her columns championed small town truths. But some lies, surely, were better left buried?

She stuffed the papers under an end table and turned to face him. "Why don't you accept I just don't like cops?"

His lids dropped, half hiding the brilliance of his eyes. "Why don't you give me a chance to change your mind?"

She saw the kiss coming. He gave her time to evade it, if she wanted to.

She didn't want to.

His lips were warm and firm. His tongue was bold and persuasive. His hands as they moved around her were confident—not clumsy, not greedy—and his chest was hot and solid. He still smelled like bay rum, but now the scent mingled with the faint heat raised by his working and the trace of her soap on his skin. Her muscles clutched inside.

Wow, could he kiss. Even after their kiss at the bar, his finesse came as a surprise. She was still subconsciously braced for search-and-seizure technique.

She slid her own palms up the rough knit of his sweater and touched the warm, smooth back of his neck. He inhaled sharply, and it was as if he took all of her oxygen, because she got dizzy then. She had the sense of being sucked into something she wasn't ready for, something big and fast and dark and dangerous, but it was hard to think of that, of all the reasons why she really did not, should not, must not want him, when his mouth was so hot on hers, and his body was warm and solid against her, and his hands were sure and a little rough.

He moved one hand between then and cupped her breast, and her blood rose. She could feel him through his jeans, against her belly, feel him rising, too. She smiled with pure pleasure against his mouth, not thinking at all, and rubbed against him. He made an encouraging sound deep in his throat and kissed her some more, hot, wet, urgent kisses, while his palm grazed her nipple through the fine ribbed undershirt she wore.

She wrapped one leg around him, desperate to get closer to his strength, to his heat, and he shifted somehow so that she straddled his muscled thigh. *Good,* she thought. *More.* He said something—she was pretty sure it was her name— and pushed down the neckline of her undershirt. Her breast popped out, all eager, and just for a moment she looked down, and the sight of Jarek's long, blunt-tipped fingers on her plump breast shocked her back to reality.

She wanted this. Wanted him.

And the realization scared her.

"Stop," she said.

His fingers flexed. "What?" He sounded distracted.

"I think we should stop," she said, hating the idea.

And he did.

Just like that, she thought, both relieved and faintly insulted. He released her, and tugged her shirt gently up to cover her breast and shoved his hands into his pockets.

"Why?" he asked.

She struggled for distance. "Is this a cop thing? Asking questions? Do I have the right to remain silent?"

"You have any rights you want. Including the right to say no. But I'd like to know why."

Her hands were shaking, and she didn't have any pockets to hide them. "I'm not what you want," she blurted.

"You're kidding, right?"

She glared.

He nodded. "Not kidding. Okay. You want a look at the evidence?"

She glanced at the front of his jeans and then jerked her gaze away. Her face burned. "I didn't mean sexually. Maybe it's possible for you to compartmentalize what you're feeling. Maybe that's part of your job, I don't know. But I can't. I won't. I have to figure out what an involvement would mean."

His eyebrow lifted. "Does it have to mean anything?"

She hugged her arms tight, covering her breasts. "Are you offering me casual sex, Denko?"

"If I do it right, there won't be anything casual about it."

The images fired her brain. The air left her lungs. Tess opened her mouth to breathe and then realized she was gaping at him like a fish and closed it again.

"Sex for sex's sake?" she said, trying to come across as cool and sophisticated and instead sounding confused. Or even, heaven help them both, intrigued.

Those clear gray eyes caught hers. "It's a place to start," Jarek said.

"But I don't know where we're going," Tess protested. "I don't even know if I want us to go anywhere. Look at this place. Look at me. You've got me picking up newspaper, for crying out loud."

He frowned. "I didn't ask you to straighten the paper."

"Well, no, not exactly. That was an example." She flapped her hand in frustration. "I just meant, you're the kind of guy who's responsible for things. You're committed to your job and your mortgage and your daughter, and I can't even commit to a house plant."

"Have I asked you for a commitment?"

"I—" Deep humiliation swept through her. "No."

"Right." He took his hands out of his pockets. "Do us both a favor. Stop worrying about what you think I want. Decide what you want. And if you want this—" he gripped her shoulders and kissed her, firmly, briefly, on the mouth "—you know where to find me."

She listened to the click of her door echo in her quiet apartment. Of course she wanted this. Wanted him. What red-blooded woman in her right mind wouldn't? And apparently she could have him, too, without guilt or expectations on either side.

The thought left her flat.

Tess sighed and went to mop her bathroom. It would be a cold day in hell before she admitted what she really yearned for to Jarek Denko.

Or even acknowledged it to herself.

Chapter 8

"What are you drinking?" Jarek asked.

Bud Sweet eyed the specials chalked over the bar at the Blue Moon. "Well, that depends. Is the department buying?"

Jarek hid his irritation. "This one's on me."

He listened impassively as his lieutenant ordered the most expensive import on the board, trying hard not to dislike the man.

Tess's voice popped into his head. *Maybe it's possible for you to compartmentalize what you're feeling. Maybe that's part of your job.*

You bet, honey.

And Jarek was not about to let his impatience with Sweet—or for that matter, his attraction to Tess—interfere with him doing his job.

"Coffee," he told Tim Brown. He glanced toward the bar. "Mark DeLucca not in today?"

"He had some training class at the hospital at four," the

bar owner said. "He'll be on tonight. Can I get you anything else?"

"We're good, thanks."

"You think that's safe?" Sweet asked as Tim left their table. "Giving DeLucca another crack at the Logan girl?"

Jarek sighed. He was here to caution Sweet, on neutral turf and out of hearing of the rest of the department. But the veteran officer seemed determined to spoil the cooperative mood Jarek was striving for. "Laura Baker's at the hospital. Besides, we don't have any proof that DeLucca's our man."

Sweet snorted. "Right. And I'm not Santa Claus, but that doesn't stop my grandkids from expecting presents at Christmastime. I say lock him up before he hurts somebody else."

"Teresa DeLucca seems to think he couldn't have done it."

"Oh, yeah. The sister. There's a character witness for you."

"I take it you two don't get along?" Jarek accepted his coffee from Tim Brown with a word of thanks.

Sweet took a pull at his beer. "Is that what she told you?"

"What should she tell me?"

"Who knows? The DeLuccas were always troublemakers. The father was a brawler, the mother was a drunk and the boy was a punk."

Holy St. Mike. Jarek absorbed this latest information like a blow, trying not to let the shock show. Tess's mother an alcoholic? But it made sense. Perfect sense when he considered Tess's protective attitude toward her brother, her lack of trust, her determination not to take on the responsibility of another family, even her habit of ordering club soda.

But Jarek still didn't see how Tess's "good child" role, which frequently fell to the oldest in an alcoholic household, jibed with Bud Sweet's verdict on her family.

"And Teresa DeLucca?" he asked quietly.

"No better than she should be." Sweet set down his bottle and leaned forward confidingly. "I busted her once for shoplifting."

"How long ago?"

"I don't know. I was just a rookie."

Sweet had been on the force almost twenty years, Jarek reckoned. Which meant Tess had to have been in her early teens.

I had my first ride in a police cruiser when I was fourteen.

Regret slid under his ribs like a knife. Ah, Tess. Oh, hell.

"What did she take?"

Sweet leaned back against the padded bench. "Some kid's toy. How should I remember?"

"You don't seem to have any difficulty recalling her family's other problems," Jarek said levelly.

Sweet scowled. "Look, don't bust my balls. Big city cops don't understand how it is in a small town. You stick around long enough and you'll see things different."

"Not so differently that I'd judge someone before I've got all the facts."

"You can't be taking their side in this."

"There are no sides," Jarek said. Okay, "Us" versus "Them" was built into the job. But the same professionalism that made cops band together was supposed to eliminate personal prejudice from their dealings with the public. "Our department serves the citizens of Eden. *All* the citizens of Eden. Whatever our personal feelings may be."

Sweet leaned over the table. "See, now, if I were you I'd want to keep personal feelings out of this discussion,

Chief. Or are you going to tell me that wasn't Tess De-Lucca seen coming out of your house on Sunday night?''

The protective rage that licked along Jarek's nerves took him by surprise. But he kept his gaze steady and his tone even. ''I'm not telling you anything, Sweet. Except that as long as you're a member of this department, you'll behave with professional detachment on the job. And I expect to be kept in the loop on this case. Do I make myself clear?''

''I do my job. I've done this job for twenty years. Nobody comes along and tells me to do it any different. Who the hell do you think you are?''

''I'm your boss,'' Jarek said. ''And on my watch, you do as I say.''

Sweet muttered something—*See how long that lasts* was Jarek's guess—and eased his bulk from the booth.

''Thanks for the beer,'' he growled, making the courtesy sound like an insult. ''Boss.''

He swaggered from the room.

Tim Brown stepped over to collect the empty bottle from their table. ''You don't want to take anything that Bud says too seriously.''

Jarek looked up at the bar owner: forty-plus, neat, with regular features and close-cropped brown hair. A ''nice guy,'' Tess had called him.

Jarek shrugged. ''After twenty years on the force, the man's entitled to his opinions.''

Tim topped his cup with hot coffee. ''I meant about the DeLuccas. Mark's all right. And Tess—''

Jarek narrowed his eyes. ''Just how much did you hear?''

Tim laughed. ''Bartenders hear everything. We're like priests that way. Or hairdressers. Anyway, the parents weren't worth much, but Tess is a good girl.''

Jarek wondered how Tess would react to hearing herself described that way. "You know her well?"

"Not as well as the previous owner. From what I heard when I bought the place, Tess was always in here, bringing Dizzy—that's Isadora DeLucca, the mama—home. Girl knows what she owes her family."

He sounded approving. Jarek just felt sad, thinking about a half-grown Tess taking on the responsibility of a drunken mother and a troubled younger brother. *I raised one family already. I'm not interested in taking on another.*

Hell, he knew that. That's why he'd suggested simple sex.

He smiled wryly to himself. Yeah, and hadn't she jumped at that offer.

Maybe it would be better for everyone involved if he concentrated on his daughter. Focused on the investigation. Keep personal feelings out of it, he'd told Sweet, and it was good advice.

Only then he got this image of Tess, the laughter in her eyes and the softness of her mouth and her body, hot and tempting in that skinny ribbed undershirt she'd had on the other night, and he thought, *I want this.*

All he had to do was keep his relationship with her neatly separate from everything else, the way he'd always divided his family life from his work, and his sex life from his family, and he could have it all. Do it all. Have her.

He took an unwary sip of coffee and burned his mouth.

She was not waiting for the phone to ring, Tess assured herself as she stood on a chair to reach the top of her crowded bookshelves. She was doing some overdue cleaning, that was all. A thirty-year-old woman, a professional, a reporter, had the right to a clean apartment.

Jarek's deep voice reverberated in her memory. *You can have any rights you want.*

Her arm jerked, and she sneezed on a cloud of dust.

She hopped off the chair to attack the next shelf. Ayn Rand was cheek to cheek with C. S. Lewis, mystery competed for shelf space with the latest chick lit from Britain. There was her Lakeland Award "For Excellence In Local Journalism" the bronze-and-black plaque read next to a rare picture of Mark at seven, scowling distrustfully at some other mother's camera. She touched the dusty glass with her finger.

There were no pictures of the two of them together, no hovering parent to capture birthday shots and vacation snaps. Of course, there had been no birthday parties or vacations in the DeLucca family, either.

Tess set the frame down with a crack. She really needed to get more pictures for her apartment.

The phone still didn't ring.

She finished dusting and ran her wheezing vacuum, emptied wastebaskets and stacked the last armload of newspapers by the kitchen door for recycling.

I didn't ask you to straighten the paper, Jarek observed.

Go away, she told him crossly in her head.

Her heart cried, *Call me.*

She struggled with the dead bolt on the back door, grabbed her garbage and stomped down the half enclosed steps to the Dumpster in the alley. Up and in with one bag. Up and in with two.

The sudden noise and movement spooked a black shadow under the Dumpster that scuttled toward her feet.

Her heart stopped. *Rats?*

But it was only a black cat, young and bandy-legged.

Tess's heart resumed beating. "You scared me."

The cat gave her a look out of pale green eyes—*Hey,*

you scared me first—sat by her feet and proceeded to wash. It was very dirty, or maybe not particularly well fed, because its coat was harsh and almost gray in places.

She bent cautiously to pet it.

It crouched away from her hand.

"My mistake," she said, straightening. Rejected by a stray, for crying out loud. "It won't happen again."

She went back for the recycling. When she reached the landing, she glanced over her shoulder. The cat was watching from the bottom of the stairs.

Tess opened a can of tuna fish and balanced it on top of her stack of newspapers. Well, she didn't want some stray eating out of the Dumpster, did she?

Dumb, DeLucca, she thought as she picked her way down the steps. That cat is probably halfway to Wisconsin by now.

But it wasn't. It was sitting right where she left it, in a patch of sun that showed up its scrubby fur and those white whiskers, startling against its little black face.

When it smelled the fish, it made a rusty sound, more squawk than meow, that surprised them both. Tess set the can on the ground by the bottom of the stairs. The cat picked delicately and then started bolting the food.

Great. She hoped it wasn't going to throw up.

She watched for a moment before turning to sort her recyclables into the fiberglass igloos provided by the town of Eden.

This time when she went back upstairs, the cat followed her. Tess stopped on the landing. "Sorry, kitty. You've got the wrong apartment."

The wrong idea.

The wrong girl.

From half a flight up, through her open apartment door, she heard her telephone ring. Just for a second, she felt the way she had in high school, when Danny Lipinski called and for one crazy moment she'd actually believed that the president of the student newspaper might ask wild Tess DeLucca to the prom.

She sprinted up the stairs, lunged for the door, and snatched the ringing phone off the wall. "Hello?"

"Tess, it's Jarek."

She leaned against the kitchen counter, trying to disguise her heavy breathing. The last thing she wanted was for him to think she was some kind of phone pervert. "Well, good morning. What can I do for you?"

"Come to the station," he said. "I have a story for you."

Tess clutched the receiver. A story was good. A story was better than a date. Wasn't it? She wanted to keep things professional, and Jarek was treating her as a professional.

But as she stood in her kitchen, feet cold against the linoleum, she had the same drop in her stomach she'd felt when she finally realized that Danny Lipinski only wanted her help with his English paper. She'd given him the help, Tess remembered, and charged him twenty bucks for it. Her first earnings as a writer.

She cleared her throat. Swallowed her hurt. "What kind of story?"

"A follow-up article."

Confusion joined the mess of emotions churning inside her. "To your profile? But that won't run until—"

"To that motorist safety tips thing you wrote."

"Another public service piece?" she asked doubtfully. Her editor wasn't likely to go for that. "I don't think—"

"I'm not going into this over the phone," Jarek said, his voice tight. "Get down here."

Tess sucked in her breath. He sounded serious. "I'm on my way."

She hung up the phone. But when she turned to shut the

door, the black cat was there, crouched low, one paw over the threshold.

In or out?

Stay or go?

Tess fidgeted. She didn't have time to wait for some alley cat to make up its mind about whether or not she could provide a suitable home life.

The cat slunk in, keeping close to her cabinets.

"Don't look so worried," Tess told it. "It's not like you can stay. I don't think the building even allows pets."

The cat sent her a deeply suspicious look and hunkered down by the refrigerator. Its shoulder bones stuck up sharply from its back.

Okay, fine. Just because it was in her apartment didn't mean she had to keep it. But there was no way Kitty was going to let her pick it up, and she didn't have the time or the heart to chase it.

She closed the back door, shutting the cat into her kitchen, and grabbed her purse and went out the other way.

"So, what's the story?" Tess demanded, planting her round, firm rear end in the ugly chrome frame chair that the town of Eden accorded to its public servants.

Jarek's mouth twitched. What did he expect, a "hello"? Did he really think she would ask how he was doing or why he hadn't called after practically jumping her bones two nights ago?

Hell, she probably didn't want him to call. Phone calls suggested a relationship, an involvement, and Tess had made it plain she didn't want to be tied to a man already bound by a demanding public job, a twenty-year mortgage and a preteen daughter.

Or was it that she didn't expect him to call? Didn't think enough of herself, or him, or that mind-blowing, blood-heating kiss to think that it warranted a how-are-you the morning after?

Maybe she hadn't even noticed. She was a beautiful, vibrant, young woman. Maybe enough men had groped her in her living room that—

Tess frowned in apparent concern. "Are you okay?"

No. He was out of his mind.

Keep the job separate. Focus on the job.

"Fine," he said.

He came around his desk and sat on the corner, so that he looked casual and friendly and still topped her by a couple of feet. Yeah. Like subliminal intimidation would work with Tess.

"But we do have a problem."

She crossed her legs. "Who's this 'we,' kemo sabe?"

He narrowed his eyes. "Do you want me to call your editor and request another reporter?"

Tess grinned. "Sorry, sorry," she said, not looking sorry at all. "What's the problem?"

He hated that what he was about to tell her would wipe that smile right off her face. He hated what he had to tell her, period.

"A local woman was on her way home last night when an unmarked car with a red emergency light signaled her to pull over."

"Who was it?"

"You know I can't tell you that." Just as he knew it was only a matter of time before Tess found out.

"How is she?"

"Fortunately she had read your motorist safety piece in the paper. She knew what happened to Carolyn Logan. She did what you suggested—flashed her lights and drove here, to the police station. The car followed her to the parking lot entrance and then drove off."

"You were here?"

"I came in." Bud Sweet, eager to pay Jarek back for his warning, had been only too happy to call him shortly after midnight to report this latest attempt. Jarek had insisted on taking the woman's statement himself. "She was okay. Shaken. Angry."

Tess nodded. "The whole town will feel the same. Folks in Eden don't like to think something like this can happen here. Especially not to one of our own."

Jarek didn't like to think it could happen, either. But he said, "Human nature doesn't stop at the city limits. Your mayor understood that when she hired me. Hatred, greed, revenge…the motives behind most crimes are the same wherever you live."

"The motives may be. But up until now, crime in Eden has been pretty tame."

"The one good thing is that this attempt makes it unlikely that the driver of the car was a member of my department."

"Why? Oh. Because a police officer could have followed her into the parking lot and pretended this was a routine stop."

Jarek nodded, impressed by her perception. "Unless he didn't want to call attention to himself."

Tess tapped one red fingernail against his desk. "Of course, if this was a copycat attempt, then your officers would still be under suspicion for the first assault."

Of course, too much perception could be a bad thing, too. "Which is why," Jarek said, "I am personally checking all of their alibis for that night."

Tess's golden eyes widened. "Ooh, I bet that's making you popular."

"It sure as hell isn't doing a lot for morale, let me tell you."

"It's not just police morale you have to worry about. The people who live here are going to be upset."

He knew that. This latest attempt, following less than two weeks after the attack on the Logan girl, could be a public relations nightmare for his department. His officers were bound to blame him for the fall out.

"That's why I called you. I don't want a panic or a witch hunt on my hands. And I can't afford to have my officers' time taken up by every outraged Joe Public calling about what he thinks he heard in the checkout line or at last night's church committee meeting. I want an official statement in the paper before the rumors start."

Tess hefted her bag onto her lap. Her dark hair swung forward as she rummaged inside. "We go to press tonight."

"Can you get something written in time?"

She brandished her notebook at him. "That depends on what you give me."

He smiled in appreciation. "Nothing that will fuel the gossip. The intended victim was driving on north Front Street at approximately eleven-thirty on Tuesday night when a police impersonator signaled her to pull over. The Eden Police Department is issuing a warning to motorists. Thanks to a similar warning in last week's *Gazette* and the woman's own quick thinking, she was not harmed."

"Gee, a compliment for the press. My editor will like that," Tess remarked.

"That's what I'm counting on." He hesitated. *Concentrate on the job, Denko.* "There's something else you need to know."

"It gets better?" she asked dryly.

"It gets worse. The victim didn't go straight home after work. After her shift ended at eleven o'clock, she stopped at the Blue Moon for a drink."

Tess's mobile face froze. But her shrug was quick and casual. "What's so bad about that?"

Jarek watched her, compassion stirring inside him. "Your brother served it to her. He was the last person the victim talked with before she drove home."

Chapter 9

Tess met Jarek's cool, gray gaze, her throat closing in disappointment. She never learned.

News flash, DeLucca. He's not letting you in. He's using you.

She swallowed hard. "Did you call me figuring I'd downplay the story because my brother is your prime suspect?"

"No," Jarek said. "I don't have a prime suspect. The investigation hasn't singled out anyone yet."

She curled her nails into her palms. "Or ruled out anyone, either, right?"

"The police are currently pursuing all leads. You can print that in your paper."

He was so calm. So careful. She felt like throwing things. "I'm a reporter. Not the police department's mouthpiece."

One eyebrow raised. "Are you saying this isn't news?"

"I'm saying, I won't write anything but the truth," she said doggedly.

"That's what I'm counting on."

She glared at him, unsure if she'd been complimented or insulted. Uncertain what his cooperation meant for Mark.

He smiled at her, and some of her hostility faded like fog on a windshield. "Come on, Tess," he coaxed. "Write the story. Don't let everybody get their news from Ed Miller at the barbershop."

And they would, she acknowledged. Talk of the attack would sweep through town like fire, crackling with self-interest and fueled by prejudice.

You know about that girl attacked on her way home from the Blue Moon?

Heard the police questioned the bartender.

And, most damning of all, *Well, what did you expect from a DeLucca?*

"How am I supposed to resist that?" she muttered crossly.

How was she supposed to resist him? He knew her weaknesses too well.

"I hope you won't," Jarek said, standing.

His knee brushed her thigh. Even through two layers of fabric, his warmth reached out to her. He looked good in uniform, disciplined strength in starched navy-blue.

She tightened her hold on her pen and reached for her professionalism. "So, are the police assuming this attempt was perpetrated by the same person responsible for last week's assault?"

He watched her for a moment, amusement and something else in his eyes. "'Perpetrated' is good. You read a lot of those true crime stories?"

She didn't want him to make her laugh. She didn't want him to make her hot. She tapped her pen against the page.

Jarek sighed. "I don't assume anything. Once something like this gets reported in the paper, there's frequently a rash of copycat crimes. But given the similarities—deserted road, time of night, red light on the visor of the car—we certainly have to consider that the incidents involve the same person.''

''You're not giving me much.''

''I don't have much.'' Frustration edged his tone.

She felt an instant's sympathy for him, which she squashed. ''Can I talk to the victim?''

''You know I have to protect her identity.''

She knew. And respected him for it. ''You can't blame a girl for trying.''

''I don't.''

She could almost believe him. It was a heady feeling. She wasn't used to believing in anybody. ''Well.'' She stood, which brought her eyes level with his chin, her breasts within inches of his starched shirt and muscled chest. ''Guess I'll go home and get to work. Can I call you? If I have follow-up questions, I mean,'' she added hastily.

''I'll be in and out, but sure. Or I could stop by your apartment. Later.''

Memories of the last time he stopped by heated her face and thickened her blood.

''Maybe that's not such a good idea. I've got to, uh—''

''Work on your story,'' he suggested.

''Yes.''

''Wash your hair.''

''Well, I—''

''Organize your sock drawer.''

No way was she confessing she'd spent the morning cleaning her apartment. She lifted her chin. ''Feed my cat.''

His laughter was a warm breath against her lips. ''You don't have a cat.''

What the hell, she thought. ''I do now.''

"What kind of cat?" he asked indulgently. He didn't believe her.

"No kind," Tess said. "It's a stray."

He drew back, his light, clear eyes studying her face. "You're serious," he said on a note of discovery.

Panic set in. "Not very. I haven't decided to keep it yet."

"How did you find it?"

"It found me," she explained. "This morning, when I was taking out the garbage. I just haven't had time to call animal control yet."

"That's my department. I can let Gail know. Although..." Jarek looked thoughtful. "Maybe Allie would like a kitten."

Another kind of panic stirred. Along with a sense of attachment? Kinship? Feelings she didn't want to examine but found hard to ignore. "It's more like a cat. And not a very pretty cat," she said.

Jarek shrugged. "I can take a look at it anyway. No sense sending it to the pound without a trial."

She wasn't sending it to the pound, Tess thought suddenly, fiercely. It was her cat. Hers.

Which was stupid, because she didn't have room in her life for a pet.

"I guess you could stop by," she said grudgingly.

"Fine. Eight o'clock?" Jarek said, so smoothly that she wondered if she'd been set up.

"Eight," she agreed.

"Do I remember who I served last night?" Her brother looked up from the knot he was tying along the boom or the beam or whatever that arm thing on a sailboat was called. The wind ruffled his dark hair, making him look young and piratical. "What the hell kind of question is that?"

Tess squirmed. "It's for a story I'm working on," she said.

She hated keeping things from Mark. But knowing too much when the police came to question him could be more dangerous for her brother than knowing too little.

"Right." Mark finished with the rope and ducked under the swinging arm. "This isn't about the attack on Sherry Biddleman last night, is it?"

"No, it's—Sherry?" Tess blurted, genuinely shaken.

He cocked an eyebrow. "You didn't know?"

"Jarek didn't say—" She stopped.

Mark was shaking his head. "God, you're easy, you know that? Is that why you're here? You running errands for the police chief now?"

"No. He called me to give me a statement for the paper."

"What's the headline? Bad Mark DeLucca Suspect in Sexual Assaults. See Lynching, page five?"

She shivered. "Don't talk like that."

Mark stared at her with black, bleak eyes, and then his face softened. He touched her cheek in a rare caress. "It's okay," he told her. "I didn't do it."

Tears stung her eyes. "I know that," she snapped. "But you served Sherry drinks last night."

"I took her order. One rum and Tab. And she spent most of the night complaining to Tim Brown how her husband doesn't like her working the late shift."

"That's it?" Tess pushed, eager to believe him.

His gaze shifted left. "That's it."

Her heart broke a little. Because she knew the signs. She had raised Mark. She'd forced his confession when he was nine and ran his bike through the Tompkins's rosebushes. She'd cracked his alibi when he was fourteen and blew off school to go swimming at the quarry. He'd lied to her then, and he was lying to her now.

"Mark," she warned, in the same tone of voice she'd used for all their lives.

"Don't worry about it, Tess."

"How can I stop worrying about it if I don't even know what it is I'm not supposed to worry about?"

"Did you understand that sentence?" Mark asked. "Because I sure didn't." He searched his sister's face and then sighed. "Okay. Sherry and I— I saw her earlier yesterday at the hospital."

Tess squinted against the glare coming off the water. "Why?"

"I had a training class."

"No, I mean what difference does it make if she saw you or not?"

Mark shrugged and tightened a line in the pointy part of the boat. "We kind of had words. I stopped by to check on Carolyn Logan, and Sherry wouldn't let me back to see her."

Misgiving clutched Tess's stomach. She took a step along the dock. "Oh, Mark. Jarek already knows Sherry was at the Blue Moon last night. If he finds out—"

"Relax. You're wasting your breath and your time. Your boyfriend was already out to see me."

Jarek's words came back to her: *The investigation hasn't singled out anyone yet.*

And her own reply: *Or ruled out anyone either, right?*

"He's not my boyfriend," Tess said.

"Good. What is he?"

"He— We— What did you tell him?"

Mark lifted his face to the wind and grinned a wolf's grin. "As little as I could get away with."

"Be careful," she said. "Jarek isn't stupid, but there's a lot of pressure on him to arrest somebody."

"Don't worry about me. I'm not the one who needs to watch out for this guy."

Tess squirmed. "What are you talking about?"

"He's taking advantage of you, the way everybody takes advantage of you. Using you to get his little public service message out."

She didn't want to believe Mark. But hadn't she suspected the same thing? Jarek already assumed she'd written her profile to win some kind of special consideration for Mark. Maybe Jarek figured she would put some spin on this story, too, as part of the same strategy.

"He could have gone to my editor," she said.

"Maybe he did. Or maybe he figured he didn't need to."

She felt slightly sick.

"I don't think that's it. He—"

Kissed me, she thought.

"—fixed my toilet," she said.

Mark grunted. "That only proves he wants something."

Tess tried to make a joke. "Maybe it's just sex."

Her brother's eyes narrowed. "Oh, that makes me feel better."

"Yeah," Tess said gloomily. "It doesn't do a heck of a lot for me, either."

Mark straightened. Water slapped the sides of the boat as it rocked under his shifting weight. "Wait a minute. It's not like you're looking for a long-term relationship, right?"

Heat rolled up her face. "Thank you. Now I feel really cheap."

He shook his head impatiently. "I just meant you know better than to get all knotted up over casual sex with some overage cop."

Jarek's voice reverberated along her bones. *If I do it right, there won't be anything casual about it.*

Tess shivered. "He's not that old," she said.

Mark raised an eyebrow.

"Forty," she said defensively. "Anyway, what does it matter?"

"That's what I'd like to know. You don't need somebody else in your life to take care of, Tess."

"I think Jarek Denko can take care of himself," she said honestly. That steely-eyed competence was one of the things that made him so attractive. And so dangerous. The balance of power was all on his side.

"Fine. And while Denko's looking out for number one, who's going to look after you?"

Uncertainty made her snap. "I don't need a baby-sitter, baby brother."

"How about a warden?"

"Very funny."

Mark jerked at the end of a line. "Yeah, it'll be a scream if he locks both of us up."

She stared at him, stricken.

Mark sighed. "Okay, maybe not. Are you going to write this article for him?"

Her hands curled into fists. "I'm going to write the article. That's my job."

"He's using you."

Her fingernails pressed the inside of her palms. "Maybe. Better me than some other reporter."

"Better for him."

"Better for us," she insisted. "I get a lead story, and you avoid that lynching headline."

Some of the tension left Mark's lean face. He reached across the narrow gap of dark water and flicked her nose gently with his finger.

"DeLuccas forever, huh?"

It was their childhood pledge, their schoolyard battle cry. Affection for her brother burned like tears at the back of Tess's throat. No unreliable and unproven attraction to the town's new police chief could be allowed to matter compared to that old loyalty.

Ignoring the whisper of her heart, Tess gulped and smiled weakly. "DeLuccas forever," she promised.

"I'm late," Jarek said to the shadowed curve of Tess's face. He couldn't read her expression through the crack in her door. But he could see his watch just fine.

It was after nine o'clock.

Late went with the job. Jarek had given up explaining it or apologizing it away. His ex-wife, Linda, had claimed his explanations bored her, and his apologies had stopped making a difference after the first rocky year of their marriage.

Tonight he'd shoveled through a stack of case reports only to be caught on his way out the door by a concerned phone call from Eden's mayor. Jarek accepted the necessity of dealing with both.

But faced with Tess's half-closed door, he felt as disadvantaged as a teenage stud rolling up for a date in his mama's minivan.

Tess shrugged. "I didn't have plans tonight, anyway. I had a deadline, remember?" She swung the door wider. "Watch the cat."

He looked down at the cat, and then up at Tess. She may not have made plans, but she was armored for a date in stiff dark jeans that showcased her amazing legs and a militantly red blouse with hidden buttons.

He got the message. *Look, don't touch.*

If her cat was in the same pissy mood, he'd wasted a trip. His daughter Allie needed warmth. Fun. Affection. All the things, Jarek reflected with a twinge of guilt, her father hadn't been around to supply.

He nodded toward the cat, regarding him disdainfully from its post by Tess's feet. "It doesn't look in any hurry to run away."

"That's because it just ate. It might change its mind."

"It must be female," he teased.

Tess tossed her hair back from her face. "I think it's learned from experience not to be too trusting."

O-kay. Definitely in a mood.

Jarek shoved his hands in his pockets and eased forward, careful not to spook the woman or the cat.

"What's going on, Tess?" he asked quietly.

Her gaze dropped. "Nothing," she muttered. "Let me get you a box. You'll need something to take her in."

Her, he noted. So the stray was female. And possibly more important to its rescuer than he'd supposed.

"Are you sure you want me to?"

One shoulder jerked in a bad-tempered shrug. She turned from him and started down the dingy hallway.

"Sure," Tess said. "What am I going to do with a cat?"

He watched the cat trot after her, its bowed legs a pair of parentheses, its tail a question mark. He strolled behind them into the kitchen.

Tess grabbed a brown grocery bag from under the sink and began loading it with stuff.

"Seems to me like you've made a good start," Jarek observed. "What have you got there? Food, water bowl, litter—"

Tess arched her eyebrows. "I may not be much of a housekeeper, but even I know not to shut up a cat for the day without a litterbox."

"So you're just providing basic care."

"Yes."

"No sentimental attachments at all."

"No."

He grinned as she dropped a yellow mouse in on top of the other supplies. "So, what's the cat toy for?"

Tess blushed dull red. "I have to protect my furniture," she said defiantly.

"Good thinking," Jarek said.

She shot him a suspicious look, her eyes mutinous, her mouth wretched. Tenderness punched his chest. And a stab of impatience. Why did it matter if he knew or guessed she was a sucker for one bandy-legged stray?

"Tess. Why don't you keep the cat?"

"I can't."

His cop's mind considered reasons why. "Against the building rules?"

"No. I don't know."

He propped a hip against her countertop. "We had a dog when I was a kid," he offered. "Black-and-white Border collie. Sasha."

"What's your point?"

He wasn't sure yet. "I was just remembering. Pets can add a lot to your life."

Tess rolled her eyes. "Yeah. Like hair on the carpet."

"Warmth."

"Dry-cleaning bills," she countered.

"Companionship."

"Trips to the vet."

Jarek shook his head, both amused and frustrated by her determined cynicism.

"They're work, all right," he agreed easily. "Seems the three of us were always arguing over whose turn it was to walk the dog or brush the dog or feed the dog... Sasha slept on my bed, so it was mostly me who took care of her. My pop used to say it taught us responsibility."

Tess's mobile mouth flattened. "I didn't need a pet to teach me responsibility."

No, probably not. Jarek reviewed what he knew of her family: *The father was a brawler, the mother was a drunk and the boy was a punk.*

He kept quiet, watching her. And the cop's trick worked, because her words spilled to fill the waiting silence.

"It wasn't that I'm an animal hater or anything, you know. Because I wanted a pet. A cat. I liked cats. They're so pretty and self-contained. Only there wasn't the money, and there wasn't the time, and our father didn't want one in the house. And by the time he was gone, it didn't really matter."

"Because you were busy taking care of other things," Jarek suggested.

"Yes."

"Your brother," he said gently.

"Yes."

"And your mother."

Her gaze slid from his. Apparently there were some secrets he wasn't allowed to share, not yet. "Sometimes," she said.

She wedged another box into the grocery bag. Attracted by the rattle of food, the skinny black cat wound around her ankles. She reached down to pat it. Kitty flinched and then rubbed its head against her hand.

Jarek regarded them, the dark-haired, defensive woman and the half-starved, shrinking cat. They were probably both more capable of supplying affection than either of them realized.

"You could keep the cat now," he said.

Her chin lifted. "No. My life is fine the way it is. A cat would change things."

She was, he thought, frozen into a habit of self-denial,

locked into rejecting the things she wanted, as if admitting the yearning would make her weak.

"That's the idea."

Tess scowled. "Look, you're the one who's into adding responsibility to your life. Take the cat home to your daughter."

He wasn't getting anywhere with her. Not on this. Not like this. So he shrugged and reached for his wallet. "Fine. What do I owe you?"

Confusion clouded that sharp, self-assured face. Good. He wanted to think he could confuse her. She sure as hell had him rethinking things.

"Excuse me?" she asked blankly.

"For the food and stuff. How much?"

"You don't need to give me anything."

"No, see, I do. You're so used to giving maybe you've forgotten how it's supposed to work. I don't expect something for nothing."

She turned from the counter and looked him up and down. "You don't have anything I want."

Under the compassion, temper sparked. "Let's see," he suggested, and moved in.

Chapter 10

Jarek felt the surprise in her tightened shoulders, tasted the heat of her mouth. He ignored the surprise and worked on the heat, coaxing that flicker into life, teasing her lips, engaging her tongue.

Tess made a sound at the back of her throat like the cat purring, and opened to him, flamed into cooperation in his arms.

Oh, baby.

He'd meant to offer comfort. He'd intended to challenge that stubborn self-sufficiency of hers. What he'd meant and what he'd intended got swamped in a rush of heat, drowned in a surge of desire.

She kissed him back, shallow and deep, pressed that firm, full body close to his, wrapped him in her long, strong arms and ran her manicured nails along the skin at his nape. He shuddered and sank into the warmth and the moment, losing his breath and a little of his mind as another wave hit him.

And then her arms loosened. He felt her struggling to get her head above water, felt her disengaging, mouth and mind and heart.

Jarek drew his head back and studied her, her half-closed eyes, the flush along her cheekbones, her reddened lips.

Her lashes fluttered. Her golden gaze fixed on his. And she said, in a sharp, self-mocking tone, "Let me get this straight. Are you actually offering me sex in return for my cat?"

Laughter and annoyance warred inside him. Laughter won.

"Let's just say I want to give you something," he said, his tone mild.

"Sex." She shook her head. "That is so like a guy."

"Don't let the shield fool you, honey. I am a guy. But this isn't about me."

Well, not entirely, he amended to himself.

"Sex is always about the man," Tess said with the authority of experience.

The flatness in her tone caught him like a blow in the dark. Unexpectedly shaken, he touched his lips to hers, striving to keep things light, to keep himself under control. "Then you've been having sex with the wrong men."

"No arguments there," she said wryly.

"Let me make it up to you." He kissed her again softly, feeling her lips warm and cling, willing her doubts away. "Let this time be all about you."

Tess was sure there was a flaw in his logic. Had to be. But she couldn't find it, not with her blood buzzing and her head humming from his kiss. His mouth cruised the line of her jaw to the sensitive place below her ear, and the nerve endings there signaled enthusiastically to the rest of her body that this was a good thing, she should go for it.

No, she shouldn't.

She wasn't even willing to take on the obligations of a cat. Spreading her legs for Jarek Denko had to be a bad idea.

His large, warm hands stroked up and down her back, and her knees and resolution weakened.

He hadn't said anything about obligation, she reassured herself, while pleasure flowed along her spine. No pressure. No expectations. This was all about her.

Sure it was.

Sex for men was always selfish. It was always about what they could get away with and, sometimes, who they could brag about it to. Didn't she have her own father as a brutal example? Hadn't she learned from her mother's sad quest for affection after Paul DeLucca abandoned them?

And to top it all off, there was her own experience at fourteen...

She shuddered, and Jarek raised his head and asked, "Problem?"

She felt a burst of gratitude for him, for his perception, for his concern. But of course she couldn't talk to him about it. She never talked to anyone about what had happened in Bud Sweet's police cruiser on that long-ago afternoon. She had put it behind her. Talking would only bring it back. Exposing herself to Jarek that way would be an act more intimate than taking off her clothes.

She shook her head mutely.

Jarek frowned, unconvinced.

She put her hand at the back of his head and pulled him down to her and kissed him full on the mouth.

"Trying to distract me?" he teased, but his eyes, his wonderful clear eyes, were serious.

"Yes," she said. "Is it working?"

"If you want it to. Whatever you want," he said. "Whatever you need."

The promise, the possibility, worked its way inside her, making some parts of her loose and warm and others tight and achy. As if he knew how she felt, what she needed, he brought his hand up and closed it over her silk shirt, over her peaked nipple, easing the ache.

No, making it worse. She bit her lip in consternation.

"Don't do that." His tongue glided along her lip, soothed the tiny sting. Her heart raced under his wide, seeking palm. "Let me," he whispered against her mouth, and bit into her like she was a jelly doughnut.

Desire surged, thick and liquid inside her. She moaned and sagged against him. And he held her, supported her with his lean, muscled arm behind her back and his hard, solid body against her front. Very hard, she thought, as he rubbed against her, but then he shifted his hips away.

She made a soft sound of disappointment, but it was difficult to protest when his mouth was hot and busy on hers and his hand squeezed and stroked her breast. Warmth lapped along all her nerves. She wanted more. She wanted all of him, the thick ridge she felt through his jeans, the exciting friction and the exquisite pressure.

He gave her more. His hand slid between their bodies, dispensing easily with her belt buckle and the snap and zipper of her jeans. She was grateful for his competence. How much experience did he have getting women out of their clothes one-handed, anyway?

He kissed her deeply, hungrily, stealing her breath and feeding her own hunger, driving her thoughts away. He felt so good, solid and warm in the places where she was empty and cold. Sensation filled her up, building, cresting, and he went on kissing her—he was a wonderful kisser—only now his hand was between her legs, against her skin.

The shock of his hot touch brought her conscience bobbing to the surface, like a body in the lake.

Oh, boy. She couldn't just stand here, propped against her kitchen counter, while he... No.

It wasn't fair.

It wasn't equal.

It was very arousing. To show her general support for all he was doing, she ran her hands over his iron biceps and made a vague grab for his butt. He obliged her by pressing closer. She sucked in her breath. Oh, that was good. But when she slid one hand around his waist and along his belt, he caught it, and kissed the palm, and replaced it on his shoulder.

Well. Okay. His shoulder was firm and warm. And when he got back to the business of kissing her, that was better than okay. He tasted like coffee and man, dark, strong flavors. He kissed her like it meant something, like she meant something, like he could go on kissing and touching her forever, his mouth warm and urgent, his hand hot and clever... Her breath came quicker. Her mind fogged.

Of course, he wouldn't be satisfied with that. No man would be satisfied with that for long.

She let her hands drift down, skimming soft cloth and hard muscle, to Jarek's belt buckle.

He took her wrist, both wrists, and moved them to the small of her back. A combination of panic and arousal balled in the pit of her stomach. Braceleting her wrists with one large hand, he kissed her throat.

She squirmed against him.

His breath hissed. He raised his head. "Honey, if you keep that up, I'm not sure how long I can last here."

She stared at him, the panic already fading. "This isn't some kinky kind of control thing, is it?" she demanded. "Because if I see handcuffs, I'm out of here."

Jarek's rare grin lit his face, and the last of her worry died. "No handcuffs," he promised. "Jeez, you're suspicious."

Despite his admiring tone, his words stung.

Tess raised her chin. "You want gullible, you're in the wrong kitchen."

He let go of her wrists to cup her face. His penetrating eyes were very warm and dark.

"I want you," he said, so simply and firmly she had a tough time disbelieving him.

"Then why don't you—"

"Do you want me to—"

"No." The answer embarrassed her, but she was far from ready for all that giving herself to Jarek Denko would imply.

"All right, then." He kissed the tip of her nose and then her mouth.

She felt herself sinking back into the soft, warm haze of desire. But doubt still blinked at the edge of her awareness, like a warning light in the fog. Maybe her sense of fairness was offended. Maybe she didn't trust him that much yet.

Maybe she didn't trust herself.

"What do you get out of this?"

Jarek raised his head again, as if he were actually considering his reply. His attention to her question made her feel validated, somehow. It made her like him very much.

"Well," he said slowly, "I get to touch you."

She struggled against the stroke to her ego, the shaft to her heart.

"Oh, and this is a thrill," she scoffed.

He gave her a crooked smile. "It'll do for now," he said. "Believe me, it will do."

His mouth brushed hers again, softly, and her heart lurched. Once, twice, a third time, lingering. Her jeans gaped open and her blouse was rucked up, but tough cop Jarek Denko was kissing her as delicately and respectfully as a boy at a seventh-grade dance.

Tess melted. She kissed him back tentatively, and then again, parting her lips. He angled his head. His tongue thrust into her mouth. She thought, Not a boy at all, and had another moment's panic. But it felt so good, what he was doing, the bold, sure claim of his mouth and the firm, unhurried seduction of his hands.

He reached around her, under her jeans, his touch exciting and a little rough. He shoved the fabric out of the way, grasping her hips and lifting her against the counter. She gasped at the sudden smooth cold under her rear, but Jarek was warm and close in front, spreading her thighs with his body.

She was all open, open and exposed. She squeezed her eyes shut in embarrassment, but his arm was steady around her, and his body was hard against her, and his shoulder was firm and reassuring under her cheek. He petted and stroked between her legs, over and over, making her arch and roll her hips against his hand. His touch seared her tender flesh. She buried her face in his neck, breathing him in, the scent of his skin and the starch of his shirt, and let his hands take her where she wanted to go.

Quick and slow, over and around, gliding and pressing, he touched and rubbed. Her breath dragged and slowed. Her heart stuttered and sped, and she almost got scared again, almost retreated in her mind from the sexual takeover of her body.

But when she opened her eyes, he was watching her, his touch hot between her thighs, his gray eyes cool on her face, *Jarek,* and that was enough to make her break, to make her cry out and shiver and shatter.

"Jarek!"

She clung to him, her body tingling and quaking, her pulse pounding like she'd just taken an aerobics class. His arm tightened around her. He was breathing hard, warm gusts on her ear, on her neck. All the little hairs on her nape rose in response.

He kissed her forehead and her hair.

"That wasn't so bad, was it?" he asked, his voice hoarse with strain.

It was incredible. He had to know it. She hadn't exactly kept her response to him secret.

"It was okay," she mumbled into his shirt.

His silent laughter rocked them both.

Tess smiled against the soft cotton knit, absorbing the steady thud of Jarek's heart and the rise and fall of his chest. His generosity stunned her. His strength cradled her. His warmth wrapped around her like a blanket. She had never felt so whole. So safe. So at home.

Not bad?

Tess blinked. It was a disaster.

She was falling—hard—for Jarek Denko.

Tess's small nestling movement ripped at Jarek's heart and just about wrecked his self-control.

He was holding his libido in check by the skin of his teeth and the grace of God. One more cute, snuggly move and he was going to forget his age and his job and his promise and jump Tess like a junkie desperate for a fix. He wanted her shirt gone, for starters. He wanted to lay her back on that Formica counter and—

Easy, altar boy.

This wasn't about what he wanted.

This was about Tess.

Jarek clamped his jaw. He stroked his free hand from her nape to the smooth curve of her bottom, over damp silk and warm skin. His fingers tightened on the curve, pressing her soft flesh, pulling her closer.

When a man found a good thing, his pop was fond of saying, he should hold on to it.

Jarek was holding on.

The good thing in his arms wiggled. Okay, so Formica had its drawbacks. Too hard. And her butt must be getting cold. Reluctantly Jarek released her, retrieved his other hand from her sweet, hot, secret places and let her tug herself to order. He hated to lose contact. He hated to lose even the shadowed sight of her. But when she fumbled with her zipper, he stepped back to make her task easier.

Tess took a deep breath and raised her chin. "Well. That was fun."

His brain woke up. Uh-oh.

"Does that mean we can do it again some time?" he teased gently.

Her golden skin turned dull red. "Well, I— Well, uh—"

It appeased his male ego to reduce quick-talking Tess to a blush and a stammer.

"When can I see you?" he asked.

Her gaze dropped. "I'm kind of busy."

Her evasion tripped all kind of alarms. "This weekend?" he asked, and then cursed himself for his schoolboy lack of cool.

"I don't know. The Knights of Columbus are having a fish boil at St. Raphael's on Saturday night—"

He wasn't going to push her. But, damn it, he didn't like whatever she was putting between them. "Got a hot date?"

That yanked her chin back up. "No. I'm covering the event for the paper. Proceeds are going to a local kid's liver transplant fund."

Not another man, then. A story.

"Sounds like a good cause," he said cautiously.

"It is," she said, her confidence returning. "Kevin Lindquist—he's only six. They're trying a living donor transplant this time, using a section of his father's liver. The family has insurance, but it doesn't cover everything."

"Wouldn't you get more people to give money if the story came out before the dinner?"

Tess shook her head. "Anybody who would come to this fund-raiser already heard about it through the grapevine. But the paper goes out to the whole county. Lots of people who won't give up their Saturday nights to drive half an hour for a church dinner. But if I dish up a good story— the brave little boy, the selfless dad, the community rallying behind them—they'll swallow that."

"And make a donation."

Tess grinned. "To the address thoughtfully provided at the end of the article."

"Nice job," Jarek said.

She shrugged to hide her pleasure. "It's what I do."

More than that, he thought. It was who she was, as much a part of her as his shield and gun were part of him. Her sharp compassion, her determination to do good, even that touch of cynicism that helped her identify her target, were better clues to her character than all her defensive words.

"So, you're tied up Saturday," he said. "What about tomorrow?"

She studied her nails. Not good, he thought.

"I've got interviews," she said.

"The kid's family?"

"His doctors."

She was stonewalling. Jarek let it go. For now.

"Okay. Tomorrow's tight for me, anyway."

That reporter's gleam entered her eyes. "The investigation?"

"That, and—" Hell. Maybe now wasn't the best time to remind her he was everything she didn't want. *I raised one family already. I'm not interested in taking on another.* "Allie's coming in."

"Your daughter?"

He nodded.

"For the weekend?"

She didn't sound upset. Just very, very cautious.

"You should meet her," Jarek ventured. "Since we're seeing each other."

Pleasure flicked across her face, followed by panic. "We are not seeing each other."

He raised an eyebrow. "What would you call it?"

Tess hopped off the counter. Probably she wanted to find her feet, but the action brought her under his chin and close to his body. His body reacted.

"I don't know," she said. "I don't know what to call it. You stop by occasionally and I let you grope me."

What the hell was her problem? He set his jaw. "You enjoyed it."

She glared. "Yes."

"But you want a date," he said, feeling his way.

"I don't know what I want."

That made two of them. And with his body hard and aching and Tess's red, confused face turned up to his, there was only one thing Jarek was sure of.

He wasn't getting what he wanted from Tess anytime soon.

"Man, you really did a number on our chief of police," Mark said as Tess strode down the dock toward his boat on Saturday morning.

She nearly dropped her doughnuts. Her heart did drop, right to the bottom of her high-heeled boots. How did her brother know about her selfish behavior three nights ago? And why was he taking Jarek's side? He was her brother. He was supposed to be on her side.

Men.

She tightened her grip on the white bag from Palermo's bakery and stopped. Water sloshed between the pilings and the side of the boat. "What are you talking about?"

Mark stretched across the narrow gap to take the bag. His free hand grabbed her elbow to help her on board. "Didn't you read the paper?"

Tess leaned heavily into his steadying grip and scrambled onto the rocking boat. "Of course I read the paper. I wrote half of it."

Well, the lead story, anyway. A just-the-facts-ma'am account of the attempted attack on Sherry Biddleman. No names, of course. She thought it had come out well.

"You read the editorial page?" Mark asked.

"No," Tess said. "Why?"

Mark balanced the bakery bag on a coil of rope and turned to the tiny half cabin. "Wait a minute. I probably have a copy around here somewhere."

"I'm flattered."

He raised one eyebrow. "I keep it to wrap fish in," he explained.

"Swell," said Tess.

She needed a doughnut. While Mark rummaged in the pilot's cabin, she dug in the bag. Her body cried out for chocolate crullers. Actually, ever since Jarek Denko had lit her up and played her like a pinball machine, her body was crying out for a lot of things, but it seemed safer to give it chocolate. Jarek could be hazardous to her heart.

Tess had written a Valentine's Day feature last year citing studies that linked chocolate with the brain chemical serotonin and with phenyethylamine, a stimulant that created many of the same bodily reactions as falling in love.

She licked her fingers. Maybe what she really needed was—

Terrified of where her thoughts were taking her, Tess reached for another doughnut.

Mark plucked the bag away and handed her Thursday's paper. "Here. You're going to get fat."

Tess scowled. What on earth had made her imagine that breakfast with her brother would cheer her up?

The sight of her byline on the front page made her feel briefly better. But when she turned to the editorial page, folding the paper to stand against the slight breeze, her mood plummeted again.

Top Cop All Wrong for Eden? the headline queried.

Tess groaned.

Mark lowered his doughnut. "Having second thoughts?"

"I didn't write this," Tess protested.

"Right."

"This is the editor's opinion. Not mine."

Mark swallowed. "Whatever. But I bet I'm not the only person in town who confuses the two."

Tess scanned the rest of the column, the chocolate cruller gurgling in her stomach. The editorial concluded, "Thanks to the responsible reporting of this paper, our latest victim foiled her attacker. But the citizens of Eden can only regret that trouble seems to have accompanied the new police chief into town."

"This is so unfair," Tess said.

Maybe she was ambivalent about getting involved with Jarek Denko, but she didn't doubt that he was a good cop.

A great kisser.

A generous lover.

He'd even left her her cat.

Tess hadn't decided whether leaving the stray at her apartment had been an oversight or strategy on Jarek's part. And now she'd never know, she thought glumly. He wasn't going to want to see her again after this.

"You bet it's unfair." Mark grinned. "He'll want my ass now."

Guilt clutched her. She hadn't even thought of that. "Oh, Mark."

"Hey, relax. He's not going to nail me for something I didn't do."

"No, but he'll hear plenty of stories about all the things you did do."

Mark shrugged. "I never got a girl pregnant—"

"—that you know of."

"—and I never took anything that wasn't offered."

Tess rolled her eyes. "Only you were offered so much."

Mark extended the open bag toward her. "You want another doughnut?"

"Are you trying to shut me up?"

"Absolutely."

"Okay."

They ate in companionable silence as gulls wheeled and cried overhead and the Saturday morning traffic chugged just out of sight along Front Street. Somewhere up the marina, a screen door slammed. Tim Brown at the Blue Moon, maybe, hauling trash to the Dumpster. The strip of park that bordered the water was almost empty. Nearby, a sail luffed in the wind as a weekend sailor headed out. A young girl, eight or nine, perched on one of the sawed-off posts that supported the pier, swinging her feet and throwing pebbles into the water.

Tess frowned. Hadn't the kid been there when Tess arrived? It must have been half an hour ago.

"Mark." She touched his arm to get his attention. "How long has that girl been there?"

He brushed powdered sugar from his sleeve. "A while. An hour?"

She handed him a paper napkin. "Anyone with her?"

"How should I know?" He took the napkin, regarding her with exasperated affection. "It's none of my business."

No. Still…

Tess watched the girl hop down to get another supply of gravel. "I'm going to go talk to her," she decided.

"You'll creep her out," Mark said. "Hey, you're creeping me out. She looks old enough to take care of herself."

He was right. At eight or nine, Tess had been opening cans for dinner and standing over her brother while he did his homework. This kid could fend for herself.

On the other hand, some sicko with a red light and a grudge was out there somewhere. Seeing a little girl alone gave Tess an icky feeling.

She stood up, making the boat rock under her shifting weight. "I'm just going make sure someone knows where she is."

"You are such a sucker," Mark said.

Tess lurched out of the boat and onto the dock.

The girl, who had dark hair, dainty features and oversize feet, ducked her chin and watched Tess sideways. Not unfriendly, but cautious.

"Hi," Tess said.

"Hi."

"Are you waiting for somebody?"

The girl stared off at the horizon. Either she thought Tess was a hopelessly uncool, interfering grown-up, or she'd been cautioned against speaking to strangers.

"Here on vacation?" Tess asked, feeling hopelessly uncool and interfering.

"No."

Tess glanced at Mark. He smiled and shook his head. No help at all.

"Well," Tess said. "If anybody bothers you, you can let me know."

The girl looked directly at Tess. She had large, light-gray eyes, cool and astute. She was older than Tess had assumed. And eerily familiar, which was dumb, because Tess was pretty sure she'd never seen this kid around town before.

"No one's going to bother me," the girl said.

Except you, the look implied.

"Great," Tess said. "But if someone did—"

"I'd call my dad," the girl interrupted. She waited a beat and then added, "He's the chief of police."

Chapter 11

Tess's world rocked, as if the marina were suddenly as unstable as Mark's boat.

This girl, with her clear gray eyes and her ragged nails and her expensive sneakers, was Jarek's daughter.

Tess took a step backward, trying to find her footing. "Oh," she said. "Okay. Well—"

A black-and-white police cruiser turned onto Harbor Street. With a feeling of inevitability weighing her stomach, Tess watched it roll to the end of the boardwalk. Jarek Denko, lean and dark and annoyed in his starched uniform, slammed the car door and stalked toward them.

Her heart fluttered. Actually fluttered.

The little girl—Allie—slid off her perch. "Hi, Dad," she said.

His gaze cut to Tess and then focused on his daughter. "What are you doing here?"

Tess was glad he wasn't using that acid-in-milk tone with her.

The girl's assurance slid away. "I went for a walk."

"I told you to watch TV while I was gone."

"You were gone a really long time."

Jarek grabbed the back of his neck with one hand, as if he had a headache. Tess felt an unexpected and not entirely welcome burst of sympathy for him.

"You're not supposed to leave the house without letting me know where you are, you're not supposed to walk alone, and—" he blew out a short, sharp breath "—you're not supposed to talk to strangers."

Allie's face smoothed into the closed mask of a child who is pretending very hard not to care. She stuck her thumbnail into her mouth.

"Actually," Tess blurted, "she wasn't talking to a stranger."

Jarek spared her a brief, unsmiling glance. "She didn't know that."

Tess tried again. "No, I mean she totally blew me off in the conversation department. I was completely intimidated."

Jarek's mouth compressed. He was really ticked off. Or maybe, Tess thought hopefully, he was trying not to smile? "I find that hard to believe."

Allie stopped chewing on her thumbnail. "Why aren't you a stranger?" she asked Tess.

Jarek frowned down at his daughter. "This is Teresa DeLucca."

"The reporter?"

Tess blinked. "He told you about me?"

Way to go, DeLucca. Now you're pumping a ten-year-old for information.

Allie's eyes sparkled with wicked intent. "Not really. I heard him arguing with Uncle Alex, and I asked Dad about you after."

Jarek had argued with his brother. Over her. Because of the article? The chocolate cruller turned queasily in Tess's stomach.

"Oh?" she asked weakly. "What were you, um—"

"It doesn't matter anymore," Jarek said.

Allie shoved her hands with their bitten nails into the pockets of her jeans. The gesture was so like Jarek's that Tess's breath caught. "Are you really going to paint clouds on my wall?" the girl asked.

Tess's gaze sought Jarek's. His was cool and unreadable. "I told her it was your idea," he said.

Oh, boy.

"Well," Tess said guardedly, "I'm not sure."

The girl nodded with the resignation of a child familiar with grown-up excuses. "Dad said you were busy."

Tess tried to ignore the surge of guilt. But it was no use. *You are such a sucker,* her brother's voice mocked in her head.

"I have to go to this fish boil tonight," she said.

"Boiled fish?" Allie wrinkled her nose. "Ugh."

"It's better than it sounds," Tess said. "It's whitefish, boiled up with red potatoes and onions and served with melted butter, lemon and coleslaw. Maybe—" she snuck a look at Jarek, but she still couldn't gauge his reactions "—maybe you should try it."

"I already planned on bringing Allie to the fish boil," Jarek said.

Because he wanted them to meet? Tess wondered. His daughter and his— She stumbled over the word. Girlfriend? Lover? Her pulse hammered.

"It's a good cause," she offered.

"That's what I figured," Jarek said. Her heart dropped with disappointment. And then he added blandly, "Besides, they might need help with traffic control."

Tess's soft mouth parted. Her eyes narrowed.

Jarek grinned, satisfied. She was so damn easy to read. He'd spent too much time out of patience with this case, out of his mind worrying over Allie, and half out of his skin with sexual frustration. It helped to know he could rattle Tess's cage.

"What is this?" she said. "Payback?"

Good guess. Too good. Not that Tess owed him a damn thing for Wednesday night, but he'd been heavy with need ever since. Oh, Jarek had had sleepless nights before. It was part of the job. But not this stubborn, grinding arousal, distracting as a toothache and a hell of a sight more obvious.

He glanced down at his daughter's interested face. "Can we discuss this later?" he asked Tess.

Her cheeks turned red, but she refused to let it go. "I just want you to know that I'm sorry for how you must be feeling. I didn't know, but I still feel some responsibility."

Didn't know? Of course she—

Jarek frowned. "What are you talking about?"

"The editorial," Tess said earnestly. "I had no idea Janice intended—"

Jarek laughed. God, he was a moron. She had him thinking with— Well, he sure wasn't using his brain. "Oh, that."

"What were you talking about?" she demanded.

He couldn't tell her. Not with his ten-year-old daughter between them absorbing every word, and Tess's brother watching from the deck of his boat like a sniper sighting down a rifle barrel.

"It's not important," Jarek said.

"You're not upset?" she asked.

"About the editorial? No."

"But—"

Jarek tugged gently on his daughter's ponytail. "Allie, why don't you go wait in the car?"

She considered. He tensed. So much between them was a battle these days. "Are you going to ground me?" she asked.

Familiar frustration locked his jaw. Why couldn't she just do as she was told? He wasn't going to bargain with her. He'd tried bargaining with her mother, and all his various deals with Linda had guaranteed was that they both felt screwed.

But he didn't want to go into a full demonstration of his heavy father routine, either. He didn't need that. Allie didn't deserve it. It would scare Tess off family life at the Denkos for sure.

He pulled himself up. Why would that matter?

"I don't know anything about grounding," Tess said. "But I think you get a reduced charge for cooperating with the police."

Allie looked at him hopefully. "For real?"

The uncertainty in her voice did him in. And by making this one concession, Jarek reasoned, he wasn't abrogating responsibility or compromising standards or doing one of the hundred other things you worried about when you were the single father of a ten-year-old girl. Not really.

"A more lenient sentence, anyway. But next time you take off—"

"I'll leave a note," his daughter promised.

He raised an eyebrow.

Allie tried again. "Call you first and ask?"

"That would be good," Jarek said, surprised and relieved by her conciliatory attitude. "At least that way maybe both of us will survive until your eighteenth birthday."

Allie rolled her eyes, but she started for the black-and-white. "Can I listen to the radio?"

Jarek handed her his keys. "You turn on the car, the radio and the police band will come on."

"Cool," his daughter said.

A little of the tension released its grip on his neck.

"Nice meeting you," Tess called.

Allie glanced over her shoulder. She lifted one hand in a half wave. "Nice to meet you, too," she said.

Jarek watched her slide across the cruiser's wide front seat and turn the keys in the ignition.

When he was sure she wasn't going anywhere, he turned and smiled ruefully at Tess. "Well, now you know why I'm not particularly concerned about one lousy editorial in the *Eden Town Gossip*."

"Gazette," she corrected automatically, but she smiled back. Something eased inside him. "Yeah, I can see you have more important things on your mind."

"She's been— It's been a tough year," he said.

"A lot of adjustments," Tess observed in a sympathetic voice.

He nodded once. "I thought it would be easier," he confessed. "Allie and me— I didn't see her as much as I should have when she was living with her mother, but we always got along."

"All the more reason for her to test you now," Tess said.

Jarek laughed without amusement. "I guess that's natural. She's definitely testing my boundaries."

"Are you a lot stricter than her mother was?"

"No," Jarek said slowly. "Linda never backed off discipline. We had our problems, but she was a good mom."

"Allie must miss her."

He knew that, damn it. Linda had always been the most

important person in their daughter's life. She'd proven it to the court when she'd fought for custody, and she'd demonstrated it over and over again through the years by her determined care of Allie...and her equally fierce criticisms of his own parenting skills.

Jarek winced. For too many years, he'd been an observer to his daughter's life. Not a participant. And not, God help them both, a father. "I've been trying to do things the way Linda used to. Same rules. Same routines."

Tess touched his arm with her neat red manicured nails. Her eyes were warm and gold. He imagined those eyes shining up at him from his pillow, those nails scraping down his back, and fought a shiver of completely inappropriate lust.

"Maybe it's not the rules Allie is testing," Tess suggested. "Maybe it's your love."

Jarek shook his head to get his thoughts back in order, and she frowned. "It was just an idea."

Great. Now he'd offended her.

"No," he said. "Allie's therapist told me that. I've been through that. I tell her I love her."

"Tell her? Or show her?"

Guilt sliced at him. Damn it. "I didn't plan on leaving her alone all morning."

Something flickered behind Tess's gaze and was gone. "I'm sure when you explain that to her she'll feel much better about it."

He stared at her, frustrated. "What are you? The voice of experience?"

"The voice of commonsense," Tess snapped. "For heaven's sake, Jarek, she just lost her mother. She wants to make sure she won't lose you, too."

He stared at her, struck. It was possible. He liked to think in terms of cause and effect. And if Tess, a rebel herself, felt his daughter's insecurity was the cause of her rebellious behavior… Well, it was possible, that's all. Jarek felt like he'd just been handed a hot tip on a cold case.

He looked through the passenger window to where his daughter slouched on the front seat, her head bobbing in time to the music from the radio. Hope and a cautious excitement uncurled inside him.

He looked gravely at Tess. "I'll think about it. Thanks."

She blushed with pleasure. "I could be all wrong. I'm the last person to give you advice. I don't even have kids."

"No," he acknowledged. "But you were one once. Maybe it helps that you can identify with her."

Tess looked away. "I don't think so. My mother's still alive."

Jarek could have kicked himself. "Sure she is. But I hear she wasn't always…there for you when you were growing up."

"You can hear all kinds of things in this town. Not all of them are true."

"But you would tell the truth," he said.

She put her head to one side. "That's very good. Is getting people to expose themselves part of your job?"

That was it.

That had to be it.

Because the other explanation—that he cared about her, that he wanted to know about her, that her past was important to him because she was becoming important to him—well, that would really screw things up.

He held her gaze. "Part of your job, too, isn't it?"

She laughed without humor. "Right. My mother is a recovering alcoholic. She always drank, and she drank more after my father bailed on us. Okay? Are you satisfied?"

"No," he said gently. "I'm sorry."

Some of the defiance left her face. "Don't be. We did

all right. She went on the wagon seven years ago, and this time she hasn't fallen off.''

"I admire her for doing what she had to to straighten up. And I admire you for holding things together. That can't have been easy. You were just a kid.''

"Kids are resilient,'' Tess said.

She shifted uncomfortably.

If this had been a real interview, that would be Jarek's clue to go for the jugular. If they had a real relationship, it would be his cue to take her in his arms.

But her brother was watching from the damn boat. His daughter was waiting in the car. And Tess didn't give any sign of wanting anything from him.

We are not seeing each other.

"Are we still talking about you?'' Jarek asked. "Or are we back to Allie?''

Tess's smile flickered. "Maybe both. And Allie will be fine. Allie has you to take care of her.''

She did. He would. He was grateful to Tess for helping him see that.

But he wondered. Who had ever taken care of Tess?

Orange sparks leaped from the fire under the blackened cauldron and danced over St. Raphael's parking lot before floating into the night.

Isadora DeLucca, her eyes as shiny as a child's, grabbed Tess's arm. "Look! Look!''

Tess nodded, intent on finding them seats along the long, paper-covered tables. Most of the crowd had surged through the food line while she was still talking to six-year-old Kevin Lindquist's family. All the places left were either on the cold outskirts by the chain link fence or dangerously close to the fire.

"Yeah, Mom. It's pretty.''

"No, over there." Isadora pointed. "Isn't that your brother?"

Tess squinted along her mother's finger to the group staked out at the far end of the table. Tim Brown was there, his arm around his pretty blond wife, Heather. George and Marcia Tompkins of Tompkins Hardware sat across from them, George red-faced and argumentative while Marcia ate her way stolidly through the contents of her plate. Mark slouched at the very end with a red-haired woman beside him.

Tess searched for her name. Julie? Judy? She did something in hospital administration, anyway. The redhead leaned forward to address the entire table, her expression amused and her gestures animated. Mark looked bored.

Danger, thought Tess. Isadora started toward them. Tess trailed behind, balancing two plates heaped with steaming whitefish and potatoes in front of her.

"—can't believe that in this day and age any woman would let her husband dictate whether or not she could go back to school," Judy/Julie was saying with an arch look at Heather.

George Tompkins harrumphed. "Well, it's her husband that pays. Pays for the classes and pays at home."

"Excuse me," Tess murmured and wedged her mother's plate next to Marcia Tompkins.

"Hi, Tess," Tim said with a wide smile. "Isadora. Great turnout tonight."

Under the cover of general greetings, Heather ventured timidly, "I really was thinking about part-time work. Elizabeth at the Silver Thimble said she could use some help."

"You ought to give Tim a hand, then, at the bar," George said.

Marcia helped herself to her husband's coleslaw.

"There's a solution," the redhead said approvingly.

"That would at least get you out of the house a few days a week."

Tim Brown squeezed his young wife's shoulders. "It would make my job a lot more pleasant to have Heather around, let me tell you. But we decided when we got married that she would take care of things at home and I would take care of her."

Judy—it was Judy, Tess had caught her name in the flurry of hellos—gave a little laugh. "Well, thank goodness there are *some* men who find a woman who can take care of herself attractive."

She sent Mark a "You and me, stud" glance through her lashes.

Mark looked blank.

"Huh," Tess said. She wiggled in beside her brother. "The only reason you date self-sufficient women is because you figure they'll make fewer demands on you."

Mark tipped back his chair. "Yeah?" he asked, equally softly. "Is that why you hooked up with the chief?"

Tess choked on her boiled potatoes. After a moment, Mark handed her his beer. Coughing, sputtering, she shook her head. Her brother was looking around the table for something else to give her when someone put a plastic cup of water in her hand.

Gratefully Tess gulped. The coughing came under control. Mopping her streaming eyes, she turned to thank her savior.

Jarek.

Her breath caught for an entirely different reason. The firelight played on his harsh features, heightening the contrast of his strong nose and deep set eyes with the surprisingly tender curve of his mouth.

"You all right?" he asked quietly.

She managed to nod.

"I thought you were going to, like, die," Allie piped up cheerfully from behind him.

"Hey, the fish wasn't that bad," Tess said. Which was pretty lame, but it won her a smile from the girl. Tess fought the glow of satisfaction that gave her.

Isadora leaned over her plate. "Teresa, aren't you going to introduce us to your new…friend?"

Judy smoothed her hair and flashed her teeth. "Please."

Barracuda, Tess thought.

"You bet," she said. "Mom, Marcia, Judy, this is Allie Denko. Oh, and her father, Jarek," she added.

Jarek's eyes gleamed at her introduction, but he kept his face straight as he exchanged greetings around the table.

"Jarek Denko," Judy mused. "Now, why is that name familiar?"

"Jarek is our new chief of police," Tim Brown said.

"Really? Will your wife be joining us, Chief Denko?" Isadora asked.

Tess groaned silently.

"I'm not married," Jarek said.

"My mom died a year ago," Allie said.

Instead of looking sorrowful, Isadora looked briefly delighted. "Oh, you poor thing."

This was awful. Humiliating. Tess stood. "Cherry cobbler for dessert. Anybody want some?"

"I do," Marcia Tompkins said, her mouth full.

"I'll take a piece," said Tim.

Tess counted around the table. One, two, three, four… Judy from the hospital was watching her weight and protested the very idea of dessert. Five, six.

"You'll need a hand with that," Jarek said.

"Unless I balance plates on my head, I'll need more than one," Tess muttered.

He smiled at her with calm eyes, and her tangled nerves

smoothed away. A tiny, warm pulse started low in her body. After her brother's brooding and her mother's fussing, Jarek's steadiness was like a port in a storm.

Jarek looked down at his daughter. "Want to come with us?"

And he already provided safe harbor and an emotional anchor for a ten-year-old. Tess didn't want to compete or interfere with that.

"Oh, no," Isadora said. "Come sit with me, sweetie, and tell me all about your school."

"Mom," Tess warned. Allie had enough adjustments in her life. She didn't need some stranger playing Grandma on her first visit home to her father.

Jarek waited for his daughter's response.

Allie chewed her thumbnail while she sized up the situation. Her cool, gray gaze—so like Jarek's—rested on Tess. Tess felt her heart beat faster, as if more were at stake here than dessert.

This was stupid. She was not asking some ten-year-old's permission to sneak off to the dessert table and make out under the cherry cobbler.

"Why don't the two of you go?" she suggested.

Allie stopped biting her nail. "No, you go with Dad," she decided. "But I want some cobbler, please."

Jarek nodded. "You got it."

Isadora beamed. Mark raised an eyebrow. Tess sighed. She was going to have some serious explaining to do later.

Her cheeks were hot, as if she'd sat too long by the fire. She threaded her way through the crowded parking lot, conscious of Jarek's presence behind her, warm and steadying as a hand on her back. There was a big knot of people around the Lindquist family, and a bottleneck by the dessert table.

Tess got in line. Under the beer and onions, she could

smell the coffee and the fire and, closer, more elusive, the scent of Jarek's bay rum. Homey smells. Comfort smells.

Half the town, it seemed, had turned out to support the Lindquists. Kids raced between the pulled out chairs and hung from the chain link fence like monkeys. Mothers lingered at the tables, their minds on their gossip, their eyes on their children. The Knights of Columbus dads patrolled the perimeter, collecting paper plates, stopping to smoke or to chat with their neighbors. Father Joe leaned down to say something to Mary Lindquist, Kevin's mother, and she smiled up at him with tears in her eyes.

"Nice town," Jarek said quietly.

"Yes," said Tess. And felt, for maybe the first time in her life, part of it all.

He took her hand. His was warm and strong. Just for a moment, she let herself imagine that they were a unit, like the young parents exchanging smiles over the head of their sleeping infant or that old couple over there holding hands across the table. An unfamiliar yearning filled her heart.

"Enjoying yourself?" a male voice asked.

Tess started guiltily.

But it was only Dick Freer, from the gun shop, and he was speaking to Jarek, not to her.

"Yeah, thanks. Good turnout," Jarek said, echoing Tim Brown.

Freer adjusted the color of his L. L. Bean field coat. "Guess you felt you had to put in an appearance. But I've got to tell you, Denko, when we hired you, I never expected you'd put public relations over public safety."

Tess blinked at the insult. And then burned.

"No?" Jarek asked in a cool voice. *Ice Man,* she thought. "What did you expect?"

"I thought a big Chicago detective would put some time

into solving crime. Don't you care that Sherry Biddleman was followed home the other night?''

''My department is pursuing its investigation,'' Jarek said evenly.

Freer jerked his chin toward the table where Allie Denko waited next to Isadora DeLucca. Mark tipped back his chair, watching them with blank, black eyes. ''And what are you doing, chief? Having a nice dinner with the prime suspect?''

Tess bristled.

A muscle jumped in Jarek's jaw, but he didn't move. ''Consider it surveillance,'' he said. ''And let me know when you'd like me to come by the gun shop and tell you how to do your job.''

Freer growled something and moved away through the crowd.

Tess's breath hissed through her teeth. ''That jackass.''

Jarek glanced down at her, his eyes unreadable behind half-lowered lids. ''Don't worry about it. I told you, the investigation isn't focused solely on your brother.''

''Forget Mark. How dare he talk to you that way?''

Jarek frowned. ''What?''

Her throat was thick with rage and shame. She swallowed hard. ''It's all the fault of that damn editorial.''

''Wait a minute. You're upset because Dick Freer doesn't think I should take a night off?''

''Of course I'm upset.''

Tess remembered the near-reverence in Steve Nowicki's tone when he spoke of his ex-partner. She recalled Jarek's calm authority as he took command of the botched-up crime scene, and his fierce protectiveness in Carolyn Logan's hospital room, and his fatigue the night he'd dropped by her apartment. To go from that to this…

"He accused you of not doing your job," she said indignantly.

"Tess, it's okay," Jarek said, his voice gentle. "I've dealt with guys like Freer before. Police wannabes, mostly. You get used to them in my line of work."

She bit her lip, frustrated by his continued imperturbability. He didn't need her defense. He didn't need her for much of anything.

Except for sex.

The thought caused a queer pang at her heart.

Although even when he'd had her unzipped on her kitchen counter, Tess thought unhappily, Jarek had managed to keep his own needs under tight wraps. It was possible, she supposed, that his amazing restraint was another indicator of his selflessness and self control.

Or maybe she should get a clue. Maybe she just didn't tempt him that much.

Someone pushed in the dessert line, and Jarek was nudged closer. Or did he move on his own? Tess was very conscious of his knee bumping her thigh, her shoulder brushing his chest.

"Of course, Freer did have a point," Jarek murmured, his mouth close to her ear. The tiny hairs at the back of her neck stood at attention.

Tess took a deep breath and turned. Mistake. She was a half step away from his broad, solid chest, inches away from his strong, stubbled jaw. He radiated a magnetism, a heat, that made her long to lean into him. "What?"

"One of the first lessons you learn as a rookie is depersonalization. Freer was really implying that my attraction to you might cloud my judgment."

Tess's heart hammered in her chest. "So?"

Jarek held her gaze, his gray eyes rueful. "So, maybe he was right."

Chapter 12

Leftover cherry cobbler was no substitute for love, Tess decided.

She ate standing at the kitchen counter, while the cat watched unblinkingly from the corner. A living, breathing, calorie-consuming cliché, she thought in disgust. She ought to get a lover. She ought to get a life.

But her would-be lover was halfway across town tucking his ten-year-old daughter in bed for the night.

Her life included a brother who just happened to be a suspect in an ongoing police investigation.

And even if Tess were willing to overlook her loyalty to Mark, it appeared that Jarek could not.

Glumly she picked another cherry from the wreckage on her plate.

The wall phone rang. She damned the way her heart jumped and then raced with possibility. It could be Mark, she told herself as she lifted the receiver. It could be her mother. It could be—

"Tess? Are you there?" a deep, irritated voice demanded.

She swallowed. "Jarek?"

"How soon can you get over here? I need you."

Her palm was clammy on the receiver. It was everything she wanted. It was everything she feared. She felt like the governess in one of those castle-on-the-cliffs sort of books, with blushes and palpitations and a brooding hero making a shameless offer she could not refuse...

"This is sort of sudden," she said. Oh, boy. Now she even sounded like the governess.

"I know. I'm sorry. If there were anyone else—"

Tess straightened. The brooding master of the castle had his lines all wrong. "Excuse me?"

"I got a call," Jarek said. "I have to go in. I'd phone my parents, but...well, they're almost seventy and over an hour away. I tried reaching Aleksy, but he's out on a case. I can't leave Allie alone, and I don't want her waking up and finding a stranger in the house."

So that was what he wanted. Her heart contracted. Her voice flattened. "You want me to come over and baby-sit your daughter."

"Yes. Please," he added as an afterthought.

"Well..." She regrouped. Grow up, DeLucca. Get a grip. "Sure. I'll, uh—" She looked at the clock over the stove. It was almost midnight. "I'll be right over."

"Thanks, Tess." The warmth and relief in Jarek's voice stirred feelings she was trying hard to ignore. "You're a doll."

She hung up the phone and looked around her silent apartment. She was an idiot.

The cat meowed plaintively when Tess went to the door. She checked to make sure it had food and water and then picked up her purse. "Don't wait up," she told it. "I don't know when I'll be back."

On the short drive to Jarek's house, Tess had time to think.

What kind of case would pull Jarek away from his daughter in the middle of the night on her first weekend in their new home? Something out of the ordinary.

Her stomach hollowed. Something *bad.*

And when Tess pulled to the curb and saw every front light blazing and Jarek watching at the door, her worst suspicions were confirmed.

She got out of the car. "What kind of a call?"

He looked weary, she saw as she approached the porch. She hardened her heart against the lines of strain that bracketed his mouth, the weight of responsibility that braced his shoulders.

She understood responsibility. She didn't need to take on any more.

"Tess, I don't have time for this now," he said.

She believed him. "You'll tell me about it when you get back?"

A grudging smile lightened his dark face. "Do I have a choice?"

She walked through the door he held open for her. "Not really."

Standing in the hall, he handed her a key to the house and the number of his cell phone. "Thanks for coming."

She tucked the key in her purse and the number in her pocket. "You're welcome. Just tell me you didn't ask me here to keep me away from your precious crime scene."

His gaze searched her face, as if he weren't sure whether or not she was joking. And then he smiled again, crookedly, and her heart eased. "I might have. If I'd thought of it."

She glanced toward the stairs. "Allie asleep?"

He nodded. "I put her to bed over an hour ago. I don't know when I'll be back. Sorry. I—"

Tess put her fingers against his mouth. "It's okay. If I get sleepy, I'll make myself comfortable on the couch."

"Suit yourself." He took her hand and pressed his lips against her palm. "But I'd rather you were in my bed."

He pressed his elbow to the gun clipped to his belt and patted the shield in his inner jacket pocket, the way another man would check for his wallet and keys. Observing his slight scowl, his remote gray eyes, Tess reflected he had already gone from her in his mind. A chill chased up the back of her arms.

He would be all right, she reassured herself. Whatever bad thing had happened out there, Jarek wasn't going into danger. Although the sight of the gun on his hip constricted her chest.

"Lock up behind me," he instructed tersely.

He was gone.

Leaving Tess with a ten-year-old girl with ragged nails and her father's shrewd gray eyes.

Not a problem, Tess thought, securing the door. Heck, she'd raised bad boy Mark DeLucca practically single-handed. How much trouble could one little girl be?

"So are you, like, my dad's girlfriend or something?"

Tess's hand bobbled as she poured the milk. It sloshed from the cereal bowl over the counter. She considered trying to explain her relationship with Jarek to his ten-year-old daughter over cereal and sliced banana.

I don't know what to call it. You stop by occasionally and I let you grope me.

Tess winced. No. Absolutely not, she thought.

"Yes," she said. "I guess you could say I was his girl-friend."

Allie inspected her like a new zoo exhibit. "I never met a girlfriend before."

Oh, boy, Tess thought, both pleased and flattered that Jarek didn't make a practice of bringing women home. So she was special.

Or just really, really convenient. He certainly hadn't introduced her to anyone as his girlfriend.

"I'm just glad to be here with you," she mumbled.

She mopped up the spill on the counter, wishing she could set herself to rights as easily. Sleeping on the couch had done nothing for her equilibrium or her hair.

"Are you going to stay long?" Allie persisted.

Tess didn't want Allie to think she was moving in on her and her father. But she didn't want her to feel abandoned, either.

"Only as long as you need me. I have to get home and feed my cat."

Something shifted in the girl's expression. "You have a cat? I always wanted a cat."

Tess opened her mouth to say, *You can have mine.* What came out was, "Maybe you should come and visit. I need help choosing a name."

"Your cat doesn't have a name?"

Tess felt inadequate. Again. "She hasn't been my cat very long," she said.

She poured herself another cup of coffee—she had a feeling she was going to need it—and resumed her seat at the counter. She felt out of her depth here. Maybe breakfast would help?

She eyed the contents of Allie's cereal bowl without much hope. Floating twigs and raisins. "Is that any good?"

Allie sighed. She had a good line in sighs, expressive

without crossing the border into outright-rude-that-could-get-you-punished. "Not really."

Tess nodded. "Then—it's none of my business, but—why are you eating it?"

Allie dug up another spoonful. "Because my father buys it for me. He thinks it's healthy, and he's trying to take care of me. I don't want to disappoint him."

Tess gave both of them points—Jarek for trying and Allie for caring. "But then he'll buy you more."

Allie let the healthy twigs drip back into the bowl. "I know."

She sounded so mournful that Tess grinned. "What do you really want for breakfast?"

Allie put her head to one side. "Belgian waffles?"

"Do I look like Betty Crocker to you?"

"Who?"

Tess sighed. "How about cinnamon toast?"

Allie nodded.

Tess got up and opened the bread box. Of course Jarek had bread. His kitchen was completely, if sparsely, stocked with everything. She put two slices in the toaster and hunted up sugar and cinnamon. After watching her for a minute, Jarek's daughter slid off her stool and silently handed her the butter from the fridge.

"Thanks."

Tess spread the toast with butter, sprinkled it thickly with sugar and cinnamon and set two plates on the counter.

Allie took a bite. "Do you have kids?" she asked through a mouthful of toast.

"No," Tess said. "I have a brother."

"I wanted a brother," Allie said. "But now I think I'd rather have a sister." She looked speculatively at Tess, as if she expected her to produce a sibling the same way she'd provided Allie with breakfast.

Tess was flattered. Terrified. What was with these Denkos?

"Eat your toast," she said.

Allie ate her toast. She ate her toast so quickly, in fact, that Tess moved the slice from her own plate to Allie's and got up to put two more pieces of bread in the toaster.

At eight o'clock the phone rang. After a moment's hesitation, Tess answered it.

"Hello?"

"Tess?" Jarek said crisply. "Did I wake you?"

"No." She smiled at Allie, who stopped chewing to listen. "We're having breakfast."

Jarek swore. "I wanted to be there before she woke up."

Tess fought a pinch of disappointment. She could use a little credit here. "Don't worry about it. She's better company when she's awake, anyway."

Jarek didn't laugh. "Yeah. Look, I'm wrapping up now. And I reached Aleksy. He'll be there any minute."

Oh, no. The last thing Tess needed was the Boy Scout's critique of her parenting skills. "Why? I mean, if you're almost finished—"

"I don't want to take advantage."

She relaxed. At least Jarek wasn't saying that he didn't trust her with his daughter. "So, we'll trade," she teased. "My time for your story."

"We'll have to talk about it."

"Hey, you promised me—"

"Tess." His voice was flat. Impatient. "Something's come up. We need to talk."

Misgiving seeped through her. "Okay," she said slowly. "We'll talk."

"You'll wait for me?"

"If your brother's coming—"

"It's Sunday. I told him to take Allie to church. Will you wait for me?"

If Jarek had used police bully tactics, Tess could have said no. But under his curt tone, she heard something else, some tiredness or trouble that made her say, "I'll wait."

She hung up the receiver, wondering sickly if she'd just made another big mistake. She was responding to someone who needed her, the way she always responded, hoping to be rewarded with approval.

With love.

Her brother's voice mocked her. *You are such a sucker.*

Allie spoke behind her. "He's gonna be late, right?"

Tess felt a tear of sympathy, for the girl and for her father. "He's sorry," she offered.

Allie stuck the edge of her thumbnail in her mouth. "He's always sorry."

"Your uncle's coming."

"Well, that's something. I like my uncle. He calls me honey in Polish. Which is kind of a crock, but I like it."

Tess cleared their dishes to the dishwasher. "You're very pretty."

"Not really. Uncle Alex goes for real babes. Like you."

Tess laughed. "I'm not in babe mode this morning."

Allie eyed her critically. "Yeah, but even with your hair sticking up, you dress nice. And your fingernails are, like, wow."

"Thanks. I think."

"I bite mine." Allie held up her ragged hands for inspection. And then, before Tess could make the mistake of offering sympathy, she added, "My grandmother Peterson doesn't like long nails anyway."

Peterson? Her mother's mother, Tess guessed. No way was Tess getting involved in this. She had no business pitting herself against the ghost of Allie's late mother. But some uncertainty in Allie's eyes tugged at her.

Jarek's frustrated voice jeered in her memory. *What are you? The voice of experience?*

Yes, Tess thought. That's exactly what I am.

"You want to know a secret?"

Allie leaned forward. Ten-year-old girls loved secrets.

"I used to bite mine, too," Tess confided.

Allie slumped against the back of her stool. "No way. Yours are, like, perfect."

"That's because I give myself manicures. And I only started the manicure thing to stop myself from chewing my nails."

Allie studied Tess's nails. "Do you think that would work for me?"

Tess shrugged to hide her enthusiasm for the idea. "I don't know. If you didn't want to mess up your polish, it might help. Do you want to give it a try?"

Allie nodded cautiously.

What a pair we are, Tess thought. Don't let anyone know what you want, and it won't hurt so much when you don't get it. "Okay," she said.

She dumped out the contents of her purse: notebook, pencils, hairbrush, gum, three shades of lipstick and her keys on a little mace key chain. Pens rolled, coins bounced.

"Wow," Allie said.

Tess swooped on a nail file and the bottle of polish she used sometimes to stop runs. "Here we go."

The girl eyed the pale color skeptically. "It's not as pretty as yours."

Tess thought of Jarek's likely reaction if he came home from a case and found his ten-year-old daughter with blood-red nails.

"It's a start," she said. "We have to start somewhere."

* * *

Tess was restuffing her purse when the doorbell chimed.

Allie hopped down from her perch. "That's Uncle Alex."

She ran into the hall. Tess heard the front door open, and a deep male voice say, "Hi, *kochanie.*"

As Tess walked in, Aleksy Denko was just straightening from a hug. His sharp brown gaze skewered her. "You still here?"

She was spared answering by Allie, who waggled her fingers at her uncle. "Tess did my nails. And she gave me some polish, so I can do them myself."

"Nice," he said, without looking. "Run get your jacket. We're late for mass."

His niece bolted upstairs.

Tess leaned against the bannister and crossed her arms over her breasts. "And hello to you, too," she said dryly.

"Sorry," Aleksy said. "Thanks for taking care of the kid."

He didn't look sorry. Or grateful. He looked hard and cold and pissed off.

"You know," Tess drawled. "If you're not nice to me, I'm going to start remembering all the reasons why I don't like cops."

He aimed a smile like a knife. "I guess you've got grounds."

Her earlier misgiving returned in force. "Like what?"

He shook his head. "Never mind."

This wasn't getting them anywhere. She lifted one shoulder. "I'll tell you my reasons if you tell me yours."

He gave her a dismissive look. "Save it for my brother. Or better yet, stay away from him."

She welcomed the flare of anger. It burned away her hurt,

distracted her from her fear. "What is it with you? I'm doing him a favor."

Jarek's brother looked briefly embarrassed. But he said, doggedly, "You're not what he needs."

He was right.

He wasn't saying anything Tess hadn't told herself. But hearing it from Aleksy touched a truth she wasn't willing to face. She wanted to be the woman Jarek needed.

"How do you know what he needs? He's a grown man."

"He's a cop," Aleksy said.

"That's his job. Jarek is more than that."

"Yeah, he's also a decent guy trying to make a stable home for his little girl. Someone like you doesn't belong in the picture."

"Someone like me?" she repeated dangerously. "You have no idea what I'm like."

"Sure, I do." He came closer, a hint of sexual threat in his stance she doubted he was even conscious of. "I know the type. Baby, I am the type. We don't do the domestic shtick."

Temper and panic drove her chin up. "You're wrong. You and I have nothing in common."

He backed off. Shrugged. "Maybe not. At least I'm not going to screw him up in his job."

All her earlier misgivings crashed in on her. He knew something. He was getting at something. Jarek's voice returned to haunt her. *Something's come up. We need to talk.*

"What's happened? What are you talking about?"

Aleksy glanced up the stairs. "I've said enough."

Oh, no. She wasn't letting him get away with that concerned uncle crap after doing a drive-by on her emotions. "I think you've said too much."

He didn't deny it. But as Allie skipped down the stairs with her jacket, just before Aleksy turned away, he leaned close again and said, softly, ''You hurt him, and you'll deal with me. And I'm not as nice as my brother.''

Well, Tess thought as the door closed behind them.

But she could handle not-so-nice, in-your-face, full-of-himself Aleksy. What she couldn't deal with were her own growing feelings for his brother.

He wanted to come home.

The realization hit Jarek as he pulled into his driveway and looked up at his modest white house.

Time was, he came off shift jazzed and impatient with his body's demands for food and sleep, with the routine that kept him from the case. But right now, with fatigue dragging at his steps and frustration dogging his soul, he wanted nothing more than to check out of the job for the next two, ten, fifteen hours.

He wanted what he supposed other guys his age took for granted. Wife. Kids. Home. Peace.

He swung open the car door. Going up the walk, he let himself picture it, imagined greeting his little girl with a kiss and a smile before he took his dark-haired wife upstairs to their room and let go. Shut out the world and lost it all in the welcoming warmth of her body.

Only his kid was gone with his brother because Jarek was late. Again.

And the dark-haired woman waiting for him wasn't his wife. Tess had no reason to welcome him home. Had no reason to welcome him, period.

Especially not after what had happened in the long hours since he'd left her.

Jarek massaged the back of his neck with one hand. What was he doing with this woman? What was he doing to her? He was a man who liked answers. He'd spent his whole adult life figuring out who and what and where and why, drawing orderly solutions out of the chaos of crime scenes.

Tess was a big black question mark in the middle of his new life.

And he wanted her there anyway.

Squaring his shoulders, he trudged up the front steps. The door opened before he could insert his key. She stood in the doorway. She didn't fit the image of what he thought he wanted, what he thought Allie needed. And yet she was so damn beautiful, with her tumbled hair and worried face, that his chest actually ached at the sight of her.

"I heard the car," she said.

He let himself breathe her in as he brushed by her, drawing in the faint warmth of her body, the scent of her hair. He was careful not to touch her. "Sorry I'm late."

She shook her head. Her golden eyes searched his face. "Was it—bad?"

She wanted the truth. He wasn't sure she could bear it. Even with all the ugly, brutal, bloody things he'd seen, this crime had left him shaken. "Yes."

Her brows twitched together. He thought she might challenge him there and then, but she only asked, "Coffee? I made some fresh."

Gratitude eased the knot at the back of his neck. "Yeah. Thanks."

He followed her down the narrow hallway to his kitchen. But he wouldn't let her wait on him. He hitched his own mug down from the shelves and poured his coffee. Black.

Tess's voice rang in his memory. *Offering you coffee is what got me into trouble in the first place.*

He took an unwary sip and scalded his tongue. Damn, damn, damn.

"What?" she asked from behind him. "What happened?"

He turned slowly to face her. "Another woman was pulled over in her car on Old Bay Road last night. And this time the rapist killed her."

Tess sucked in a breath. "Oh, God. I'm sorry."

He set down his mug. "So am I."

"At least you have homicide experience. That has to be a help. In finding her killer, I mean."

"Maybe. Tess—"

She hurried on, as if she didn't want to hear what he had to say. He wished to God he didn't have to say it.

"If you're worried about Allie, she's fine. We got along fine." Tess smiled, inviting his participation. "I did her nails."

Jarek felt even worse. "Sorry I had to leave her with you."

"Well, it's too bad you got called away on her first weekend here, but I'm sure if you explained to her—"

"Tess." He made his voice as gentle as he could. "This isn't about Allie. It's about Mark."

Her face closed, instantly and absolutely. "No."

"The victim was seen with him at the church last night."

Tess hugged her arms against her. "So what? I was there, too. You were there. Four hundred other people must have been at that church last night. Including Father Joe."

"Only none of them is dead." Frustration and pity churned in Jarek's gut. But he couldn't give expression to them, any more than he could vent the anger that rose in a slow, hot tide. Anger with her brother for getting into this mess. Anger with Tess for her blind, stubborn loyalty. Anger with himself for doing his job.

In a voice picked clean of emotion, he said, "The woman who was raped last night—the woman who was killed—was Judy Scott."

Tess's face went as white as the dead woman's. "My

brother wouldn't rape anybody. He certainly didn't need to rape Judy Scott.''

Jarek was inclined to believe her. Which made it even more critical that he stick to the facts. Hang on to his objectivity. ''He admits he had sex with her last night.''

''Which only goes to prove— Wait a minute.'' Tess's head snapped back as if he'd slapped her. ''He *admits?* You talked to him?''

''I had to. He was the last person we know of to see Judy Scott alive.''

''Except her killer,'' Tess said.

''Her killer would have been the last,'' Jarek agreed carefully.

''But Mark didn't have any reason to kill her!''

Jarek hoped Tess was right.

Freer was really implying that my attraction to you might cloud my judgment.

He made himself say, ''Unless Mark didn't know who was in the car until he pulled her over. Unless she recognized him.''

''He wouldn't do that. He didn't do it.''

''Then he doesn't have anything to worry about.''

''Excuse me, are you asking me to have some great faith in our justice system now?''

''No, I'm asking you to trust—'' Me, he thought. Trust me. ''—my department to do its job. Judy Scott fought her attacker. We recovered blood from under her fingernails.''

Tess glared. ''Not Mark's blood.''

''You could help us prove that,'' Jarek suggested coolly, while his gut burned and churned.

''How?'' She shot the word at him.

''It'll take several days to get the lab results from DCI. If the blood type is consistent with your brother's, then any judge would give us a warrant to obtain a blood sample from him. We probably have sufficient cause to get one anyway. But the whole thing would be resolved a lot quicker if Mark volunteers a sample now.''

''You want me to talk my brother into letting you stick him so that you can compare his blood to the blood under Judy's fingernails.''

''To rule him out as a murder suspect. Yes.''

''You go to hell,'' Tess said, and marched out of his house.

He went to church instead.

Waiting in the shelter of the arched double doors for mass to let out, for his daughter to come out, Jarek wondered if God would forgive him for the way he'd just tried to manipulate Tess. God knew she never would. But here, in the shadow of God's house, he let himself hope that maybe Mark DeLucca hadn't raped and killed Judy Scott.

He prayed, as he hadn't prayed since he was an altar boy at St. Wenceslaus, for Tess, with her quick, hard loyalties and soft heart, and for her mother. Even for her brother.

Mercy for the living, Jarek thought.

And justice for the dead.

Chapter 13

"Fine," Mark said bitterly. He tossed his first responder's jump kit into the back of the Jeep and slammed the door. "I know I'm innocent. But if you want me to prove it to you, I will."

Tess winced. She'd known Mark wouldn't miss his Monday night trauma care class. She'd figured she'd catch him afterwards in the hospital parking garage, away from an audience and before he reported to work at the Blue Moon. But despite her correct guess, she'd obviously caught him at a bad time.

Right. Like there was a good time to tell your brother you wanted him to donate blood to eliminate himself as a murder suspect.

"You don't have to prove anything to me," she protested. "If I thought you were guilty, I'd never suggest you give a blood sample. But since you're not, it would make things a whole lot easier—"

Mark's lip curled. The overhead garage lights threw his

face into dramatic light and shadow, making him look more like a fallen angel than ever. "Easier for who? For Denko?"

Hot blood surged up her face and neck. She would not feel guilty. She didn't have any reason to feel guilty, damn it. She was looking out for her family, the way she always had. The way she always would. The thought was vaguely depressing.

"Easier for you. He'll get a warrant to force you to give a sample anyway, Mark. By going in voluntarily, you can get this whole thing over with sooner."

Mark crossed his arms and leaned against the side of the Jeep. "Why bother? Why should I help the police chief do his job?"

"Do you really want half the people in this town thinking you killed Judy Scott?"

Mark's face was hard and expressionless. "I can live with it."

"I don't want to."

"It's a little late to start worrying about the DeLucca family name, big sister."

"It's not that." Frustration sharpened her voice. "I'm worried about you. I'm afraid you'll get hurt. Mark, I went into the *Gazette* office today, and it was scary. Everybody's talking. Everybody's too terrified to stop and think."

Some of the frightening blankness left Mark's eyes. "I can take care of myself, you know."

"Not if you get jumped on a dark road by a gang of vigilantes. Mark, the people I heard talking are looking for someone, anyone, to blame. Why make yourself a target?"

The silence stretched out in the deserted garage, measured by the slamming of Tess's pulse in her throat. In the distance, the elevator dinged.

"All right," Mark said at last. "I'll think about it."

"Thank you." She hugged him.

After a moment his arms came around her. He patted her back awkwardly. "Poor Tess. You always did want the family we never had."

Filled with relief, she pressed her cheek to her brother's lean, hard chest. "You're all the family I need," she said.

But she didn't believe it anymore. If she could choose... But when had she ever had a choice?

Mark gripped her upper arms and gave her a little shake. "Uh-huh. Is that why you're playing house with the chief now?"

"I am not— Who told you that?"

"Grapevine goes both ways, Tess. I heard you spent Saturday night at his house."

Driven on the defensive, she said, "I was baby-sitting his daughter."

"While he investigated your brother for murder. How cozy. Not to mention convenient."

His words forced her to confront her own fear that Jarek was using her. Had been using her all along. "I didn't know— I don't think Jarek even knew the victim's name at that point. He only asked me to come over because Allie hasn't met that many people in Eden yet."

"And you said yes out of the goodness of your heart."

"Yes."

"Kind of like you agreed to talk me into getting a blood test."

"*No.* Don't be a jerk, Mark. Just give the damn sample."

He studied her a moment with dark, unreadable eyes. And then he smiled. "Okay. DeLuccas forever. I'll let your boyfriend draw my blood."

"When?"

"Tomorrow soon enough for you? Because I've got work now."

"Tomorrow will be fine." She wasn't in that big a hurry to give Jarek Denko his victory.

And in a couple of days, when the test results came back from whatever lab the police sent them to and Mark was completely cleared, she would wave the proof around and thumb her nose in Jarek's face.

Tess drove out of the parking garage feeling as good as any woman could who had half-lost her heart to the Ice Man. Worse, to a man who saw her as a roadblock. Who wanted to use her as a shortcut.

In her rearview mirror, she could see Mark's Jeep following her compact. Another car lurched down the ramp behind them and then a third glided out of the shadows. Funny. The level Mark had parked on had been almost empty. She hadn't expected this much traffic leaving the garage.

The caravan proceeded on the wooded road toward town. Tess expected Mark to pass, but his Jeep maintained an even speed behind her. Well, the rapist was still out there somewhere. Mark probably thought he was protecting her. She smiled at his headlights in the mirror, remembering Jarek's dark blue Crown Victoria tailing her from Chicago.

Her heart squeezed. Her smile died. There was nothing personal about Jarek's protection. He'd just been doing his job then. He was only doing his job now.

The road edged the brightly lit Gas-N-Go and plunged into the woods again. One of the other cars sped up and pulled even with Mark's Jeep. Tess frowned as it cut in front of him and then slowed abruptly. Jackass driver. It was too dark to play bump cars. She eased up on the gas to negotiate a bend in the road by the old ranger tower and checked in her rearview mirror.

No headlights.

No Mark.

Her hands tightened on the steering wheel as she drove on, dividing her attention between the road ahead and the road behind. Mark was a reliable driver. He knew this road like the lineup of bottles behind the bar. He wasn't sixteen anymore, out testing his new license and her patience on a Friday night. He never talked about his time in the Marines, but she knew vaguely he'd been a squad leader in Afghanistan. He could take care of himself.

But as another mile crept by, marked by the flash of the broken yellow line, the prickle of unease at the back of her neck would not go away. Suppose he'd had an accident? Or car trouble? She could turn around right now and he would... Well, laugh at her probably. Tess pulled a face at the windshield. Or get ticked off. She'd already made him late.

She turned around anyway, with an instinct for trouble honed by years of late-night phone calls and trips to the jail to post bond.

She drove back a mile or more to the zigzag around the old fire tower. Her headlights caught Mark's Jeep—off the road and at an angle.

Her heart pumped. Her first thought was that he'd had an accident.

And then she saw five or six other vehicles pulled onto the shoulder and parked in the graveled strip at the tower's base. Relief weakened her. One car—an SUV—had its engine running and its headlights on. So help had already arrived. She saw a knot of men standing in the glare of the lights, their backs to the road. How many? How serious was it?

She didn't see Mark. Was he hurt?

Mark's Jeep half-blocked the entrance to the weedy strip. She looked frantically for a spot. There. Behind that truck. She pulled in. The car bounced as the tires bumped from

the pavement and sunk in the mud. The night air rolled
through her open back window, the heady scent of a Great
Lakes spring cut through with car exhaust.

Her gaze scanned the group under the tower. She thought
she recognized her brother's sharp profile between several
other dark figures. His head hung down. They appeared to
be holding him up. Two men on each side.

And then a fifth man crowded close to Mark and punched
him hard in the stomach.

Her breath stuck in her chest. Oh, God.

They weren't supporting Mark.

They were beating him up.

She fumbled for her purse on the passenger seat, dumped
out the contents to grab her cell phone. What were you
supposed to dial in an emergency? Star? 911?

She punched in 911, thanking God when the dispatcher's
bored voice came over the hissing air waves.

"Help," Tess said. Her hands shook. Her voice shook.
"I'm on Old Bay Road, about a mile south of the Gas-N-
Go by the ranger tower. They're beating my—" No. What
would get Jarek here fast, no questions asked? "Someone's
being attacked. Hurry."

"Your name?" the dispatcher asked, wide-awake now
and urgent.

But Tess had already thrown the phone down on the seat
and backed her car onto the road.

This was crazy. She knew it was. But she could no more
hold back from helping Mark now than she'd been able to
hold back from the playground bullies twenty years ago.

Jamming the heel of her hand on the horn, she steered
her compact one-handed through the trees and straight at
the men holding Mark.

Her car jolted through a rut and crashed through a screen
of bushes. Heads turned. Her brother's startled white face

flashed in her headlights. Blood ran in a dark line from his nose. His attackers' faces were black and blank as figures in a nightmare. Ski masks?

She expected them to jump. She expected them to scatter. They didn't. They turned, dragging Mark like a shield into the path of her oncoming car.

She had no time. No choice. She stomped on the brake and skidded to a stop.

"For God's sake." Her brother's voice was thick and hoarse. "Get out of here!"

She groped for the stick shift. Reverse. Reverse. But bodies pressed around the car. Something—someone?— thudded against her hood. A man's hand thrust through her back window and scrabbled for her door lock. Tess clutched her door handle. It tore from her grasp, burning her palm, as the door jerked open.

She flung herself away, across the seat, but a man's hand grabbed her thigh. She screamed. He hung on, seizing her knee, dragging her from the car. The vinyl seat scraped her stomach. She hugged the seat, clung to the steering wheel. A weight pressed her thighs, her back, and then her fingers were peeled from the steering wheel and she was hauled from the car.

She was surrounded by bodies, overwhelmed by the scents of stale beer and wet wool and male excitement.

This was it. Fear tasted flat in her mouth and churned in her stomach. She was going to be gang raped. She was going to be killed, just like Judy Scott. Mark was going to be killed, and she couldn't do a damn thing to stop it.

Her breath rasped. Unless Jarek got here. Please, God, let Jarek get here in time.

She kicked desperately behind her, and heard the man holding her swear.

"Aw, hell," he said. "It's his sister."

Another man cursed. "Tess?"

Someone growled an obscene suggestion that sparked and ran through the circle of men like flame through a line of gun powder. Ugly laughter hissed. The threat of violence billowed and built like smoke leading to an explosion. Fear rose sour in the back of Tess's throat. She gagged on it.

Mark lunged and strained against the four men holding him. Someone slugged him in the kidney. His body jerked, then slumped. Tess struggled and cried out.

"Hey." This voice was younger, less certain. "This isn't what we're here for. She didn't do anything."

"We can't let her go."

Tess swallowed terror. She knew that voice. Didn't she?

"Not till we're done with him."

"Then get her out of here." The young voice grew more confident. Tess was sure she'd heard it before, too. These were locals. Neighbors.

Her brother's careless assurance played back in her mind: *I can take care of myself, you know.*

And her own warning: *Not if you get jumped on a dark road by a gang of vigilantes.*

Outrage burned in her gut and spilled like tears from her eyes.

"I'm not missing my chance to teach the jarhead a lesson," the man holding her objected.

"Give her to me, then."

Someone sniggered. "Better hope Connie doesn't find out you're snuggling up with Tess DeLucca."

"Shut up," the man said, his voice savage with embarrassment.

Connie. Larsen. Tess's brain ticked over. The young speaker was Officer Paul Larsen, and the other man was Carl Taylor. She was almost sure of it.

If she identified them, would it put Mark in even more danger? She was afraid it would.

But she could appeal to Paul, she thought frantically. Couldn't she? He *knew* Mark, they had played together in the park as kids, he couldn't stand by and watch while a bunch of thugs beat her brother to a bloody pulp...

Maybe he could.

Rough hands shoved her. Hard hands clutched her arms above the elbows and spun her around. She scratched at them with her nails. Paul Larsen swore and wrapped his arms around her to grab her wrists. He half marched, half dragged her away from the tower, toward the trees.

"No," she said. "Wait! Please."

He held her tighter. "I can't stop them."

She heard a muffled impact—a punch, a grunt—behind her and sobbed. "They'll kill him!"

"No." Paul's voice was too low and shaken to be reassuring. "It's just a warning. They'll let him go. After. I swear."

She struggled against his hold as horrible sounds drifted with awful clarity through the spring woods. Terrible sounds—threats and thumps—interspersed with even more terrible silences.

The playground taunts of childhood fights sang mockingly in her head. *Sticks and stones may break my bones, but names will never hurt me.* Tears ran down her face.

Mark groaned.

Tess wrenched her body from side to side, striking out with her feet. Paul grunted and gripped her close. *Better hope Connie doesn't find out you're snuggling up with Tess DeLucca.* She tried to bite his arm through his dark sweater. She hoped she left marks.

"Ouch." He shifted her roughly.

A light cut across her vision. Tess lifted her head in hope.

And saw a police car pull up to the edge of the graveled strip.

Jarek, she thought. Relief, warmth, triumph expanded her chest.

The cruiser's door opened, and Bud Sweet got out.

Her heart plummeted.

By the time the second police car showed up—three minutes later? five? a crawling eternity?—Tess barely had energy left to raise her head. She was blinded by tears, strangled by snot and the handkerchief Paul Larsen had stuffed in her mouth to keep her from screaming. Her cheeks were abraded. Her wrists were bruised.

Mark sagged between two men. He'd stopped groaning a while ago. Some of the energy had gone out of his assailants' punches.

A red light flashed from the turret atop the second car. A single blip sounded before the cruiser glided to a stop just outside the angled beam of the SUV's headlights. The door slammed, and a lean, compact figure stood backlit by the rotating red light.

"Oh, God," Paul Larsen said in Tess's ear. "I'm screwed."

Bud Sweet hitched his belt over his ample stomach and spoke for the first time since his arrival. "Okay, boys. You've had your fun. Now move along."

"No one goes anywhere," Jarek said in a cold, flat voice.

The group by the tower froze in the lights. Paul shrank deeper into the shadows. Jarek stood, his dark, disciplined figure flickering in the devilish red glow. Unmoving. Immovable.

Tess gulped against her gag. She wanted to cheer. She wanted to shriek a warning. What did Jarek think he was doing? He wasn't going to save her. He was going to get himself killed. He was in as much danger as Mark. What could he possibly do, one man against—

Sweet bridled. "'Scuse me, Chief, but I don't think you understand—"

Jarek angled his body. His hand was out of sight, behind his leg, but his stance made it clear he had his gun. Maybe he made it clear in some silent way that he would use it, too, because Sweet shut up.

"You can explain it to me," Jarek said mildly. "Back at the station." He pitched his voice to the trees. "Officer Larsen? That your vehicle I passed on the way in?"

Paul cursed softly and fervently. "Yes, sir," he called.

"I want a report on the victim's injuries. Do we need an ambulance here?"

"He's okay," volunteered one of the men still holding Mark. "We just beat the crap out of him."

"Larsen, get his name," Jarek snapped. "Take all their names. And if any of your pals isn't feeling particularly communicative, please remind them that I have already recorded their license plate numbers. Unless they all intend to report their vehicles as stolen within the past twenty-four hours, I already know who they are. Now…" Jarek's voice roughened like winter ice. The temperature in the clearing dropped by another ten degrees. Paul was sweating. "Where is Miss DeLucca?"

Paul dropped her like a burglar caught with an armload of stolen goods. Tess fell down and staggered forward. Her knees were weak. Her heart threatened to pound out her ears. It took her half a dozen paces to work her fingers around the gag and tear it out of her mouth.

"Here," she choked out. "I'm here."

She wanted Jarek to take her in his arms. She wanted to breathe him in, his confidence and his calm and his strength. But he didn't reach for her. If anything, he became more still, a frozen statue of a cop. She couldn't even tell if he was looking at her.

"Can you drive your car?" he asked.

She could barely walk. But she stumbled somehow to Mark's side. The men who had been holding him turned their faces away.

She worked saliva from her numb, dry mouth and spat. "I hate you," she told them. "I hope you die."

"Tess." Impatience edged Jarek's tone. "Can you drive?"

She sank by her brother. His breathing was loud and shallow. "Yes. I think so."

She fumbled for the pulse under Mark's jaw. It stuttered under her fingers. "Mark? Honey, can you hear me?"

His eyes opened, shining slits in his swollen face. He mumbled something.

She leaned closer to hear. "What?"

"You…alrigh'?" he slurred.

Her eyes filled. Her nose dripped. "I'm fine."

"Get your brother in the car," Jarek instructed. "Take him to the hospital."

"I don't know if I can move him," she blurted.

"I'll help you," Paul said.

She didn't thank him. Together, they loaded Mark into her car, careful of his ribs and his head.

She looked back once over her shoulder. Jarek stood braced in the flickering red light, a solitary figure against seven angry, sullen men.

How could she leave him with nothing but Paul's uncertain support and Bud Sweet's self-serving explanations? But how could she stay? Mark needed a doctor. Needed her.

She drove off with Jarek's reflection wavering in her rear

view mirror. One guardian against chaos, like a warrior angel in the mouth of hell.

Her heart splintered. But her faith, which had shattered years ago, or maybe just been worn down by rough handling, formed like a tiny diamond in her chest.

Jarek wanted to pound something. Specifically he wanted to sock Bud Sweet.

He stared across the metal chief's desk at his second in command. With an effort, he kept his eyes level and his voice even. "I have preliminary statements from witnesses. I'm turning them over to the prosecuting attorney in Fox Hole. And until her investigation is concluded, you and Officer Larsen are suspended with pay."

Sweet's face was red. "You can't treat me the same as Larsen."

"I just did."

"You need me," Sweet insisted. "You've got a murderer on the loose. You get rid of me now, and I'll see the town turn on you."

He probably would, Jarek thought grimly. He probably could. Jarek was the interloper here. Sweet was the hometown operator, a twenty-year veteran of the force...

Jarek's jaw clamped. None of which could be allowed to matter. "This town's already turned on one of its own. You're no good to me or anybody else if you don't follow procedure."

"Protecting the likes of Mark DeLucca?" Sweet sneered.

Contempt burned in Jarek. He exhaled carefully, trying to release it on his breath. The lieutenant honestly didn't get it. "Protecting the rights of all its citizens. Upholding the law means following the law. You blew it with DeLucca when you let personal feelings interfere with you doing your job."

Sweet put both hands flat on Jarek's desk and leaned forward. "You mean like you're doing with his sister?"

Jarek crossed his arms deliberately. "My relationship with Tess DeLucca has no bearing on my handling of this case."

"Bull," Sweet said. "She's putting out so you'll ease up on her little brother."

Jarek didn't realize he'd reached for Sweet until he saw his own hand fisted in the fat man's shirt. He released him in disgust, his own restrictions binding as a Kevlar vest. Upholding the law meant following the law, damn it. Plus Sweet, while he outweighed Jarek by sixty pounds or so, was a good ten years older.

"Turn over your gun and your shield," he said, soft and real precise. "And get out."

Bud Sweet straightened his creased shirt. He shot Jarek a vindictive look. "She's not worth it, you know. This isn't the first time the DeLucca girl's used her body to reduce a charge."

The words alerted Jarek like a creaking floorboard in an empty crack house. "What do you mean?"

"He means," Tess said from the doorway, "that he groped me in the back of his police car when I was fourteen. And said he would get the shoplifting charges against me dropped if I promised not to tell anybody."

Chapter 14

Tess shrugged, but the careless gesture did not hide the pain in her eyes or the tremble of her chin. "So I promised to keep our dirty little secret. Though I'd disagree with him now about which of us was using the other."

Jarek's blood ran cold and then hot with fury. His hands clenched by his sides.

"Is this true?" he demanded of Sweet.

His lieutenant's gaze slid sideways. He smirked. "I'd say she got the best of the bargain. I hardly touched her. Anyway, she was a real skinny girl."

Red rage erupted through Jarek's cool.

One hand hauled Sweet across his desk. The other hit him hard in the jaw.

There was a thunk, a gasp from Tess, the scrape of steel legs across linoleum as Sweet fell back against a chair. His meaty arms flailed before he grabbed the chair seat and dragged himself upright.

Jarek stepped around his desk and waited for Sweet's return punch.

But the veteran cop only pressed the back of his hand to his bleeding mouth and sneered, "Upholding the law means following procedure, huh?"

"Get out," Jarek said through his teeth.

"You can't take that bitch's word over mine on something that happened sixteen years ago."

"Yes, I can. You're through. Give me your gun and your shield. Now."

Sweet laid his .38 flat on a stack of reports. He unclipped his shield's leather holder and flipped it onto the desk. "You're going to be sorry," he warned.

"Not for this," Jarek said. No, not for this.

He watched his former lieutenant lurch from the room and then turned his attention to Tess. She stood to one side of the door, hugging her elbows, and all the regret he hadn't felt before crashed over him in a wave. Her golden skin was nearly gray. Her eyes were smudged with makeup and fatigue. He wanted to help her, shelter her, protect her.

He wanted to take her in his arms, but nothing in her expression or her posture hinted she would welcome such a gesture.

So he asked instead, roughly, "You all right?"

He thought her eyes filled with tears. She looked away. "Fine."

She was still keeping her secrets. His disappointment surprised him. But it was his job and his nature to seek answers. And Jarek wanted the key to the riddle of Tess DeLucca more than he'd wanted anything in a long time.

"What was it you took?" he asked.

"A rubber football," she said. "From the five and dime."

Jarek made the connection. "For Mark?"

"It was his birthday," she explained. As if she needed to defend her action to *him*. "He wanted one so much, and there wasn't anything—" Her voice wavered. She bit her lip to get it back under control.

There was his cue. Jarek crossed the room in two quick strides and took her in his arms. And maybe that was the signal *she* needed, because instead of shrugging him off, Tess turned her face into his chest and clutched his shirt and started to cry. First slow, leaking tears that soaked his shirt and then big, gulping sobs that shook them both.

He wrapped his arms around her tight and held her while she cried out the fear and frustration of this long night against his chest.

"It's okay," he murmured over and over into her soft hair, even though he didn't know if that was true. Didn't know if he could *make* it true, could make things up to her somehow. Make up for the hurts of her neglected childhood and the pain of her abuse and the loneliness of responsibility that she'd taken on too young.

Oh, yeah. Like that could happen. Look at the way he'd messed up his own family. He'd already demonstrated he was not exactly prime husband and father material.

But because he was trying, because she was warm and soft and her crying was tearing him up inside, he swallowed the lump in his own throat and stroked her dark hair and said stupid things like, "Shh, honey, it's okay," and "Everything's going to be all right."

After a while the sobs stopped. Her grip loosened. She sniffed against his shirt.

He reached into his back pocket and used his handkerchief to dry the tears from her warm, flushed cheeks. For some reason that nearly set her off again.

She used the heel of her hand to wipe her eyes and said,

"If you tell me to blow, it's going to really spoil the mood."

Jarek's arms tightened around her involuntarily. He loved her humor. He loved the strength that allowed her to laugh at both of them even when things were tough and emotions were high. He loved— He caught himself abruptly.

"I'm not going to tell you to blow," he said.

She gave him a watery smile. "Good."

"How's your brother?" he asked quietly.

"Three cracked ribs and some internal bleeding from where the fractures tore muscle tissue. They put a chest tube in in the E.R. The doctor said he was lucky. He'll be out of the hospital in a couple of days."

He hadn't protected her brother. But he could see to it that his attackers were brought to justice. "I'm charging Carl Taylor, Earl Willard, Walter Hotchkiss and Tom Dewey with aggravated assault."

"What about Paul Larsen?"

"Suspended with pay pending an independent review," he told her honestly. "He'll probably be fined and suspended. If he keeps his job—which is a big if at this point—I'm busting him back to traffic control. It's small payment for what he did to you, but—"

"It's enough," Tess said. "His wife will make him pay, believe me."

A silence fell. Not uncomfortable, but...awkward, Jarek decided. It felt good holding her like this. Maybe too good.

Tess gave this little smile that twisted him in knots. "Hell of a night," she said.

He thought of the reports he had left to write, the follow up calls and interviews he had to make tomorrow. "Yeah, well, it's not over yet."

Tess leaned back in his arms and gave him a look. The

angle of her body pushed their hips together, close enough that she had to feel how her nearness affected him. The look was the kind that even a rookie detective could identify as, well, significant. Jarek's blood left his brain and surged to his groin. The contact between their lower bodies became even more revealing and dangerous.

"It doesn't have to be," she said, still looking directly into his eyes. The warmth shimmering in her gaze stopped his breath. "Over, I mean."

Holy St. Mike.

The beautiful, sexy young woman in his arms had just made him an offer—Jarek was sure it was an offer, he might be out of practice, but he wasn't out of his mind—and he was considering saying no.

Okay, maybe he was out of his mind.

He asked, "Why?"

Tess blinked at him. "You need reasons?"

Yes. The drive for answers was part of who he was, of what he did. But this new need had nothing to do with his job. It left him vulnerable in a way that scared him. Carefully he reminded her, "You're the one who wanted to wait until you decided what an involvement between us would mean."

"And you were the one who said it didn't have to mean anything."

He stuck his hands in his pockets. "That was before."

"Before what?"

Before I figured out I could fall in love with you.

Don't tell her that. That was the one thing guaranteed to send commitment-phobic Tess running.

"Before all this business with your brother."

Her full lips pressed together. Was that disappointment in her eyes? "Mark's getting a blood test. He agreed to it tonight."

"That's not what I meant. Tess—"

"It's not a problem," she assured him. But she was already withdrawing from him, Jarek saw, his irritation barely masking his fear. Maybe not physically—he was the one who had set that distance between them—but in her mind. She lifted one shoulder in a shrug. "Hey, he's in the hospital anyway, right? What's the loss of a little more blood?"

"Look, what happened—" He stopped, frustrated. Never apologize to a civilian. Never explain. Every cop knew better than to lay himself open to charges of liability. And no police chief in the world handed ammunition to a reporter. But Jarek's own integrity—not to mention his sense of what he owed Tess—forced him to it.

"The attack on Mark should never have happened," he said stiffly. "Not in my department. Not on my watch. I'm trying to tell you I'm sorry."

She shook her head. "There are too many people in this town who remember Mark the way he was seven years ago."

"And more than a few who probably resent what he made of himself once he left," Jarek guessed.

Her eyes widened. "Exactly. So, you see, you weren't at fault."

"But I am responsible."

"No," she said. "You stopped them. You saved him. Saved me. And I appreciate it."

"You have every right to resent me for what happened tonight."

"Well, I don't. I'm grateful."

She meant it, Jarek saw. His heart contracted. Her gratitude was harder to bear than shouted accusations. If he accepted her offer now he'd be guilty of taking the worst kind of advantage.

"That's what I'm afraid of," he said.

Her eyes narrowed. "Wait a minute. You honestly think I want to go to bed with you as a way of saying thanks?"

"Basically."

"Boy, are you out to lunch," Tess said.

He almost smiled. Except that he was tired and turned on and losing control of the conversation. He wanted her, damn it. And it was taking every ounce of discipline he had not to take what he wanted. "It's not unreasonable," he said. "It's easy to mistake feelings of, well, gratitude for—"

Her eyes flashed. "Easy for you, maybe." She poked a finger in the center of his chest. "I know what I'm feeling. I know what I want. If *you've* changed *your* mind—"

She wanted him. She'd said so in no uncertain terms. Rejecting her now would humiliate her.

And damn near kill him.

Relief rolled through him. He took the hand that was stabbing at his chest and held it in both of his.

"I haven't changed my mind," he said quietly.

"Oh." She swallowed.

He watched the movement of her throat and the pulse fluttering under the angle of her jaw. She didn't look like a woman claiming a lover, he thought with tender amusement. She looked...apprehensive.

He leaned forward, still holding their clasped hands against his chest, and kissed her gently on the mouth.

Her lips were warm and stiff with surprise. Patiently he kept his lips on hers until they softened and relaxed. Until she softened, opening her mouth with a little sigh, closing her eyes.

He kissed her again, a slow, soft kiss that promised more than it took.

When he raised his head, she sighed again and rested her

forehead against his shoulder. It felt good there. Her dark hair slipped forward, hiding her face.

"I don't want you to think I'm doing this to get Mark off," she said.

Jarek froze. And then he recognized the ugly echo of Bud Sweet's insinuations. Fury at the man who had abused her youth and her loyalty and her fear slammed into him. But he kept all traces of it from his touch on her cheek, all shadow of it from his voice. Tess needed to lay this particular ghost to rest. And he needed to be the one to help her do it.

"I don't. As long as you don't think all cops are after one thing."

She made a sound against his chest that could have been a laugh or a sob. "Deal," she said. She lifted her head, and her golden eyes were glowing. "Your place or mine?"

He wanted her under his roof, in his bed. He wanted to stake his claim so deep she wouldn't have time for ghosts or comparisons. "Mine."

Still she hesitated. "Allie—?"

"Is at my parents' house."

Yesterday, miraculously, Allie hadn't spent the drive to Chicago slouched in her seat, hiding in her headphones. She actually volunteered comments. She liked her new room, she said. She showed off her new nail polish.

Tess did it, she'd confided, with a sideways glance at her father. *Do you like it?*

Jarek wasn't sure. Wasn't ten too young for nail polish? But his daughter was smiling and talking to him, and if her new manicure was responsible, then he would take the nail polish and be grateful. If Tess was responsible... Well, there was time ahead to decide how he felt about that.

Tonight he only had to think about Tess. Selfishly he

was glad. Tonight was for the two of them. Only for him. Only for her.

Tonight he would show her.

Jarek's bedroom was like his car, dark and practical. Tess stopped just inside the door, her heart threatening to pound its way out of her chest. The only personal items she could see were a picture of Allie on Jarek's dresser and a crucifix on the wall by the bathroom.

He entered the room quietly behind her. "All right?"

She wasn't sure. On the ride over, despite the warmth of his hand on her knee and the simmer of her own blood, she'd had time to worry. Time to cool. All the doubting voices of experience had snickered in her brain like unwelcome back seat passengers. And the voices in her head sounded suspiciously like his brother. Disturbingly like hers.

You're not what he needs.

You are such a sucker.

Shut up, she told them fiercely.

"I'm fine," she said. "I'm looking."

Jarek kissed the side of her neck, and the kick of her pulse temporarily drowned out the voices. "At what?"

"Your room. It's very…" Grown-up, she thought. Intimidating.

"Very…?" he prompted.

She moistened her lips. The solid furniture and plain walls made her feel like she'd intruded on a priest's cell or a warrior's tent.

"Functional," she said.

His laughter was a vibration against her back, a warm breath against her ear. It stirred the fine hair at her nape and something else low in her belly.

"It's been a long time for me," Jarek said. "But I think the bed still works."

His self-deprecating humor and his honesty gave her the courage to turn in his arms. "I don't know what you've heard about me. I don't know what you expect. But I'm not a big mattress tester, either."

His hard mouth curved. But his eyes were serious and very steady. "I'll keep it in mind."

"You believe me?"

"Yes."

Just that one word. She wasn't used to unqualified...anything, let alone acceptance. She poked at it, cautiously, like a suspicious housewife with a fresh tomato. "Why?"

"I'm a detective, Tess. Used to be a detective. I go on the evidence."

She was surprised she could still be disappointed. But she was. Oh, she was. "You checked me out?" she asked, indignation rising in her voice.

He frowned. "No. It's a personal observation. The truth is important to you. That's one of the things I admire about you—your honesty. The way you do your job." He reached to smooth a strand of her hair behind one ear. His touch lingered. The back of his fingers brushed her jaw. "I didn't figure you'd lie to me, that's all. Not about this."

The gift of his words, the warmth of his touch, made her squirm inside with pleasure. She turned her cheek into his palm. "Oh. I thought maybe you meant some other kind of evidence."

"Hmm..." He kissed one eyebrow. She closed her eyes. "I did notice you don't travel with an overnight bag."

"No toothbrush," she agreed breathlessly as his mouth cruised the side of her face.

He bit the point of her jaw, and she melted. "I can give you a toothbrush."

His chest was warm and solid under her seeking hands. He was warm lower down, too, and more solid by the second. She moved her hips experimentally, and he grasped her rear end in both large hands and pulled her firmly against him. Oh, boy.

"No condoms." She gasped.

"I've got condoms."

"I didn't even bring—" the hot ridge rubbing between her legs felt so good "—a change of underwear."

He eased her legs open with his knee and moved between her thighs. "You're not going to need underwear," he said. "Not for a long time."

He stroked a line of fire from her hips to her waist. Tugging her shirt free of her slacks, he slid his hand up and inside, across her quivering back and around to her front. His fingers skimmed her breast. Desire bolted through her.

She gasped. "We could get rid of it now. The underwear."

She felt his smile against the side of her face. "Now would be good."

Despite his agreement, he didn't seem to be in any particular hurry. He kissed her softly, and then not so softly, and then hard and deep. She swayed and sagged against him, opening her mouth wide, urging him on, urging him in. He palmed her breast, teasing her nipple to an aching point.

He rubbed and made her sigh. He squeezed and made her moan. He kissed her, his tongue thrusting boldly into her mouth in a way that melted her knees. And then he went back to his light, delicate tracing through the lace of her bra.

Tess inhaled in frustration. This all felt good. Wonderful, in fact. But it wasn't enough.

Leaning back against his supporting arm, she dragged her T-shirt over her head and dropped it on his tidy floor. Self-consciously she combed her hair with her fingers. But Jarek wasn't looking at her hair, she realized. He was staring at her breasts in their bright red demibra.

He raised his gaze, and she jolted at the heat in his eyes. Jarek cleared his throat. "I may change my mind. About your underwear."

Distracted by the hard, almost primitive cast of his face, it took Tess a while to absorb his words. She grinned. "Like it?"

"Yeah. Is the rest of it that—" He gestured with one hand, apparently at a loss for words.

"That what?" she prompted, filled with a new, delicious sense of her own power.

Humor and hunger warred in his eyes. His gaze traveled from her face to her breasts. To her belly and the zipper of her jeans. Her insides clenched. Her thighs loosened.

"That…red?" he asked.

She was dizzy with delight, drunk with confidence, swooning from the look in his eyes. "Why don't you find out?"

He reached for her. Snagging a finger in the front closure of the jazzy red bra, he tugged her forward. It snapped open, and he smoothed the lace cups back from her breasts with his long, blunt-tipped fingers. Her heart stuttered. His hands stilled.

"Beautiful," he said.

She squirmed, uncomfortable with compliments. "I thought you liked the bra."

His voice thick, he said, "I like you better."

He kissed the slope of her breast above her shaking heart.

He kissed the outside curve, his hair brushing her arm. He ran his tongue along the heavy underside, and her nipple puckered. He touched it with just the tip of his tongue, and she gasped.

"Hot," he said, and took her into his mouth, tasting her fully. He pushed her breasts together and feasted on her nipples, drawing out her response, making her twist and sigh.

He unbuttoned her jeans. His hands slid everywhere, stroking, commanding. He nuzzled and sucked. Through the pulse pounding in her ears, drumming in her blood, she heard an unfamiliar, needy moan. Hers. She bit her lip.

She touched his jaw. She tugged on his short hair. He straightened and wrapped his arms around her, so that she could feel him hard and reassuring all along her body. Her bare breasts rubbed his rough cotton shirt front. He kissed her, his mouth hot and possessive, and backed her toward his bed.

Like dancing, she thought, and laughed in pure pleasure.

Jarek raised his head. He lifted an eyebrow. "Want to let me in on the joke?" he asked mildly.

"No joke," she assured him. And then thought, why not tell him? It was true, and he didn't mind it when she told the truth. "I'm happy, that's all."

His rare smile broke, dazzling as the sun on snow. "Honey, I haven't begun to make you happy yet."

He was as good as his word.

He tumbled her back on his bed—it bounced—and came down on top of her. His arms braced beside her head. His weight pinned her to the mattress. He felt strong. Solid. Incredible. Tess sighed in relief. They were getting somewhere now. But he went back to kissing her mouth. He kissed her throat. He savored her breasts and burned a hot trail down her stomach, using his lips and teeth and tongue until her skin was tender and her emotions were raw.

Tess arched mindlessly as he slid one finger along her zipper. His hands spanned her waist, shoving her jeans over her butt, grazing her bare skin.

She sucked in her stomach. What if he didn't like—?

"Thong panties?" Jarek groaned and rested his forehead on the curve of her belly. "Red thong panties. Honey, I'm a dead man."

She relaxed. Smiled. Opened her arms wide and let them fall against the pillows of his big, hard bed. "Gee," she said. "I feel terrible. Maybe you should, I don't know, punish me or something."

Jarek laughed, a short, surprised sound that did nothing to relieve the tension pulsing through him. He looked down again at Tess, at her pale gold skin and the shadow of dark curls. At the strip of scarlet silk that taunted him like a red flag in front of a bull.

Red. Holy St. Mike.

He took a deep breath. He was not going to lose it, he promised himself. He was going to make it good and slow for her. So slow she would never forget it. So good she would come back for more.

He worked her jeans down her thighs. Both of them shuddered as he paused to touch, to taste. He stroked her long, sleek legs. He kissed her smooth, curved belly. She tasted like woman, like scented soap and sex. He really had died and gone to heaven.

He eased his fingers along the edge of red elastic, his touch delicate, flirting with the soft curls, following the tender crease of her thigh. And when she made a sound of sweet excitement, when her hips rolled and lifted in invitation, he pulled that skimpy triangle of silk out of the way and put his mouth on her.

He wanted to learn her body like her responses were a puzzle he had to solve.

But he never had a chance. He was caught up in her response, her scent, her cries, the twisting movement of her hot, sleek body. She swamped him, surrounded him, towed him under and carried him out to sea. She shuddered as she crested the first time, gripped his shoulder and tugged his hair and dragged him up to her. They rolled across the mattress, while his blood roared in his ears and her hands wrestled with his clothes.

"Take it off," she said through her teeth.

It. His mind, pummeled by sensation, whirled uselessly. His shirt? His pants?

Tess solved his dilemma. She grabbed the edges of his shirt and pulled. She yanked the button free of his slacks and grasped the tab of his zipper.

"Hey." He was startled to a moment's sanity. "Watch the teeth, honey."

She froze. "Sorry."

He swore. "Never mind."

He took her mouth with urgent greed, and she made this little sound at the back of her throat—*heaven*—and ravaged him back, capturing him in her arms, parting her warm, smooth thighs. For him.

Her fingers wrapped him, and his mind went blank. His vision blurred. While her hands streaked over him, he groped for the box of condoms, fumbled with protection. He wanted to be inside her. He needed to be inside her now.

He felt her open for him, saw her lips part and her eyes widen as he took her hands, as he laced his fingers with hers and pressed inside her. One long, slow stroke into the heat and the heart of her. Home.

She stretched to welcome him, arched to receive him.

They moved together, in a simple rhythm that drew him in and drove him on. Everything he was, everything he wanted, was here in this bed with her now. Her hands clasped his. Her gaze held his. She tightened around him with a soft, shuddering sigh, and his world exploded. He lay on her, deafened, breathless, his heart hammering and a dozen red-on-black suns dancing behind his eyelids.

Chapter 15

The more things changed, the more they stayed the same, Tess thought.

She was naked between the sheets of Jarek's bed. Last night the earth had moved, the stars stood still, and Jarek Denko had made her feel like a natural woman. Any and every clichéd love song playing on the radio had suddenly made sense.

And she still woke up alone.

Surprise, surprise.

She eased onto her side, trying not to feel Jarek in every delicious ache and twinge, and squinted at the bedside table. Was it really three in the morning? Had to be. The clock was one of those digital display models, as practical as everything else in this room. Well, everything except her. Tess looked at the floor, where her red bra made a bright spot on the carpet. She definitely did not match the rest of Jarek's decor.

She sat up and started patting down the sheets at the

bottom of the bed for her panties. At the last moment, she grabbed another foil packet from beside the bed and folded her fingers over it.

In her underwear and Jarek's shirt, she padded barefoot down the stairs, following a dim glow from the living room. The television? Tess frowned. Maybe Jarek wasn't a cuddle-me-close kind of guy, but she'd never have guessed he'd give up his bed to watch late night truck racing.

But what else was keeping him up in the middle of the night?

She stopped in the doorway. Jarek sprawled on the big leather couch, a laptop balanced on his thighs, his intense face lit by the blue glow of the computer screen and the slanting yellow light of a lamp. He wore jeans. Nothing else.

Just the sight of him—those broad, bare, powerful shoulders, the vulnerable hollow above his collarbone, his hair-roughened chest and the smooth, tender skin of his neck—did something funny to her insides. He looked tired and preoccupied and very, very sexy. Every single spot on her body he'd touched or kissed or licked, every stretched muscle and satisfied nerve ending, came alive and shouted *Mine*.

As if he could hear that silent chorus, he looked up, his gray eyes dark and distracted. And then he smiled. "Hi."

She flushed at being caught mooning over him like a fourth-grader with her first crush. He was busy. She shouldn't have come down. "Hi. I woke up and you, um, weren't there."

Great. She wasn't only intruding, she was whining.

"Sorry." Jarek rubbed his face with one hand. "I thought I'd get some work out of the way while you were sleeping."

She tried a joke. "You write a lot of traffic tickets at three in the morning?"

"Actually I'm trying to get the interviews typed up to turn over to the state's attorney in Fox Hole."

He sounded weary.

She took a step closer, holding the edges of his shirt together, drawn more by the need in his voice than the desire clamoring in her own body. "What will he do with them?"

"She," Jarek corrected her absently. "The prosecuting attorney is a woman. She'll turn them over to the sheriff to investigate police misconduct in the attack on your brother. I can't be involved. The integrity of the review process has to be above question."

"There's no question about your integrity," Tess said fiercely.

"Well, there will be," Jarek said with a touch of bitterness.

She sat on the arm of the couch, tugged by guilt and concern. Jarek's gaze fell to her exposed thigh and darkened. Flushing, she fussed with the hem of the shirt, trying to keep the condom hidden in her hand. "No, there won't. The mayor and the town council hired you because they knew the police department needed new leadership. New discipline. New standards."

"The new broom sweeps clean?"

"Absolutely."

"And how are they going to react when the new broom knocks a hole through their floorboards?"

She didn't know. "Do you regret it?" she asked.

"Regret what? Stopping half a dozen drunk vigilantes from beating the crap out of a former serviceman?" He shook his head. "No."

"No, I meant…hitting Sweet."

Jarek grinned, a brief, sharp grin that made him look disconcertingly like his brother Aleksy. "The only thing I regret is not breaking the bastard's jaw. But this whole incident has forced me to reconsider what I'm doing in this town."

She risked a touch on his bare arm. "What do you mean?"

"I've always defined myself by my job. And I haven't done my job here very well."

"You've done everything a man could do."

"I don't know." He rubbed the back of his neck with one hand. "At least if I'd put your brother in custody for the murder of Judy Scott, the way Sweet wanted, they wouldn't have jumped him."

"But Mark didn't do it."

"I haven't proved that."

"You will," Tess said. "When the blood tests come in."

"You have that much faith in him." His voice was flat.

"I have that much faith in both of you. You'll find the person who did this, Jarek. And you'll stop him."

He met her eyes, and something deep and decent flowed between them. A question asked. A reassurance given. Tess felt the warmth of it well in her chest, saw it surge in his eyes.

"Maybe," he said, still holding her gaze. "Thanks."

And even though Tess knew it was a mistake, even though she knew it was an illusion—she couldn't give him what he wanted, she'd never been able to give anyone what they wanted or needed. She hadn't stopped her father from leaving or her mother from drinking or her brother from getting into trouble. Anyway, even though she knew all that, that look made her feel mighty good.

Jarek exhaled and looked away, breaking the link. Leaving her shaken and aching with possibility.

"I just need to focus on the right connection," he said with an edge of frustration. "There is one. Two of the three attempts occurred after the women left the Blue Moon. Two of the targets worked at the hospital. And both Carolyn Logan and Sherry Biddleman described a dark, unmarked car with police-style lights."

Tess tried to gather her thoughts back from places they had no business wandering. Jarek didn't need her stupid daydreams. He needed her knowledge of the town. "*Could* it be a police connection?"

"We've been over this. God knows I've been over it. I'm tracking down every man in town with any connection to the police or the fire department or emergency rescue. I checked out every officer's alibi for the night Biddleman was stopped. And I'm going back over every one of them now. Particularly Sweet's."

"Because he groped me sixteen years ago?"

"Because he's a pervert and a predator. Yes."

A part of Tess wanted Sweet—the man who had shamed and scared and scarred her—to be guilty of the assaults, too. But Jarek had told her he prized her ability to tell the truth. So she said, honestly, "A pervert maybe. But not a violent one. Whoever attacked Carolyn and killed Judy was angry. I don't think Bud Sweet is capable of hiding that kind of rage all this time."

Reluctantly Jarek nodded. "Rape is usually about anger. Or power. I'm betting our guy feels threatened in some way, and the rapes are his attempt to re-establish control. Over his victims and over his own life."

As the child of alcoholics, Tess understood the longing for control. There were years of her childhood when the safest way to handle emotions was not to acknowledge them and the only good memories were repressed ones. Still, the idea that someone was out there managing his emotions by attacking, degrading and killing women gave her the creeps. She thought of the way their neighbors had turned on Mark, their friendliness a mask for violence, and shivered.

Jarek's gaze sharpened. "Cold?"

"No. Scared," she said without thinking.

Worried about the attacks.

Afraid for her brother.

And terrified that the protective skin she'd grown over her emotions was about to be stripped away. Because she wasn't in control anymore. Jarek Denko had wrested control from her. And taken her heart.

He shifted the laptop to the floor and stretched his arm to her. The yellow lamplight slid over the well-defined muscles of his arm and exaggerated the harsh planes of his face. She trembled with lust and longing and fear.

"Come here."

Bad idea, she thought.

I know what I'm feeling, she'd boasted to him a few hours ago. *I know what I want.*

Only the more she was with him, the more she wanted. How much longer until she wanted it all, and Jarek decided he didn't have any more to give?

Her mouth was dry. Her entire life, Tess had been the one who gave—to her mother, to her brother, to her job. There was power in that, in being the one who was needed.

Now the power was on Jarek's side, and she was afraid.

"I should let you get back to work," she said.

"I'd rather take you back to bed."

Desire jolted her heartbeat. But she shook her head, held back by her fear and her pride. "That's okay. You don't have to."

His eyes narrowed. "Don't have to?" he repeated carefully.

"I just meant—" He looked dangerous, she thought. What had she said to upset him? "You're probably tired, so—"

"I'm not tired."

"Sure, you are," she said, pulling his shirt more tightly around her. The edges of the packet bit into her palm. Why didn't he let her go with her excuse and her dignity intact? He was the one who couldn't wait to hop out of bed with her, wasn't he? "We both are. It's been a long day, and—"

"I'm not too tired to make love to you, Tess."

A thrill ran through her. Her body sent up another chorus of tweaks and twinges, reminding her how good it had been. How good he had been.

And yet Jarek, she thought resentfully, was as cool and unruffled as lake water. His voice was patient. His eyes were steady. Only a muscle jerking at the side of his jaw indicated that they were discussing anything more significant than where to go for dinner or whose turn it was to take out the garbage.

"Thanks," she said, backing toward the hall. "But I've changed my mind."

He moved so fast she didn't have time to evade him. One hand wrapped her waist and pressed her to his hard, half naked body. The other caught her chin.

"Let's see if I can change it back for you," he said, an edge to his voice. And his mouth swooped down on hers.

He was anything but cold now. He was hot and hungry. Provoked.

She'd intended to provoke him, she realized, as his hands took, as his mouth plundered. She wanted to shake his calm control, to make him as needy as she was.

Even if it was only for sex.

But even as that thought arrowed through her brain and

quivered in her heart, her body responded to his. Now that it knew what he could do for her, it was already melting, tightening, adjusting to his. She felt him harden against her, and her thighs loosened. Her pelvis tilted, seeking more. The kiss of his body hair, the smell of his skin... They overwhelmed her, tastes, textures, sensations, sliding over her, bursting through her.

When he reached between the panels of his shirt and cupped her, she was wet and ready for him. He groaned in satisfaction. She quaked with need.

"I want—" She moaned as he touched her. "I need—"

He gave. His zipper rasped. She tugged his jeans down, her hands frantic. He took the condom from her as her fingers flexed, as she felt the lovely muscle of his buttocks bunch under her touch.

Elastic cut into her hip as he wrapped his hands in the skimpy red strip and ripped it off her. She cried out in protest and excitement. He transferred his grip to her buttocks and lifted her, backed her against his living-room wall. When the cool plaster hit her back, she jarred in shock. And then she felt him, thick and hot and seeking at her body's entrance, and softened in surrender. She would give him...anything. Whatever he wanted, as long as he didn't stop.

She braced on his shoulders, wrapped her thighs around his waist, and felt him come into her. He possessed her. Impaled her. And there was nothing she could do, no way to hold back her body or her rioting emotions. He completely supported her, touched every part of her. Every movement drove him deeper. His legs were rock solid. His breathing was harsh and shallow. His arms trembled.

His hands gripped her hips, lifting, pulling. Her body bowed as he thrust into her, harder, faster, demanding. She throbbed around him as he pounded into her, strength to strength, need to need, matched. Mated.

He kissed her, licking into her mouth, while his fingers pressed tight on her behind, and his body rubbed warm and rough against her front. He was hot and solid, and he filled her again and again. His breath was hot on her face, in her ear. He said, "Come on," tightly, impatiently, and then he groaned her name, "Tess," and then he said, *"Now."*

At his command, she shattered, and he erupted.

It was hard to regret head-banging, mind-blowing, heart-stopping sex, but Jarek was giving it a shot.

He set the drugstore bag next to the full mug of coffee on the nightstand and turned to see if the soft crinkle had disturbed Tess. She stirred and sighed, but she didn't wake up.

She was so damn beautiful. And she looked really good in his bed, her full, soft mouth relaxed in sleep, her dark hair tangled on his pillow, her arms faintly golden against his sheets. She looked like a princess in some fairy tale.

Yeah, and he was the overage, oversexed caveman faced with convincing her he could replace Prince Charming.

Jarek shoved his hands into his pockets. "Tess?"

Her shoulder hunched. Her lashes fluttered and lifted. Just for a second, before thought and caution woke, he imagined the sun shone in her eyes. And then she raised a hand and covered her face.

"Oh, God. Do I smell coffee?"

"Yeah. I brought you a cup. On the nightstand."

She hugged the sheet to her breasts and reached. He could see the outline of her nipples, the curve of her hip, and his body, which was forty years old and ought to know better, reacted hotly and instantly.

"How did you sleep?" he asked like a polite host instead

of the Neanderthal who had ripped her underwear last night.

She cradled her mug in both hands. "Fine, thank you," she said, just as politely. Was it the steam that brought that faint, irresistible flush to her cheeks?

"I brought you some other things, too. In the bag."

She looked doubtful, but she put down the cup and anchored the sheet in place with her arms to take the bag.

"A toothbrush." She smiled. Jarek felt some of the tension ease from his shoulders. "And...lotion?"

"I don't know what you like. My sister uses that stuff."

"It's very nice." Tess put the bottle on top of the sheet next to the cellophane wrapped toothbrush. "And what is—" Her voice flattened. "Underwear."

Jarek's jaw set. He'd wanted to buy her something special to replace the stuff he'd torn. Wanted to buy it someplace special—Marshall Fields, maybe, or even Victoria's Secret—to atone for his lack of finesse. But at seven o'clock on a rainy Tuesday morning, he'd had to settle for the discount drug chain on Highway 12, where his options were limited to skimpy nylon knockoffs and oversized cotton numbers that looked like something Baba, his grandmother, would wear.

In the end, remembering the mind-boggling, fantasy-inspiring red thong, he'd gone for one of the skimpy knockoffs.

Mistake, he thought now, looking at her stunned face. The purple lace panties dangled from her hand. She thought they were sleazy. Hell, they were sleazy.

"They're very...bright." Her mouth quivered. Oh, God, she wasn't going to cry, was she?

"I had to get you something." He took his hands out of his pockets and then jammed them back in. He didn't trust himself with all that golden skin so temptingly close.

She raised an eyebrow. "Trying to buy my silence?"

"What the hell are you talking about?"

"You don't need to bribe me. I'm not going to go home and write 'Police Chief Beds Murder Suspect's Sister' for the *Gazette*."

His jaw set. He didn't think he deserved that. "Listen, I don't care who knows I took you to bed. Write us up for the damn paper. Take out an ad. Send in an engagement announcement, if you want."

She winced and studied her nails. "That seems an equally extreme and unnecessary response. I'm a big girl, Jarek. I don't expect things—I don't expect you to buy me gifts just because you—just because we slept together one time."

Bribes, she called them. Gifts. Like no one ever bought her anything before.

And maybe no one had.

Maybe that was her problem, Jarek realized. She didn't expect anything from anyone.

Or maybe it was his problem now.

Slept together one time? he thought. Get used to it, honey.

Frustration roughened his voice. "Damn it, Tess, it's no big deal. I wanted to do something for you, that's all."

Her wide gold eyes were serious and uncertain. They tore his heart. "That's it?"

"That's it." If he left out a couple of little facts. Like he was falling in love with her. "Well, and I never ripped off a woman's clothing before."

She grinned, as if his discomfort gave her confidence. "Never?"

"You're the first."

"Thank you." She touched his wrist lightly with her red-tipped fingers. "I think I like that. Being your first."

She could be his last, he thought, if she wanted. He covered her hand with his as he bent to kiss her. She could be his one and only.

But if Tess couldn't accept a pair of cheap panties from him, she sure as hell wasn't ready for a proposal of marriage.

He had to go slow, Jarek thought, even as her lips warmed and parted under his and his blood hammered in his ears. He had to stay in control. Protect Tess. Clear Mark. Do his job.

"I've got to get to work," he said, straightening up, away from temptation.

Tess drew back, her hands tightening on the sheet. "I'll get out of your hair, then."

He knew her well enough now to hear the hurt under the careless tone.

"No," he said. "Take your time. Take a shower." He liked that, liked imagining her wet and naked in his bathroom. "Take the day off, if you want. I'll be home by six. Seven," he amended.

"Tess!" She heard the dead bolt lock snick back. The door to the Blue Moon opened, and Tim Brown stood framed in the dark entrance. "I didn't expect to see you this morning."

She smiled apologetically from the stoop, hugging her arms against the chilly lake breeze. "Hi, Tim. Got a minute?"

"For you, sure. You taking the day off?"

Take the day off, if you want. I'll be home by six. Seven.

She was not waiting around on the fringes of Jarek's life until he had time for her. She had her own job to do, her own family to take care of. She was on her way to the hospital now.

But she smiled at Tim and said, "Sort of."

"Must run in the family. I don't want to tell tales, but your brother never showed up for work last night."

She fingered her purse strap. "I know. That's what I wanted to talk to you about."

Tim frowned, but swung the door wider. "Coffee?"

She'd had coffee. Jarek's coffee. The memory and the caffeine churned in her stomach and thrummed in her blood. "I don't need anything. Thanks."

"Orange juice?"

Why was everyone suddenly so determined to offer her things? Coffee. Orange juice. Underwear.

Oh, boy. Tess took a deep breath, trying not to think about the unfamiliar purple panties hugging her rear end. "Orange juice would be fine."

"You got it," Tim said. "Come on in."

Their footsteps echoed on the plank floor as he led the way to the main room. The blinds were still closed, the chairs still up on the empty tables. Tim slipped behind the bar, where a big stuffed fish—a pike—leered over the rows of polished glasses. When he reached for one, his sleeve pulled back, and Tess could see a long red scratch on his arm.

She slid onto a stool and propped her elbows on the bar. "Ouch. Hurt yourself?"

"What? Oh." He glanced at his wrist. "Cut myself in the kitchen. It's nothing." He tugged his sleeve down and whisked the orange juice out of the bar refrigerator. "So, what's up with Mark?"

She watched him splash juice over ice. If she concentrated really hard, she could get through this conversation without breaking down into tears. Without screaming accusations against their neighbors. "Mark won't be in to work today. In fact, he won't be able to come in for a while.''

Tim set the glass on a napkin and nudged it toward her. ''Is he sick?''

She toyed with the edge of the napkin. ''He's in the hospital, Tim.''

''My God.'' He looked shaken. ''I'm sorry. What happened?''

Tess appreciated his sympathy. But then, Tim had always been willing to give Mark a chance. She liked to imagine his friendliness stemmed from genuine liking, and not just because her brother was good at quelling the drunks on a Saturday night.

''Mark got beat up last night. By a bunch of drunken yahoos who thought he was responsible for the attack on Judy Scott.''

''I can't believe it. Mark?''

She nodded. ''It took six of them, but...'' Her voice trailed off.

''That's terrible. Is he going to be all right?''

She was grateful his first question was about Mark's health and not his guilt. ''I think so. I'm on my way to see him now, actually. They took the chest tube out this morning.''

''Well, that's good,'' Tim said. ''So he'll recover?''

''Physically? Yes. But emotionally...'' Her throat closed. She forced a sip of orange juice. ''I just can't get past the idea that people I thought I knew could do something like this. I feel like I can't trust our neighbors anymore. I don't trust my own judgment. What will happen when Mark's released from the hospital?''

''Well, you know he always has a job here.'' Tim rubbed a rag over the polished surface of the bar. ''Do they still think he did it?''

Tess held the cold glass to her hot forehead. "I don't know what people think anymore. I'm just hoping the blood test will prove he's innocent."

The rag paused in its circles. "What blood test?"

"The police collected blood from under Judy Scott's fingernails. If Mark's not a match, that would rule him out as a suspect."

"Gee, I didn't know that. So, everything's going to be all right." Tim smiled. "Isn't it lucky you have an in with the police."

Jarek leaned back in his chair, adjusting the phone under his jaw. He'd spent the last several hours alone in his office, shuffling and arranging his facts like cards in a mental game of solitaire: red on black in changing sequences, trying to line up the evidence in just the right order to solve the puzzle and win the game.

Now he jotted another note and asked Aleksy, "He retired in '96? You sure he wasn't fired?"

"Nope. But here's where it gets interesting." Even through the telephone line, Jarek could feel his brother's excitement. "You told me to ask around. So, two months before the retirement went through, guess whose ex-wife's house burned down under questionable circumstances?"

Jarek's attention sharpened as another card fell into place. "Arson?"

"Could have been. Real professional job."

"So, what happened?"

"Your guy's got twenty years in the department with no previous disciplinary action. What do you think happened?"

"The union negotiated a deal," Jarek concluded grimly. It made sense. The firefighters' union in Chicago had some of the best and bravest in the city. And almost as much clout as the police. They would protect one of their own.

"You got it. Well, there were no fatalities," Aleksy said. "And no proof."

"So the city paid him off and settled for him leaving town." Jarek made another note. "Okay. Thanks, bro."

"You owe me."

Jarek stood and reached for his jacket. "Fine. If this pans out, you can be best man at my wedding."

His brother swore, disgusted. "Hell, I've done that already."

Jarek tried not to let his brother's words get to him. "Maybe we'd both make a better job of it this time."

This time.

With Tess.

Just for a minute, as he hung up the phone and headed to his car, Jarek let himself feel really good thinking about it. He'd never figured when he moved to Eden that domestic bliss could come packaged in black leather pants.

But maybe they could pull it off. This time. It wasn't just that his prospective bride was different. The groom...well, he was different, too. Older, for sure. Wiser, he hoped. More attuned to what really mattered.

Jarek turned into a neat little subdivision of tidy lawns and semidetached garages.

What mattered now was Tess. Not just her happiness, but her safety. Because before Jarek could concentrate on being the man she wanted, he had to be the cop she needed.

He checked house numbers and pulled up in front of a small brick house with white trim, black shutters, and a bright wreath of plastic flowers on the door. He went up the swept walk to the curtained door.

A young blond woman—he recognized her from the

church fund-raiser—answered his knock, her pretty face creased in puzzlement.

He showed her his shield. ''Mrs. Brown? Heather Brown? Is your husband at home?''

Chapter 16

Tess shifted on the bar stool in embarrassment. "I wouldn't say I had an 'in' with the police, exactly."

Tim raised a knowing eyebrow. "Right. What would you call it? Exactly?"

"It—I'm…"

—*sleeping with the chief of police.*

Hot blood swept her cheeks. She hid behind her orange juice. "For heaven's sake, Tim, I'm a reporter. You hear things in my line of work."

"Mine, too," the bar owner said promptly. "And one of the things I hear—and this isn't necessarily my opinion— is that our new police chief is more interested in chasing tail than catching bad guys."

Tess winced. What she had experienced with Jarek was too new, too private, too precious for sharing. Even with a nice guy who had taken a chance on her brother.

Or maybe she was simply too confused to talk about it

yet. Maybe she wasn't sure yet how this new relationship would fit into her life. How she fit into his.

But she didn't have any doubts at all about Jarek's integrity. Or his devotion to his job.

"He's a good man," she said, more sharply than she intended.

"Hey." Tim raised both palms in mock surrender. "I said that's what I heard. I didn't say I agreed with it. As far as I'm concerned, the chief is like Dick Tracy. He's Dudley Do-Right. Okay?"

She smiled. "Sorry. I guess I'm a little—" *insecure,* she thought "—touchy on the subject."

"Not a problem," Tim said. He slid a plastic bin of limes and lemons out of the refrigerator and set it next to the cutting board. "So, are you two serious?"

She didn't have the experience to judge. She didn't have the confidence to say. She watched the fruit fall into neat wedges beneath Tim's knife.

"He likes my underwear," she joked.

The knife—it was a big kitchen knife, a chef's knife—paused. "Only your underwear?"

Tess had a sudden memory of Jarek saying thickly, *I like you better,* and her body flushed with heat, and her muscles clenched deep inside.

But she was already regretting her flippant comment. She didn't want what she felt, what she shared with Jarek, reduced to a snigger over drinks in the bar.

So she said, more or less honestly, "I don't know how he feels."

"You have to have some idea," Tim said.

She shook her head.

"Hopes? Expectations?"

She didn't expect anything from anyone. If you let yourself hope, you could be disappointed.

"We're sort of taking things one day at a time," she said. "He was married before, you know."

The knife bisected a lemon with surgical skill. The two halves fell and quivered on the cutting board. "No, I didn't know that," Tim said.

It was remarkably easy to unburden herself to him. Bartenders were like priests that way, she supposed. Was this what her mother had been looking for all those years? Absolution?

She shook the thought away. "I get the feeling he'd like to put me in one kind of box and the rest of his life in another." Tess took another slug of juice. "I don't like it."

"You have to figure he knows best," Tim said gently.

"Best for him, maybe. He's a cop. He's had practice compartmentalizing his feelings." Tess stared morosely into her glass. "But I don't want to be relegated to some safe little niche he has picked out for me."

"You don't mean that," Tim said.

She was afraid he was right.

She was terribly afraid that she wanted Jarek, needed Jarek, so much that she would accept a future with him on any terms.

Her fear and her pride twined together like a braided lash. The impact made her flinch. She lifted her chin. "I like to think I've got more going on in my life than keeping his bed warm and his socks clean."

Tim smiled wryly. "You mean like Heather does?"

Oh, boy. She'd really put her foot in it this time.

Tess had enough trouble planning her own life. She was in no position to criticize someone else's choices. And she certainly hadn't intended to insult Tim. Or his cheerleader wife.

"No, Heather does—" Very little, Tess remembered. She thought back to the last time she had spoken with

Heather, at the benefit dinner, with her mother and brother and the Tompkins and poor Judy Scott all sitting around the firelit picnic table. What was it Heather was talking about? "Well, she's going back to school now, isn't she?"

"No."

"But I thought—"

"That's your problem, Tess. You think too much."

Wow. Tim was really offended. She offered him a quick smile and a joke. "And here I always thought I just talked too much."

But he didn't smile back. "Heather belongs at home. She's happier there. Safer."

"Yeah, well…" Tess shrugged. "Maybe."

"I take care of her," Tim said, holding the knife motionless against the cutting board.

He was starting to creep her out.

"That's good, Tim. Whatever works for the two of you. I guess I'm just used to taking care of myself."

"You took care of your mother."

"Well, I tried."

He nodded. "And your brother. I admired you for that."

"Gee, thanks." Tess felt like she was hauling something slippery from the bottom of a pool. Something heavy was under the surface, and she couldn't quite get a grasp on it. She slid from her bar stool. "Listen, speaking of Mark, I've got to get to the hospital before visiting hours are up. Thanks for the juice."

Tim came around the bar, still carrying the chef's knife. "Don't go."

She backed toward the door. "I really should."

It was stupid to feel nervous.

It was ridiculous to think that Tim—*Tim,* the original Mr. Nice Guy—could mean to hurt her or harm her in any way.

But he kept coming after her, a small, set smile on his face.

Holding that big knife...

Ignoring reason, going on instinct, Tess turned and ran. Two steps, three steps to the door. Her head jerked back as Tim yanked her by her hair. Her scalp screamed. Pain shot through her neck. He dragged her back against his body and pressed the knife in his other hand against her stretched throat.

Fear arced through her like an electric current, stopping her breath, shorting out her brain.

"You can go ahead and scream if you want," Tim said, sounding amused. "There's no one here to hear you."

The duct tape hissed as Tim wrapped the roll around her ankles.

"I'm sorry to do this, Tess. I liked you. You fooled me for a long time. But I have to take care of you now."

Tess was all for being taken care of. Preferably by someone who wasn't holding a large kitchen knife.

But there was nothing she could say. Nothing she could do.

She was sitting on the cold linoleum floor of the Blue Moon's utility closet, with her legs stretched before her and her arms strapped behind.

It was amazing how quickly duct tape went on. It was amazing how uncomfortable it was. Too tight at her wrists, it pulled at her skin and the fine hair of her arms. Stretched across her mouth, it dragged at her cheeks and burned on her lips. Tim cut it with his knife.

She had whimpered as the blade approached her cheek, the point dangerously close to her eye.

"Oh, Tess. Don't worry about the knife. I use my hands." He'd cupped her face in a parody of tenderness, his fingers trailing over the tape. "I always use my hands. I want to touch you."

Images of Carolyn Logan's battered, violated body flashed on her brain.

Tess couldn't scream. She struggled not to vomit. She tried to kick, and Tim pricked her with the knife.

"Oops," he said. "Careful."

She watched, disbelieving, as blood welled beneath the tiny rent and stained the leg of her jeans. The pain came after, burning her calf and catching her chest.

"I guess this knife is useful after all. There, that should hold you," Tim said cheerfully, slicing the tape by her ankles. "I don't have time to play with you now, but we'll have lots of time later. I'll move you tonight, after the bar is closed."

Tonight.

Tess's heart raced. Jarek would miss her tonight. She grabbed the thought like a lifeline. *I'll be home by six,* he'd promised her. *Seven.*

Oh, God, that was hours away. But if she wasn't there... If he cared enough to call... If he came looking for her...

Her hope unraveled like a fraying rope, too slender to support the weight of all those "ifs."

Tim checked her wrists a final time and stood. "I have to go move your car now. We wouldn't want your friend the police chief to find it parked in front of the bar. Be very quiet back here. Because if he comes looking for you—"

He turned in the doorway and smiled. "—I'll kill you both," he said.

Jarek knocked on the window. Behind the bar in the shadowed room, Tim Brown looked up, surprised. He crossed the room, wiping his hands on a rag.

Jarek heard the dead bolt click, and then the door swung open.

"Hi, Chief. We're not serving for another half hour."

"I didn't come for coffee," Jarek said. "I was hoping you could answer a couple of questions for me."

"About Mark DeLucca?" Tim shook his head in seeming regret. "What a shame. He won't be working here again, if that's your concern. Not that I believe everything I hear, you understand, but the women who visit my establishment have to feel safe."

Slick son of a bitch.

Anger licked through Jarek. With an effort he kept it from his face and voice.

Aleksy's background check on Brown had provided one connection. As a former Chicago firefighter, Brown could own red signal lights. Heather Brown's artless disclosures about her marriage and Brown's comings and goings on the nights in question had yielded a possible motive and a slim opportunity. But without reliable physical evidence, all Jarek had so far was an educated hunch. He didn't have the "reasonable belief" required to obtain a warrant and arrest the bastard.

"I have several concerns," he said. "I'd appreciate you coming down to the station to talk about them."

"We could talk here." Tim smiled and threaded his way through the tables, back toward the bar. "And I could get you that cup of coffee."

Jarek followed, his senses on full alert. "No, thanks." He wasn't drinking anything Brown set in front of him now. "Actually I'm a little shorthanded. It would be easier all around if we could do this down at the station."

Brown raised both eyebrows. "Do what?"

"Well, I hoped you might volunteer a blood sample," Jarek said. "Just as a matter of routine. We can get one without your consent, of course, but I figured you'd want to step forward."

Brown went very, very still. Something flickered behind his eyes and was gone. And then he shrugged. "Sure. Whatever will help you out. But right now I'm getting ready to open, and with DeLucca out of the picture, I'm shorthanded myself. What do you say I come by tomorrow?"

Jarek didn't like it. But he didn't have any real grounds to object.

Taking a suspect to the police station against his will constituted an arrest, whether Jarek charged Brown with a crime or not. And if a court decided the arrest was unlawful, then the evidence obtained as a result of that arrest—the blood sample that Jarek hoped could nail Brown for the rape and murder of Judy Scott—could be inadmissible for prosecution.

Jarek frowned. "I guess tomorrow would be—"

Crash.

From somewhere down the dim hallway that led to the kitchen, metal clanged, followed by a couple of staccato thumps as something—somethings—hit the floor. The clatter affected Jarek like an alarm and wiped Tim's face clean of expression.

"What was that?" Jarek asked.

Tess lay on her side on the cold linoleum floor, feeling the warm blood seep through her pants leg and stick the fabric to her skin. Her hip and shoulders ached. Her leg throbbed. The floor smelled bad, and Tess felt worse.

In the dim light that came from around the edges of the door, she could see shelves packed with cardboard boxes and plastic gallon jugs of cleaning solution. A rolling mop bucket stood next to some sort of shower cubicle.

Nothing she could use for escape, unless she could slide down the drain or Tim was obliging enough to free her and hand her a broom as a weapon.

Hot tears leaked from the corners of her eyes and ran across her nose and into her hair. Her hands started to go numb—first at the wrists and then in her fingers.

With dull hope, she heard someone come into the bar, heard footsteps cross the floor and the murmur of conversation. Maybe she could make a noise, kick the door, knock something over... And then she recognized Jarek's deep even voice, and hope died.

If he comes looking for you, I'll kill you both.

She couldn't take that risk. Her heart turned stone cold within her. Jarek was armed, but Tim was prepared. Jarek had no reason to suspect the bar owner, no reason to be on his guard. She had to accept responsibility for him, the way she had accepted responsibility for everything and everyone she'd ever loved.

Because when Tess weighed the certainty of Jarek's safety against the slim possibility of her own rescue, she realized she could not risk him.

She loved him.

But the realization brought her no joy. This is what love led to, she thought, as pain knifed through her constrained shoulders and adhesive pulled at the edges of her jaw. Once you let yourself love somebody, you were trapped. Screwed.

Murdered.

And yet lying on the floor, she felt a tiny spark of rebellion flicker in her chest, coaxed to life by the sound of Jarek's voice, by the memory of his hands. Long, blunt-tipped hands. Strong, capable hands.

The recollection of her own words infiltrated her consciousness, more persistent than the cleaning fumes that rose from the drain. *I have that much faith in both of you.*

She took a tight breath. Did she really?

You'll find the person who did this. And you'll stop him.

Could she trust Jarek that much? Trust him to do his job, to be a cop, to rescue her and protect himself?

Could she put the control of their future in his hands?

She rolled across the floor, shutting out the numbness of her legs and the pain of her shoulder blades. With her chest heaving and her arms doubled uncomfortably under her, she raised her bound legs over her head and brought them down against the wheeled mop bucket.

It crashed to the floor. Brooms thumped. Her heart pounded.

Tess lay on her side in the silence, squirming away from the trickle of dirty water, and prayed.

Tim Brown froze.

"What was that?" Jarek asked.

Brown's shoulders relaxed. He shook his head. "God knows. This is an old building. We get all kinds of noises. Creaking floorboards, mice in the kitchen—"

"It would take a mighty big mouse to make that kind of noise."

Another, smaller clatter drifted from the hall.

Brown forced a laugh. "Maybe you're right. I guess I should check it out."

All Jarek's instincts were screaming at him to beware. No way was he letting Brown out of his sight. He eased back from the bar, his elbow automatically checking for the butt of his gun.

"Let me do it for you. Trust the job to a professional." Jarek smiled. "Just in case your mice are armed and dangerous."

"No, that's okay, I—"

"Or we can go together," Jarek suggested smoothly.

Brown pulled his lip as he considered. And then he nodded once, shortly. "I guess that would be okay."

He reached under the bar and pulled out a baseball bat, an old wooden Louisville slugger.

Jarek braced.

Brown grinned. "For the rats," he said, flourishing it. "I keep it handy in case the boys at the bar get a little too rowdy on Saturday night."

Damn. Jarek's heart was doing about a hundred and ten. He followed Brown down the poorly lit hallway, trying to control his breathing and his overactive imagination.

The case against Brown was circumstantial at best. At this point, Jarek was grasping at straws. Jumping at shadows.

Brown stopped outside an ordinary interior door: fiberboard pressed to resemble wood, with a simple lock and one of those machine lettered signs that read, Utility Closet—Staff Only.

Brown unlocked the door, leaving a dark, uninviting crack, and moved back a couple of paces. "You go ahead. It's dumb, but with everything else that's been going on, I guess I'm a little nervous after all."

You and me both, Jarek thought.

He took one step forward. Two. And then, alerted more by the silence than by any sound or change in the air behind him, Jarek ducked.

The baseball bat swung over his head and cracked into the opposite wall.

Holy St. Mike.

Crouching, Jarek pivoted. His emotions shut down. His training took over. Brown staggered, his body twisting, thrown off balance by his missed swing. Jarek launched up, jabbing at exposed kidney. His fist connected, hard, with soft tissue, and Brown grunted. The bat clattered to the floor.

Jarek followed through with a drive. Brown's hands came up, trying to push at his face, trying to gouge at his eyes. Jarek wrenched his face away, wrapped his arms around the big man's waist and tackled him to the floor. His shoulder slammed the wall as they went down. Brown's head hit the door with a thump like a ripe cantaloupe. The door crashed half open before it bumped against something on the floor.

Brown scrambled in sick desperation, pushing weakly at Jarek's arms. But the kidney punch and the dive into the door had finished him.

Panting, Jarek hauled and rolled the bar owner's heavy body out of the dark doorway. "I hope your head hurts worse than my damn shoulder."

Straddling the other man's thighs, Jarek reached behind his waist with one hand for his cuffs.

And heard a sound that chilled his blood.

A muffled whimper from behind the door.

Chapter 17

"**Y**ou took ten years off my life back there," Jarek said in the elevator going up to Tess's apartment. "And, honey, at my age, I don't have that kind of time to spare. Don't do it again, okay?"

"It's not like I had a choice," Tess said, indignant, and then staggered as the elevator lurched to a stop. She gave Jarek a shaky smile. "Uh-oh. Guess I'm not as recovered as I thought."

"Tell me something I don't know," Jarek muttered. He scooped her up and cradled her against his hard, muscled chest.

She sighed and wrapped her arms around his neck. "Are you sure you should do this? At your advanced age and all?"

"Don't mess with me, Tess. I'll lock you up."

"Promises, promises." She traced the crease in his cheek with one finger. "How's your shoulder?"

"It's fine. I'm fine. Where are your keys?"

She maneuvered to get them out of her purse. He unlocked the door and carried her over the threshold like a bride.

"Bedroom?" he asked succinctly.

This could be good, Tess thought, her heart quickening hopefully. She waved a hand toward the hall. The cat trotted after them as Jarek carried her through the apartment and laid her on her bed.

But he didn't join her there.

He knelt on the floor beside her bed and slid off her shoes.

He rolled down her socks. "Nightgown?"

"Uh—"

He stood and pulled open her top dresser drawer. "In here?"

"Yes."

He disregarded the tumbled satin and lace in favor of her old comfort cotton, the one she kept for lonely Friday nights and lazy Sunday mornings. "Arms up," he said, approaching the bed.

He undressed her with impersonal care, as if she were his patient. He pulled back her covers and tucked her in as if she were his daughter.

Tess was hurt and confused. Sickened by Tim's deception and shaken by his crude handling, she was physically sore and emotionally tender.

She wanted cosseting.

She wanted closeness.

She wanted Jarek's solid body naked next to hers, and he was withdrawing behind this wall of imperturbable care.

"That's it?" she said.

"Do you want a drink?" Jarek asked.

"No, I do not want a drink," she snapped.

"Do you want your pills? The doctor in the E.R. said you could have another one at seven."

Tess sighed. If she couldn't have Jarek, she could drug herself to sleep. "Fine. I'll take a pill."

Jarek pulled the bag with her prescription out of his jacket pocket and shook one of the super strength painkillers into his palm. He fetched her a glass of water from the bathroom and stood over her while she swallowed her medicine.

"There," he said with satisfaction. "That will take care of you."

The words awoke a sour echo of Tim Brown's threats: *I have to take care of you now.*

Tess shuddered.

Jarek frowned. "Do you want another blanket?"

She was cold, but not from the temperature in her room. She was cold and sick and lonely at heart, and she wanted Jarek to warm her. But he had already done so much. She didn't have the right to expect more. She didn't have the right to ask.

The black cat crept from the doorway and jumped up on the corner of the bed. It slunk forward until its nose just touched Tess's arm. Prompted, she rubbed its hard, sleek head, and was startled by its rusty, unfamiliar purr. Tears filled her eyes.

"Your cat's happy to have you home," Jarek said gruffly.

Tess cleared her throat. "Relieved," she said. "She knows where her food comes from. Did I thank you for coming to my rescue? Again?"

"Only about twelve times. You can stop now."

"I really am grateful," she insisted.

He shoved his hands into his pockets. "Tess, I don't want your gratitude. I was only doing my job."

She didn't want to hear that. She didn't want to be a part of his job to him, like an unpleasant duty he was forced to perform.

"Lucky for me you're good at your job."

"Your brother doesn't think so. I thought he was going to punch me out at the hospital."

"Given that he's still hooked up to about three machines, I think you were safe."

"He was worried about you."

"I was worried, too." She tried to joke. Good old Tough-As-Nails Tess. "I was afraid the hospital was going to keep me overnight and make us share a room like we did when we were kids."

"They should have," Jarek said harshly. "They should have kept you more than a couple of hours for observation."

She liked being home in her apartment, in her bed, with him. Even if he was insultingly reluctant to join her.

"Sherry Biddleman said I was fine. I didn't need to be admitted to the hospital."

"You have no idea what you need," Jarek said.

She was afraid she did. She needed him. Too much.

So of course, she crossed her arms on top of the covers and stared him straight in the eye and lied. "I don't need anything."

Jarek rubbed the back of his neck. "You know what your problem is?"

"I feel sure you're going to tell me."

"You're too independent."

The injustice of his accusation robbed her of breath. But not for long. "*I'm* independent? What about you? You didn't even tell me you suspected Tim."

Jarek blew out a sharp breath. "I suspected everybody. Tess, be reasonable. I can't tell you every lead in an on-

going investigation that might not pan out. You're a reporter.''

She didn't want to be reasonable. She didn't want his
logic. She wanted his love. She wanted his energy and passion. Even his anger was preferable to his Officer Frosty
routine.

She said, nastily, ''I am not *a* reporter. I am *the* reporter
you're sleeping with. Or maybe that's not important to
you.''

His mouth compressed. ''You're the one who set the
limits on this relationship.''

Maybe he was right, and she was just too miserable to
care. Or maybe not. She thought of him kissing her hot and
hard on her living room sofa and then saying in his cool,
deep voice, *Have I asked you for a commitment?*

And her ego shattered, and all her insecurity and temper
spilled out.

''Oh, and you've been totally up front with me,'' she
said. ''Chief Does-It-Have-To-Mean-Anything Denko.
You've held out on me from the beginning—about your
family, about your job, about my brother being a suspect.''
She felt the hot tears well in her eyes and willed them back.
''You can go to hell.''

''Tess—'' Jarek took a step toward her. Stopped. ''I
think at least I should go home,'' he said gently. ''You're
tired. You've had a couple of really tough days. We should
discuss this when you're rested.''

''Discuss it, hell,'' she said. ''I'm not even speaking to
you.''

He studied her a minute with cool, gray eyes. That be-
traying muscle ticked beside his mouth. She held her breath
in hope.

''I'll see you in the morning,'' he said, and walked out

of the room. She heard him lock the apartment door behind him as he left.

Isn't that just fine, she thought.

And burst into tears.

Isadora DeLucca frowned at the television screen, where the author of *Losing the Losers in Your Life* was extolling her program and selling her book to a fascinated and mostly female audience.

"I know this was filmed in Chicago," Isadora said, "but I just cannot agree with that woman."

Tess looked up from applying a last coat of polish to her nails. "What woman, Mom?"

"That—that author." Isadora sniffed. "I mean, does wanting someone always have to be wrong?"

Tess squinted at her new color. Deep blue, to match her mood. "It is if they don't want you back," she said dryly. At least, it was supposed to come out dryly. To her astonishment and shame, Tess heard her voice quaver. Her eyes filled. Her nails blurred.

"Oh, baby." Her mother left her chair and sat by Tess on the couch. Folding Tess in her thin arms, Isadora laid her cheek against her daughter's hair. "What is it? What's the matter? You can tell me."

Tess hadn't told her mother anything—anything significant, anyway—since she was nine years old and making excuses to Mark's kindergarten teacher about why Mrs. DeLucca couldn't attend a parent-teacher conference.

What good would it do?

What had her mother ever done to heal her or rescue her or make things all better? What could she do now?

And yet there was comfort in her mother's thin, fierce embrace. There was genuine invitation in her voice.

And Tess, like the confiding teenager she'd never allowed herself to be, blurted, "He didn't call."

"Who didn't call, sweetie? Jarek?"

Tess nodded miserably.

"But—" Isadora twisted her head to look at the table next to the sofa, where a bouquet of bright daisies nodded from a blue enameled cup. "He sent you flowers."

Tess sniffed. "A get well bouquet." With a note that read, *Can't get away.* And signed simply, *Jarek.*

Isadora smiled. "What did you want? Red roses?"

The humiliating thing was that was exactly what Tess wanted. Red roses, white lace, four bridesmaids and the whole nine yards.

"I don't know," she muttered.

"Don't know?" Her mother eyed her shrewdly. "Or won't say?"

Tess picked at a fleck of blue polish along one nail. This confiding business was not going exactly as she hoped. "I'm not sure what you're talking about."

Isadora sighed. "Tess, all your life you've pretended that what you wanted isn't important. It seems to me that this would be a good time to figure it out."

Right. Tess had had nothing but time. All the long and lonely sleepless hours of the night. "I guess I want— I guess I need him to tell me I'm important."

"Have you told him that?"

"Well…" As if she could. "No."

Isadora's back straightened. "Tess, you're a wonderful girl. You've been a wonderful daughter. But for someone who's always made a big deal about honesty, you haven't been very honest with Jarek about your own needs."

Tess stopped fussing with her nails. "Shouldn't he know?"

"He's a detective, sweetheart. Not a mind reader. You should tell him."

You haven't been very honest.

Tess took a deep breath. "I'm afraid to," she admitted.

"Afraid? Sweetie, you've never been afraid of anything in your life."

"I'm afraid I'll tell him, and he'll say no."

"Oh." Isadora looked sadly at her hands. "That's my fault."

"Oh, no, Mom, I—"

Her mother reached over and took Tess's freshly manicured hand between both of her own. "You grew up being disappointed. That's my fault." And then she added, firmly, "But it's your fault if you let that disappointment shape the rest of your life."

Tess's mouth jarred open.

And the doorbell rang.

Isadora gave her daughter's hand a final pat and stood to answer the door. "I wonder who that could be."

"Wait!" Tess unfolded her legs and reached for her hair. She needed a brush. She needed lipstick. She needed—

"Jarek," Isadora said warmly. "How nice to see you."

"Mrs. DeLucca. How's—"

"Tess?"

That was Allie's voice, Tess thought, confused. That was Allie, pushing past the grown-ups at the door to stand in front of the couch with worried eyes and a truculent expression.

"Are you all right?" the ten-year-old demanded.

Something loosened in the region of Tess's heart, and she had to fight to keep from grabbing the kid and hugging her hard.

"I'm fine," she said, and it was almost true.

Allie nodded. "Good."

She launched herself at the couch, and Tess, despite her surprise, managed to catch her.

"Dad said everything was fine, but that's what he always says. So I made him come and get me so I could see."

Was that why he was here? Or was that why he was late?

"I was kind of worried," Allie said, the words muffled against Tess's chest.

Tess swallowed the lump in her throat and cuddled the girl closer. "Well, your dad was right. Everything's good. Everything's great, in fact."

At least, it would be if she had anything to say about it.

"Hey." Allie lifted her head. "Your nails are blue."

"I guess they are."

"Can you do mine blue, too?"

Tess refused to meet Jarek's eyes. "You bet."

Allie squirmed around on the couch, so that her slim shoulder butted Tess's side. It felt good, Tess decided. It felt right. "Is that your cat?"

Over by the bookshelves, the black cat crouched, watching the action with wary green eyes. "It is now," Tess said.

"Cool. Does it have a name yet?"

"Not yet," Tess said.

Allie sighed with satisfaction and said, "I could help you pick one out."

"Allie," Jarek said warningly from by the door.

His daughter shot him a mutinous look from under her lashes.

"Why not?" said Tess, feeling reckless.

"Maybe we could discuss naming the cat later?" Jarek suggested.

She made the mistake of looking at him, and the warmth in his eyes bumped her heart into her throat.

Isadora held her hand out to Allie. "Do you like ice cream?"

"Are we trying to leave them alone?" Allie asked.

"I think now would be a good time," her father said, never taking his gaze from Tess's.

Her breath stuck in her chest.

"Okay." Allie hopped out from under Tess's arm. "We'll see you guys later, then." Tess heard her say to Isadora, "I like mint chocolate chip."

The door closed behind them. The apartment seemed very quiet.

Jarek looked at Tess huddled on her couch, with her brave blue nails and uncertain mouth, and felt his world shift and right itself, with her as its center.

"How are you holding up?" he asked quietly.

She lifted her chin. "Okay."

"I spent the morning with the D.A.," he told her, since some words seemed required. "We put a rush on the lab and got a match linking Brown to Judy Scott. We're still working out the timetable for his attack on the Logan girl—he may have swiped her wallet, and then called her to come pick it up. At the very least, he'll be charged with aggravated assault and murder in the first degree."

"Is this for the record?"

Jarek grinned. He should have known that nothing—not abduction or attempted murder, not his daughter's embarrassing attempts to co-opt her cat or Jarek's own damn clumsiness—could keep her down for long.

"That's for you," he said. "I'll give you a formal statement for the paper later."

She still looked unconvinced. So much for talking.

He crossed the room and sat on the couch beside her. His weight already had her tipping toward him even before he took her in his arms. He felt the slight resistance in her shoulders, and then she relaxed and leaned into him.

That was better. She smelled terrific, a combination of soap and scent and Tess. His brain shut down as he held her, just held her, for long moments. She felt wonderful. Warm and alive and real and right.

She turned her face up for his kiss. His hands tightened on her arm, at her waist. He kissed her, kissed that soft, full mouth. So warm. So giving.

He gave and took in equal measure, filling his hands with her, with the cloudy darkness of her hair, the soft curve and dip of hip and waist, the slope of her breast.

She sighed and sagged against him. And then she pulled away. "Wait a minute."

Her lips were red and parted from his kisses. Her eyes were miserable and determined.

Jarek's heart squeezed. "What?"

"There's something I have to say."

Hell.

"Now?"

Tess's courage almost failed her. Jarek was so gorgeous, with those little lines of impatience between his brows and that combination of amusement and heat simmering in his eyes.

What they had was good. What they had was great, in fact. Why screw it all up by asking for more?

But she wanted more.

Her mother's words jabbed her with their honesty. *It's your fault if you let disappointment shape the rest of your life.*

"Yes, now. There's something you've got to know."

She thought he stiffened. "I'm listening."

Here goes, she thought.

"I love you," she said baldly.

"Tess—"

She put her fingers against his lips. If he interrupted her now, if he put her off, however kindly, she might never have the guts to continue. "Let me finish. I love you, and I think you care about me. I mean, you *act* like you care about me."

She realized she still had her hand over his mouth and pulled it back.

"But—?" he prompted.

"But I need the words," she said. Why did this have to be so hard? "I need you to tell me."

"Tell you." He wasn't just expressionless. He looked stunned.

"What I— If I mean anything to you."

"Fine. I'll tell you," Jarek said slowly. "On one condition."

A condition. Well. Tess struggled to hide her disappointment. She had fallen in love with a logical man with multiple responsibilities. It only made sense that he would negotiate terms for their relationship.

"What sort of condition?" she asked. Maybe it was something she could live with.

Jarek took her cold hands in his strong, steady clasp. "I want to tell you in church. In front of God and Allie and your mother and both our brothers and all the witnesses I can find. Marry me, Tess."

Hope welled in her chest. Tears started in her eyes. She had never in her life cried as much as she had these past two days. But these tears were different. Warm. Happy. Healing. "That's it? That's your condition?"

Jarek's smile dented his cheek. "It's a pretty big one. Will you? Will you marry me, Tess?"

With all her heart, she wanted to say yes. But his

brother's words still plucked at the edge of her mind. *You're not what he needs.*

"Why?" she asked.

"Because you're honest and dedicated and loyal."

"So's a dog."

He laughed. "Because you make me feel alive. Because you painted my daughter's fingernails. Because you stood up for your brother and stood up to mine. Hell, I don't know. Because you wear red underwear." His hands tightened on hers. "You're what I want. You're all I need. Will you marry me?"

Her heart answered him before she could form the words. But when she could speak, she said, "Yes. On one condition."

"Anything," he said.

"Tell me."

And this time he understood. His eyes steady on hers, he said, "I love you, Tess."

Joy swept through her and spilled out in tears. She leaned toward him and rested her forehead against his strong, sheltering shoulder. She felt his kiss against her hair.

"About damn time," she said.

* * * * *

Alex is about to meet his match in

ALL A MAN CAN ASK

*coming from Intimate Moments
in January 2003—and
look for Mark in April!*

I N T I M A T E   M O M E N T S™

presents:

Romancing the Crown

With the help of their powerful allies,
the royal family of Montebello is
determined to find their missing heir.
But the search for the beloved prince
is not without danger—or passion!

Available in November 2002:
UNDER THE KING'S COMMAND
by Ingrid Weaver (IM #1184)

A royal mission brought Navy SEAL Sam Coburn and Officer
Kate Mulvaney together. Now their dangerous mission—and a love
that never died—might just keep them together forever....

This exciting series continues throughout
the year with these fabulous titles:

Available only from Silhouette Intimate Moments
at your favorite retail outlet.

Where love comes alive™

Visit Silhouette at www.eHarlequin.com

SIMRC11

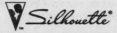

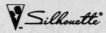

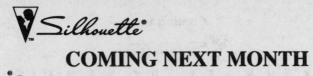

COMING NEXT MONTH